AN. WILLIS

DOORS OF GOLD AND RUST

Doors Of Gold And Rust (Byrne House #2)

Produced by Observatory Books
Denver, Colorado

First edition August 2020
Ebook ISBN 978-1-7343597-2-5
Print ISBN 978-1-7343597-3-2

For my nieces and nephews

DOORS OF GOLD AND RUST

PART 1
REFLECTION

1

THE LETTER ARRIVED ON A FRIDAY. THE CREAM envelope shone like a beacon on Evelyn's front porch step. She slowed when she saw it, the strap of her school bag sliding down her shoulder. She didn't know who'd sent it—*couldn't* have known—didn't even know it was addressed to her. But already she had a weightless sensation in her stomach. Like the sidewalk was disappearing from beneath her feet, and she was falling.

She concentrated on moving forward, hitching the bag back into place. She marched up the steps and stood over the envelope. It waited there so innocently. Resting on the flagstone. A couple of brown maple leaves drifted past. Already December, and still no snow.

Miss Evelyn Ashwood, the envelope read in looping cursive. Nothing else. No address. No postmark, no stamp.

She scooped up the letter, dusted off a stray leaf, and turned the envelope over. No return address. But there was a name. A name that she had hoped to never see or hear again, though she hadn't expected to be so lucky.

Daniella Byrne, the back of the envelope said in the same elegant script.

Her breaths came shallow and fast. Feeling eyes upon her, Evelyn whirled around to face the street. But all was quiet. Walter Park was deserted. No cars drove past. Her mother Vivian wouldn't be home from work for several more hours. Evelyn was alone.

These days, she hated being alone more than almost anything. Yet she had been avoiding her friends' invitations. Because the thing she hated most of all was pretending.

Evelyn let her gaze move to Byrne House. The massive Victorian mansion was built of rough grey stone, surrounded by overgrown gardens. The setting of her childhood nightmares and dreams. A house full of dark memories and hidden, underground passageways.

The place she'd barely escaped alive four months ago.

That day—in that underground lab—was the last time she'd seen Daniella Byrne. When the police got involved, Daniella ran. Where, nobody here in Castle Heights knew. Evelyn had figured that Daniella would come back eventually. Byrne House was her home. Her inheritance, along with all the Byrne family's many secrets.

But a letter, after everything that had happened? It was a more direct overture than Evelyn had expected. And at the same time, disappointingly passive. Daniella owed her more than this.

The paper was satiny beneath her fingers. For a brief moment, Evelyn thought of tearing it up. Out of anger, mostly. Or maybe just fear. The two emotions had taken up residence in her heart these last few months, her most frequent companions. She'd also given voice to these emotions in therapy, though she couldn't tell her therapist what really happened to her in the tunnels beneath Castle Heights. The truth about what she'd done.

She found her keys, unlocked the front door, and slammed it behind her. Her bag dropped onto the floor. She tore open the flap of the envelope.

10th December
San Francisco

Dear Evelyn,
Memory is a funny thing. I've thought about our last conversation often, and wondered how much of it you still recall. In some ways— assuming you do remember, which is far from certain—you know me better than anyone ever has. Even William, as much as he and I love each other. But love is far less intimate than hate.
Not that I hate you now, no matter what you must have done to Darren. I haven't heard from my brother since that day that we were all together in August, so I assume that he's dead.
I want you to know that I forgive you.

Evelyn stopped reading. She crumpled up the letter and threw it against the wall.

Alex, she thought.

Her phone had settled to the bottom of her bag, beneath a paperback copy of *Wuthering Heights* and a Snickers bar. The phone didn't recognize her print. Her fingers were trembling too much. So she fumbled through the passcode. She thumbed to the name *Alex Evans*—her boyfriend of a little over four months—in her messages. But as she stared at their last exchange from that morning, she remembered he'd still be at school. He was on East Coast time, two hours ahead, but he didn't have early dismissal on Fridays like she did. And he didn't get reception in his school's main building.

Cursing to herself, she texted him, *FaceTime asap? urgent.*

Today was the last day of school before winter break. She'd been hoping that Alex would come to Castle Heights for the holidays. But even yesterday he'd been vague about his plans. Ever since the summer, Alex had been focused on healing the breaches within his family. She understood, and she would never have asked him to do anything different. But she'd been struggling to heal, too. Whether she liked it or not, she had to do that without him.

Other names stared up at her from her messaging app: *Milo Foster. Silvia Reyes.* Two of her closest friends, both of whom knew the truth about all that had happened at Byrne House over the summer. But that was the very same reason that she hesitated to write them. Milo and Silvia clearly wanted to move on. They'd supported her and comforted her countless times, but they'd also told her—in not so many words, of course—that she should move on, too.

I could call Jake, she thought. Her thumb tapped against her phone case.

But she wasn't quite that desperate. Yet.

How dare Daniella write that: *I forgive you.* She didn't want Daniella's forgiveness. She wanted some kind of justice for what Daniella had done. Her fists clenched and unclenched as she paced the living room, trying to calm down. She kicked the leg of the couch as she passed.

That day we were all together in August, the letter said.

"You mean the day Darren almost killed me?" Evelyn shouted into the empty room. "The day you left me down there to die?"

She was too jittery to stay still. She went to the living room window and glanced out. The street was still quiet. Over at the mansion, the windows were dark like they'd been since the end of summer. The round tower window mirrored the clouds drifting past. If anyone was in there, she wouldn't see.

Suddenly a figure appeared, stumbling out of the park. Out of the *past.* Milo Foster. His cheeks were gaunt. He'd lost his glasses, and he tripped as he stepped off the curb. She reached toward him, her hand hitting the window.

It was just a memory—the night that Evelyn and Alex had found Milo after he'd been missing in July. She squeezed her eyes closed. When she opened them, the vision of Milo was gone. She backed away unsteadily from the window.

Another one of the flashes. They'd been more frequent lately.

Finally she sat down and put her head in her hands. She wouldn't cry. She wouldn't give Daniella the satisfaction. It was all a ploy, anyway. Daniella was adept at playing sweet and innocent, but she always had an ulterior motive. She hadn't written that letter just to spread peace, love, and understanding. No, Daniella wanted something. Evelyn needed to find out what.

But she couldn't do it alone.

She grabbed her phone and started to text.

∼❧ ❧∼

It had all started in July, with Milo Foster's disappearance. He'd been inside Byrne House at the wrong time. Reginald Byrne—Daniella and Darren's father—had collapsed, and Milo had only wanted to help.

Reginald was Darren's first victim. And that same day, Milo became the next.

Darren had been re-creating the experiments that his ancestor, Walter Byrne, conducted at Byrne House over a century ago. Walter, and later Darren, had been searching for a cure to a debilitating disease from which they both suffered. Since childhood, Darren had experienced intense visions that would leave him with migraines and gaps in his memory. He didn't realize until later that these so-called "hallucinations" were actually real: visions of past events. But these episodes were often terrifying and overwhelming, too vivid with emotion. He rarely remembered them afterward. Daniella hated her role as her brother's caretaker, though in truth she herself was responsible for Darren's illness.

But Darren's experimental serum didn't cure his disease. His research came to a standstill. He needed another one of Walter Byrne's journals—one that had long ago gone missing from Byrne House. Darren came to believe that Evelyn had that journal. He kidnapped her and took her through the passage beneath Byrne House to the secret laboratory.

That was where Daniella found her—strapped to a table, under the influence of Darren's powerful drug. The serum allowed Evelyn to experience not only past events, but to see the emotions and thoughts emanating from a living person. Evelyn had read the truth in Daniella's mind that day: she had known all along about her brother's experiments.

Daniella only ever did what served her. Nothing more.

She'd left Evelyn to face Darren alone. Perhaps Daniella had hoped that, if Evelyn survived, she'd have no memory of the entire incident.

But Evelyn remembered.

She could still see the dark pool of blood that poured from Darren's body. Hear the sounds of his last breaths as they echoed against the tunnel walls. She hadn't wanted to kill him. But only one of them was ever going to make it out of those passages alive. Trapped in the tunnels afterward, Evelyn had just barcly held onto her sanity.

Yes, Daniella. I remember it all.

Those unbearable memories would stay with her for the rest of her life.

2

J AKE WAS WAITING BY THE STATUE IN THE PARK. He'd insisted they meet here; they rarely met at either of their homes. *I don't do parents,* Jake had said. But Evelyn knew he preferred the statue for other, more macabre, reasons.

"How are you?" She always asked first thing with Jake. He rarely told her outright, but his expressions usually said enough for her to know whether to brace herself.

Today he grimaced comically. "I'm breathing."

"I'd guessed that much."

"You're the one who texted *me*." He ruffled his fingers through his spiky hair. Streaks of grey marked his temples, making him look far older than seventeen.

"So what's the emergency?"

"I heard from Daniella Byrne." Evelyn held up the letter.

"Why's it all crumply?"

She plopped down near him on the grass. Leaves crunched beneath her vintage Levis. "Because I got mad when I started reading it."

He took it from her hand and glanced over the first few paragraphs. He whistled. "Yeah, I can see why. Daniella doesn't know for sure that her brother's dead? Maybe that's a good thing. You jammed a screwdriver in his neck."

Evelyn flinched. "Thank you, master of subtlety."

The statue marked the location of Walter Byrne's—and later Darren's—laboratory. When Darren took Evelyn down there, she'd woken to find Jake already strapped to a table beside her. Like her, Jake had been injected with the serum.

Since that day, Jake's moods had grown much darker. Unpredictable. Sometimes, it was just his sense of humor. But he had a habit of texting during all hours of the night. He'd send her rambling descriptions of his nightmares, stream-of-consciousness accounts of the worst things he'd ever done. Things that belonged in a journal or a therapy session, though he'd refused to talk to an actual therapist.

And yet—he managed to make her laugh on days when no one else could. At least she didn't have to pretend with him. He understood, at a fundamental level, what she'd been through. Like her, Jake remembered that lab. How it felt to be strapped to that table.

"What about you?" Jake asked, turning serious for a moment. "Any more of those, you know, flashback things?"

"Nope," she lied. "I'm fine."

Despite their shared memories, she felt more comfortable keeping him at arm's length. Jake already knew too much about her. She'd known him since childhood, and he'd grown up to be a pompous, self-centered jerk. He'd dated Silvia and treated her cruelly. Just a few months ago, Evelyn and Jake had despised one another. But after Darren Byrne's laboratory…Jake was different. Not necessarily better. Not a friend, exactly. But different. Wounded.

Maybe Daniella was right. Sometimes, love was less intimate than hate.

Jake stood up and dug a plastic baggie from his pocket. He held it out to her. Chocolate chip cookies. "My mom made these. You look like you need them more than I do."

She glanced over at him. Same bruise-like shadows under his dark eyes. Patches of grey at his temples, where his glossy black hair had faded after the ordeal in the tunnels. He hadn't texted her about any of his nightmares in a couple of days, but he still didn't look like he'd gotten much sleep.

"Nah, keep your cookies," she said. "You're way more pathetic than me."

That got a half-hearted smile out of him. He took a bite and said, "Read your letter then. Let's hear what Daniella has to say."

A gust of wind blew through the park, a breath of the coming winter. Evelyn looked toward Byrne House, though from this vantage point, she could only catch glimpses of stone here and there.

She smoothed out the letter as best she could and began to read aloud.

I want you to know that I forgive you.

I'm willing to put all that ugliness in the past. We have a common interest: Walter Byrne. When I was younger, I studied his journals obsessively. You probably already know that about me, don't you? I was so lonely as a child. Mentally, I was far beyond my cohort. I was taking college classes at thirteen. Yet I couldn't make true friendships with my classmates, either. To them, I was just a little girl. And Darren —you already know the difficulties I had with my brother.

Sometimes I felt as though Walter Byrne was my only friend.

A long time ago, I gave up on his wilder claims: astounding inventions, discoveries that would amaze the world.

But then I saw the mirror that you found. And I started to hope.

"So that's what she wants," Jake interrupted. "The mirror."

Evelyn hesitated. It made sense. Daniella had been shocked when Darren showed her the mirror in the underground lab. Told her what it could do.

At first glance, the mirror looked like nothing more than an antique with a small handle and a gold frame. But Walter Byrne had created it using a certain crystal from the mine beneath his home—the same crystal that had caused Walter's sickness and that Walter later used in his experiments. He'd wanted to show his wife, Ada Byrne, the same miraculous visions that he witnessed during his episodes. But unlike the powdered form of the crystal, which—when inhaled or ingested—caused such horrible side effects, the mirror's visions were relatively gentle.

Evelyn had discovered the mirror in one of the tunnels beneath Castle Heights, and she'd used it multiple times to solve the mystery of Ada Byrne's disappearance over a hundred years ago.

The irony? Evelyn didn't care one bit about the mirror anymore. Daniella could have it back, if that would make her go away.

She picked up reading where she'd left off.

I'd like to examine the mirror, if you'd let me. But Evelyn, there could be something even more incredible waiting for us. In fact, I'll let you keep the mirror entirely in exchange for one, simple thing:

Your help.

Walter spoke in his later writings of another invention—his greatest achievement, one that he never had the chance to show his wife. He did mention the mirror too, though I didn't fully understand those references until I saw the mirror for myself. But no, this grander invention is something else entirely. Something that would allow the user to not just see the truth of the world, but to change it.

I lost my faith years ago. I thought that Walter's writings were just madness. But now, after seeing the mirror, I believe. It's real, Evelyn. He left clues to its hiding place. You and I could find it.

We will find it.

I realize that, right now, you might not trust me. But I'm going to prove myself. I know exactly what you want, and I'm going to deliver it to you. And once I do, once you believe that I'm right about Walter's greatest invention, you'll be begging me to come back to Byrne House.

With best wishes,
Daniella Byrne

3

JAKE SHOVED THE LAST COOKIE INTO HIS MOUTH. "Daniella knows how to bring the drama. I'll give her that."

Evelyn set the letter aside and stood up. Dampness had seeped from the grass through the seat of her jeans. "She thinks I'll be 'begging' her to come back? She'll be waiting a long time."

She was still unnerved by Daniella's message. But more than anything, she was confused. Another of Walter Byrne's inventions? What could possibly be more impressive than the mirror? Maybe the "invention" was entirely Daniella's, some elaborate means of revenge for Darren's death. Or maybe Daniella was really chasing shadows. She could go right ahead. Evelyn was never going to help her.

Jake picked up the letter, examining it. "'*I know exactly what you want, and I'm going to deliver it to you.*' What do you think that means?"

"It means nothing. She's playing games."

He dropped the letter, fixing her with a stare. "What do you want most, Evelyn Ashwood?" he asked darkly.

Daniella probably thought that Evelyn wanted money, or admission to some fancy college, or maybe a collection of original Diane von Furstenberg dresses. She probably couldn't fathom that Evelyn would actually want something mundane: to be with the boy she loved. Because to Daniella, love was a means of manipulation. A path to an end.

I want to be with Alex, Evelyn thought. *That's all.*

He'd gone back to New York at his mother's request shortly after the fall semester started. Alex said it was just for a few weeks, to smooth things over and make sure his mom was okay. And then weeks became months. Evelyn spoke to him almost every day, yet the ease between them had turned to effort. Every conversation, there was more and more that she left unsaid. He had enough difficulties with his family. Alex needed her to be okay. She wanted to give that to him. Even if it wasn't quite true.

But if he were here, she assured herself, *things would be the same again. Just like before he left.*

"What do you want?" Jake asked in a sing-song voice. "Is it Alex Evans? Or are you tired of waiting for him yet?"

Evelyn walked a few steps away, kicking fallen leaves. She didn't discuss Alex with Jake. Ever. "How's unpacking going?" she asked instead.

The Oshiros had just moved over to a smaller home a couple streets away from Evelyn's. They'd given up their big house to help pay his dad's legal fees; his father had been arrested last year for some kind of white collar crime, but then worked out a deal. They'd sold Jake's car, too, the beautiful classic Camaro that Evelyn had admired. He drove his mom's minivan now. Or walked. Not that he went much farther than Walter Park these days.

"If I unpack," he said, "then I might find my physics textbook, and then I might have to finish my assignments and actually pass the class. It's a slippery slope."

"Mr. Peterson isn't going to let you make up all that work now. I doubt you'd pass even if you found that book. Even if I helped you study."

"You'll help me study?" He tilted his head to look up at her.

Bending toward him, she pushed his cheek with her palm, making his head turn back in the other direction. "God, no. I hate you, remember?"

"Oh good," Jake said, laughing. "I was afraid you'd finally lost it."

"Not yet." She smiled, glad to see a tiny glint of happiness in his eyes, however small.

Then he ruined it. He grabbed her hand. She'd just been playing around, trying to lighten the mood, but Jake was squeezing her fingers too tightly. His dark-ringed eyes were too intense.

"If Evans really wanted to come back to Castle Heights, he'd find a way," Jake said. "But he doesn't want to. Not even for you."

"Let me go. That hurts."

She knew that Jake was a little too attached to her. There were the texts, the calls. But his overtures had been more explicit, too. *Why didn't we ever hook up?* he asked once. *We could have fun together.* She'd shut him down. Jake had laughed like it was all a game. A joke. But sometimes, he looked at her in a way that made her wary—like he was a lonely, starving animal peering out of a cage. She didn't know if he saw her as a savior or a meal. Maybe he didn't know, either.

Deep down, a lonely part of her liked to be wanted. Even though Jake's neediness also sometimes scared her.

Jake turned her palm upward, staring at it. "If you looked under a microscope," he murmured, "do you think you could still find Darren's blood on your skin?"

She yanked her hand away. "Goodbye, Jake. I've had enough for today." She stooped to pick up Daniella's letter. It crinkled as she shoved it in her pocket.

Evelyn walked back towards her house. But then she noticed the guy at the other end of the park, sitting on a bench. He had his elbows propped on his knees, apparently lost in thought.

He looked up. She stopped abruptly, unable to breathe.

It was Alex. Here. Alex was here in Walter Park.

She opened her mouth to shout to him. She started running. He was looking straight at her. But he wasn't smiling. Something was off. He was the wrong one—the Alex from early in the summer. Hesitant, inscrutable. Back when he'd still been lying to her.

Then he started shimmering at the edges.

Suddenly the bench was empty. He'd vanished. A shudder charged up and down her body. Her knees weakened and she stumbled, catching herself against a tree.

Jake appeared beside her. "You just had another flash, didn't you?"

"No."

"You did so. What did you see?"

She pressed her thumbs into her temples. "None of your business."

But she didn't object when he touched her shoulder—gently—and led her back to the statue. He helped her sit on the concrete base. She bent over at the waist, head in her hands. Hiding the tears in her eyes.

Jake had been with her the first time it happened. That was why he knew. Nobody else knew. Not even Alex.

A few days after Alex left town, she and Jake had been walking around the neighborhood. Back then she'd responded every time that Jake texted, spent time with him whenever he asked. He'd helped rescue her from the tunnels, so she'd felt that she owed him. And he had no one else to talk to.

That day, she was still on crutches so it was a slow walk, but mostly she was just listening to Jake vent. They'd been walking on the opposite side of the street from Byrne

House. All in one instant, Evelyn had seen a little boy appear.

The boy was on the ground in front of the mansion's front gate, screaming and crying and cradling his leg. His skateboard had rolled away into the street. She knew this boy. She'd seen his picture countless times—the red helmet with white stars, the yellow Mario Brothers t-shirt.

It was her Uncle Sammy on the day he'd badly broken his ankle. He'd been eight years old. She had a photo of him, wearing those same clothes, in her keepsake box.

Evelyn's Nana had told her the story. Vivian—Evelyn's mother—and Sammy weren't supposed to play near Byrne House. Nana forbade it. Nana had always taken the rumors about Byrne House seriously. It was a place where bad things happened: children got lost, families turned against one another. But the sidewalk in front of the mansion was also just the right kind of uneven to make it fun for skateboarding.

Back then, Viv and Sammy hadn't listened to the warnings.

Sammy's ankle had healed, and to Evelyn, it was just a minor incident in the Stanton family history. But that afternoon with Jake, she'd felt Sammy's pain in her own leg, as if his injury and hers were the same. She'd cried out, like her uncle was speaking through her. She didn't understand what was happening.

The crying boy seemed so immediate, as if he were right there in front of her. Yet he wasn't—this was a vision of something that had happened years ago. It was exactly like she'd been gazing into the mirror. Or under the influence of Darren Byrne's serum.

One of her crutches had slipped out from under her. She fell into the street. Jake had bent over her, asking what was wrong. Her head was clouded over with Sammy's emotions, and she couldn't stop herself from telling Jake everything. They'd sat there on the curb for a while, in the shadow of Byrne House, Jake holding her as she cried.

She'd had similar visions many times since then. Flashes, she called them. They weren't like the nightmares about Byrne House she'd had growing up—those nightmares had followed her into real life only once. The "sleep hallucination" when she was fourteen. That episode had so disrupted her life that Evelyn spent years trying to get past it.

But now, she was seeing flashes of other people's memories and emotions every single day.

She guessed the flashes had something to do with the drug that Darren had injected her with, and possibly her other past exposures to the crystal from Walter Byrne's mine. At first, she'd feared that she had the same sickness that plagued Darren and Walter. But her flashes, though upsetting, didn't cause her to convulse or black out. They were usually over within a few seconds. She'd lived through so much already. She could handle this, too.

I am strong. I am not broken on the inside.

"You sure you're okay?" Jake asked, pulling her out of her thoughts and back to Walter Park.

Her head pounded. She glanced over at the park bench. Still empty. She longed to see Alex again, even just a faded memory of him, and that made her even sadder.

"I just wish the flashes would stop," Evelyn said. "Makes it a little hard to concentrate in trig class." She tried to smile.

Jake leaned back against the statue. "Maybe *that's* what you should want from Daniella. A cure. Then, I bet you'd help her. Just like she said."

He spoke flippantly. But Evelyn sat up, her eyes widening. Daniella had an antidote to Darren's serum. It couldn't cure Darren's illness. But what about the flashes? Daniella's antidote was, at the very least, worth a try.

But Evelyn didn't feel hopeful. Now, Daniella's letter worried her in a way it hadn't before. She unfolded the paper from her back pocket and looked at it again. *I'm going to prove myself... You'll be begging me to come back to Byrne House.*

Now, she was afraid that Daniella could be right.

4

EVELYN SAT BY THE STATUE WITH JAKE UNTIL THE sky started to darken. He was playing a game on his phone, so she could just sit and enjoy the quiet. Cars turned onto the street; neighbors returning from work. Kids came and went in the park. Strings of holiday lights blinked on. Tables were set for dinner in the windows, families gathering and hugging each other hello. Evelyn glanced over at her own home, wondering when her mom would be back.

What she saw made her stand up, her shoulders tensing.

There was someone on her front porch. A man. She immediately thought of the way the letter had appeared earlier: no stamp, no return address.

She'd forgotten to turn on the porch light. She could only see the outline of the figure standing there. It was more a sense of movement than a clear picture. But it looked like he was peering into the windows.

Then he went around the side of the house.

Jake looked up from his screen. "What is it?"

"Somebody's at my house."

"I don't see anyone."

She walked briskly across the park. The figure was back on the porch now. He turned and started down the steps. She could see him better: a tall, lean frame. Dark hair.

A scar ran from his eyebrow to his mouth along the left side of his face. Another flash of Alex. Again. Was her mind in control of the visions, somehow? Was her subconscious so cruel?

She stopped walking. She heard Jake catching up behind her.

The vision of Alex smiled, and she felt it in her heart like a sliver of glass. He looked so real that she could almost believe he was here in Castle Heights instead of thousands of miles away. He crossed the street and walked toward her. But she couldn't read any emotions from him, the way she usually could with the flashes. And the way he kept glancing over at Jake, and chewing his lip like he didn't know what to say—that didn't seem like just a memory.

"Hi." Alex tilted his head, his hair falling to one side. His green eyes had turned uncertain. "You don't exactly look happy to see me," he said.

Jake snorted. "I'm not."

Alex grinned like he appreciated the joke, but his eyes weren't laughing. "I wasn't talking to you." He opened his palms toward her, asking a question.

She ran over to him and jumped up, cinching her arms around his neck. He caught her around the waist. "I can't believe you're here," she said. "You're *here*. Why didn't you tell me you were coming?"

"It was spur of the moment. I wanted to surprise you."

She let go of his neck and slid down until her feet met the grass. She touched his face, his hair, still proving to herself that he was real. Alex dipped his head like he might kiss her, but then she remembered Jake was there. He would probably make some disgusting comment about it later.

She pulled back and whispered, "Not here."

Alex frowned. His eyes moved over her shoulder. "Hey, Jake. How've you been?"

"Amazing. I'm sure Ev's told you all about how fantastic my semester is going."

"Not so much, actually." Alex's arm drew around her waist.

She hadn't mentioned Jake to Alex in a while. He never responded well when he heard Jake's name, and he'd be furious about Jake's neediness and the late-night texts. She hadn't wanted Alex to feel jealous, especially when there was absolutely nothing to be jealous of.

"Don't be mad," she said quietly.

"I'm not," he whispered back.

She wiggled out of Alex's grasp. "Jake, I'm gonna go. You good?"

Jake shrugged and walked toward a bench to sit down. "Peachy. Have fun."

On her porch, she couldn't help glancing back. Jake was still sitting there, slumped in the same position. She couldn't see his eyes from here. Shadows spilled a gauzy layer of grey over his face. But she imagined she could feel him watching anyway.

5

EVELYN DIDN'T KNOW WHAT TO DO FIRST.

She wanted Alex to tell her everything, and to tell *him* everything, and hug him and kiss him and stare at him until her eyes started to water. She wanted so many different things at once that she just stood there in her entryway, hardly able to meet his gaze. He'd parked his suitcase to one side of the door, his coat laid over the handle.

"Hi," Alex said.

"Hi."

Alex used his fingertip to lift her chin. "I'd really like to kiss you now. If that's okay."

He was smiling with his head bowed a little, almost like he felt shy, and she realized how awkward she felt, too. She'd imagined this so many times, built it up so much in her head. She'd thought that the moment she saw him, the last four months would simply melt away. But that hadn't happened yet. That distance was still between them, though Alex stood right in front of her.

Maybe it was like coming in out of the cold—she needed to warm up first. To get used to the idea of him being here.

"I think I need a minute," she said.

Disappointment darkened Alex's expression for a second, but then it was gone. "Of course."

They went to the living room and sat on the couch. Alex put his arm around her, holding her tight against his side. His fingers wound into her hair.

"I love you, Evelyn."

"I…love you too."

There was so much unsaid in that pause—and Alex heard it. "What's wrong?"

She remembered the first time Alex told her that he wanted her, over the summer at the kickoff dance. He'd said everything that she wanted to hear, and still it hurt. Happiness and pain in equal parts. They shared so much history, and not all of it good.

Evelyn put her hand on his cheek, over the scar that stretched from his eye to his chin. His skin was hot, burning into her palm. "I'm sorry. I'm happy, I promise. Is your mom here, too?"

"In a few days. For now, I'm all yours." Alex leaned over and kissed her gently on the cheek. She rested her head in the curve between his shoulder and neck.

"When I showed up in the park I thought you were upset," he said. "You were looking at me like I wasn't even there, like you could see through me or something."

Tell him about the flashes, she thought.

She'd tried to tell him. She really had. A few days after the first one—of her Uncle Sammy as a kid—she'd broached the subject during one of their calls. "What if something changed in my head, because of everything that happened in the tunnels?" she'd said.

Instantly his manner had shifted. The change was subtle —his shoulders tensing, pupils dilating.

"What do you mean?" he'd asked.

"I see things differently. The past…it's not gone. Not for me. It's like you wake up from a nightmare, but then you realize the real world isn't there anymore. And days pass and you start thinking the nightmare won't ever end."

She knew she wasn't making much sense. She was groping for the right words to capture what she'd experienced, why it worried her so much after all the things she'd already seen. But Alex had seemed to shut down, going silent on the screen.

Then he'd whispered, "What do you want me to say?" Pleading with her. He wanted to fix this—fix *her*—but he didn't know how. And that overwhelmed him.

For so long, he'd been trying to protect her.

For years, Evelyn had suspected that she had a deeper connection to Byrne House than sheer proximity could explain. When she first met Alex over the summer, she'd felt that same intuition: that she already knew him, though she couldn't explain how. Yet he denied that he'd met her before.

Then, the night of the kickoff dance, Alex had revealed the secret that everyone—Evelyn's parents, her neighbors, even Alex himself—had kept from her.

She and Alex had met at Byrne House when they were six years old.

On that long ago day, Alex and his brother William had been visiting their relatives at the mansion. Evelyn had gone there with her Uncle Sammy—who still hadn't listened to Nana's warnings about the place, even when he was grown —and she'd befriended Alex. They'd been climbing a tall tree on the grounds when they fell and crashed into one of Walter Byrne's old mine shafts.

It was dark down there, and there'd been thick dust in the air. Alex had been injured all along his left side. At the time, Evelyn had pressed her jacket to his face to staunch the bleeding, the way her mom would've done. The dust and dirt made her cough as she tried to breathe. She could hardly see. The space around them had been almost pitch black. But soon, shapes had begun to appear out of the dark.

Voices had begun to speak. Yet Alex couldn't hear them.

She didn't understand until a few months ago, when she learned about the strange mineral that Walter Byrne had discovered beneath Byrne House. When she was six years old, in the mine shaft, she had inhaled the same crystalline substance that Darren later used to create his serum. She had seen people from the past, experienced their emotions. They'd looked like ghosts. There'd been terror in that underground place, still lingering like an unseen poison. Even now, she didn't know what those people had been so afraid of. But as a child, she'd been so frightened that her mind completely blocked the experience. It had taken her over a decade to finally remember.

Sitting here now, in her living room with Alex, she couldn't help thinking of that day in the mine shaft. And fleeing through the tunnels this past summer, feeling so afraid. She didn't want to look at Alex and always think immediately of those terrible memories. She wondered how much longer she'd have to wait before she only felt good with him.

Stop it, she told herself.

She wouldn't let the past control her. And she didn't want Alex to feel compelled to protect her, either.

"I was just surprised to see you," she said. "Tell me about the flight." *Anything but Byrne House*, she thought.

Alex told her about the annoying woman he sat next to on the plane, the new sci-fi book he started reading. Evelyn tried to let everything else in her mind go quiet. She'd missed the rich sound of his voice in person. No technical issues, no dropped calls, no distance. Finally. In turn, she recounted about half a dozen completely irrelevant things, just enjoying his presence beside her.

Night was settling over the street by degrees. Neither of them got up to turn on the lamp in the living room. After it turned really dark, Evelyn got up on her knees so that they were eye-to-eye.

"I think I'm ready to kiss you now."

"Yeah?" His breath was soft against her cheek.

"Yeah."

She gently ran her fingers across his forehead, around the edge of his ear. She traced her thumb over his profile and his cheekbones, relearning the shape of his face in the dark. His smell she knew by heart, citrus and musk, so familiar it made her ache to think of how long she'd been without it.

She barely brushed her lips over his, anticipating how they'd fit so perfectly with hers.

"You're trying to drive me insane, aren't you?" Alex said.

She laughed, and Alex dove forward to kiss her. Their mouths moved together, each of them remembering what the other liked. When to go fast and intense, how to shift into soft and slow, tilting their heads at just the right angles. Their hands were next, fingers dipping under clothes to reach skin, rediscovering how it felt to be this close.

A car door slammed outside. Heels clacked against the front walk. Evelyn jumped out of Alex's lap and switched on the light just as the key scratched in the lock.

"Mom, guess who's here!"

Vivian lifted her eyebrows as she walked in, pulling her keys from the door.

Alex had gotten up from the couch and followed Evelyn into the entryway. "Hi, Mrs. Ashwood. Hope you didn't miss me too much."

"Alex! Of course we missed you." Vivian dropped her purse and rushed over to give Alex a hug. Alex silently mouthed "wow" over Viv's shoulder.

Evelyn was just as shocked as he was. Her mom hadn't exactly been sad to see Alex leave at the end of summer. After Evelyn's childhood accident on the Byrne House grounds and subsequent memory loss, Vivian had forbidden anything related to the Byrne family. There'd been some drag-out fights between Evelyn and her mom over the summer, and Viv had eventually eased up. But only a bit.

"Here for Christmas?" Viv asked. "Or back for good?"

Alex's eyes darted to Evelyn's, but he didn't hesitate. "Yes to both."

Evelyn's heart rose.

"Should we get some dinner?" she said.

Vivian waved her hand, already heading toward her home office. "You two go ahead. I have a few more things to do. Just be responsible, stay out of trouble. Be home by ten."

Evelyn smiled, a little relieved that her mom sounded like her overprotective self again. Viv had seemed more distracted lately, ever since Evelyn's parents had agreed to separate. Evelyn's father was now permanently living in Baltimore, making official an arrangement that had been the norm for nearly a year.

"I'll keep Ev in line," Alex said.

They walked over to a Thai place a few streets away for dinner. The night was chilly, so they got cups of hot cocoa for the walk back. Houses twinkled with multi-colored lights, and Christmas trees stood proudly in windows.

As they were passing Walter Park, Evelyn saw a figure moving in parallel between the trees. A familiar figure. It took her a moment to be sure she wasn't having a flash.

She let go of Alex's hand. "Can you wait here a minute?"

"Why?"

"I'll be right back. Just wait." She walked onto the grass and into the trees. Jake turned away when he saw her coming and went deeper into the park. Leaves crunched beneath his feet.

Evelyn followed him. "What are you doing?" she asked.

She couldn't see Jake's face where he was standing, out of the reach of the streetlights, but she saw one of his shoulders go up and down. "I dunno. Am I not allowed to be in the park anymore, now that he's back? Does his family own it or something?"

"Could you not follow us around? It's creepy."

Jake laughed harshly. "So just because I'm here in the park when you happen to walk by, I'm stalking you?" He sat on the ground, leaning back against a tree. "I get it, you have the real thing now and you don't need me anymore. Go. Be happy. You don't have to rub it in."

Great. Now he was guilt-tripping her. Evelyn walked over to the tree and stood above him. "You know it wasn't like that. Nothing's changed, we're still…whatever. *Friends*, I guess. Okay?"

He looked up, a feral glow in his eyes. "Wow, thanks. I feel so special."

"I'll see you later, if you can stop acting like a—"

"You do realize she just feels sorry for you, right?" Alex stepped in front of her, looming over Jake. "When are you going to leave her alone?"

"Alex, stop," she said, tugging his arm.

"I should leave her alone? Like you did? I always seem to be the only one around when Evelyn really needs someone."

"She didn't need *you*," Alex said. "She's the one who saved *your* ass from Darren Byrne."

"You're right, she did save my ass. And then I went to get you, like she asked me, because without me telling you where to go you'd never have found her in those tunnels." Jake leaned his head so he could see her behind Alex. "You and I know what happened down there, right Ev? We're the only ones who do. Just like I'm the only one who knows what the past few months have really been like for you."

Alex didn't say anything. Evelyn tried to pull him away, back to the sidewalk, but he resisted. "If you really think you're her friend," Alex said, his voice deep in his throat, "you'll stay away from her. That's the only way she'll get over what happened."

"This is what you've been waiting for?" Jake asked her. "For Evans to show up and talk about you like you're not even here?"

She let go of Alex's arm and started walking across the park toward her house. She didn't want to listen to either of them anymore.

"If you won't leave her alone," Alex said, "I'll make sure that you do. And you'll regret it."

"You hear that, Ev?" Jake yelled. "He's going to protect you from me. He's never protected you from any real threats, so he has to make up new ones."

Evelyn started running and skirted around the house to the backyard. She sat on the patio and waited for Alex to find her. Something that she did far too often, it seemed.

6

IT DIDN'T TAKE HIM LONG. ALEX'S SILHOUETTE appeared around the side of the house. He sat down beside her on the concrete, both of them staring into the darkness of the backyard. Evelyn tucked her cold hands inside her coat sleeves.

"Why didn't you tell me about Jake?" Alex asked.

"Tell you what? I mentioned that I see him sometimes. I guess we're kind of friends." Though friendship wasn't the right word. It was more a type of symbiosis. A dependance that wasn't entirely healthy for either of them. She liked to tell herself that it was all one-sided, that Jake was the one who needed her. But she'd texted him. She'd found comfort in Jake's presence, however fleeting.

"You said earlier that you weren't mad," she said.

"You believed me?" he asked.

Alex reached past her shoulder and gathered up her hair into his hand. The strands slipped gently between his fingers. "I was trying really hard not to be mad this afternoon, even though I wanted to punch that smirk off Jake's face. I can't blame you for wanting to talk to someone, though I don't get why you couldn't pick Milo or Silvia. I just...I thought you were okay here. That things weren't so bad. And then I see you with him in the park—that weird expression on your face—and I realize the only reason you'd be there is if things are still really not okay at all. And I didn't know."

She had no idea what to say. She hated pretending. But with Alex, she was afraid to do anything else.

"You were gone," she said. "You had other things to deal with."

"Like my mother." He sighed, looking up at the sky. "She hasn't had a drink in weeks. She's going to AA meetings, and she has a sponsor. But it's hard for me to know how she's really doing." Alex had only recently discovered that his mom had a problem at all. "Things haven't been easy for any of us since my dad died last year."

"I know." She touched his hand. Their fingers wound together.

"Anytime I brought up Castle Heights, she closed off. But it's hard to blame her. As far as my mom knows, this place has been bad news for everyone in her family."

"Am I included in her definition of 'bad news'?" She'd met Alex's mom a few times when she came to stay at Byrne House in August, and Mrs. Evans had seemed distant. Her eyes had always skimmed past, like Evelyn was just part of the scenery.

"Evelyn, I don't mean you. She likes you. She just wishes that William and I had never inherited part of the estate. If it wasn't for Byrne House, then Will would still be living his old life. At least, that's how my mother sees it. She didn't want me coming back here at all."

When Darren had kidnapped Evelyn, Milo Foster and his grandmother had called the police to Byrne House. William had been the one to answer the door. The police never found any evidence of wrongdoing—since Evelyn and Jake had chosen to stay quiet about the secret lab—but the attention had been enough to send Daniella packing. And when Daniella ran, William had followed her. William had blamed all the trouble on Alex.

In the months since, Alex had seen William just once in New York. The rift between the brothers had only widened.

"Then how'd you change your mom's mind about coming?" Evelyn asked.

Alex grimaced. "Well, I didn't. When I got the message from Will last night, with the flight reservation, I just—"

Evelyn shifted on the grass. "Wait, what message?"

"William e-mailed me out of the blue. He said he was sorry we argued over Thanksgiving and wanted to make up for it. He said he was heading back to Castle Heights, and he asked me to meet him here. He'd already booked my flight. He promised he'd handle everything with my mother. So I just…left. I skipped school today. All I could think about was seeing you."

Evelyn was struggling to process his story. After months of estrangement, William suddenly bought Alex a plane ticket? "Does your mom know you're here?"

"Well…now she does. I called her when I was in the Lyft from the airport. She's been staying off and on with a friend who knows she's sober—I think he's her boyfriend, but of course she won't tell me. She agreed to come here in a couple days. She wants to see Will, too."

"When does he arrive?"

"The message said by Christmas. Why does this matter? I'm *here*. This is what we wanted, right?"

Christmas. That was just over a week away. Evelyn stood up, rubbing her face. None of this made sense. First that letter from Daniella, and now this message from William…

"*Right?*" Alex asked, an edge to his voice. "You're not upset that I interrupted your night with Jake, are you?"

She spun to face him. "Seeing you is *all* I wanted." Her voice was cracking. "Practically all I've thought about since the day you left. I would've—"

She was about to say, *I would've agreed to almost anything*. That's when it hit her: Alex hadn't come here today by chance. And it certainly hadn't been his brother's generosity.

Alex had been delivered here, right to her doorstep, just as surely as that letter was hand-delivered earlier.

7

"WE DON'T KNOW FOR SURE THAT DANIELLA'S behind this," Alex said.

Evelyn had gone inside to get the letter. She'd walked back and forth across the patio while he read the whole thing, using his phone to light the page. Daniella's admission was right there, written in blue ink. *I know exactly what you want, and I'm going to deliver it to you.* Alex just didn't like to believe that he'd been deceived.

"If it was William's idea, why did he write to just you, and not your mom? You don't know when he'll be here because *she hasn't decided yet.* She's trying to manipulate us."

And dammit, Daniella was succeeding. In less than half a day, Daniella had already made good on her promise. Evelyn felt like a pawn, and she didn't even know what game Daniella was playing. If Daniella could deliver Alex here so easily, couldn't she take him away again, too?

Alex threw up his hands. "I don't like it either. But she can't do anything to us. I won't *let* her."

He got up and put his hands on Evelyn's shoulders, stopping her pacing. "You don't honestly believe this stuff in her letter. About Walter's amazing new invention?"

"No, but clearly she wants something from me, and she's trying to use you to get it." Which she should've expected. Evelyn had underestimated Daniella before. "I showed Jake the letter earlier, and right away he thought—"

"*Jake thought?* Sure, if Jake said it then it must be true." He laughed through his nose, a sound devoid of humor.

"Sometimes I feel like I never know what's going on inside your head. But apparently Jake does."

She groaned inwardly. Why had she said his name? What had possessed her?

"Jake doesn't know me. He knows things that happened to me, and yes, sometimes I talk about stuff and he listens."

Alex huffed. She rested her hand on his arm. "But you know *me*, better than anyone." If she kept saying it, maybe she could convince herself that was still true. "Can we just forget about Jake?"

"Tell me you won't see him anymore," Alex said.

"*What?*"

"He just wants to f—" Alex shook his head. "He just wants to sleep with you, Evelyn. It's obvious."

That, she already knew. But Alex was overreacting. "You're being ridiculous." *And about as mature as Jake*, she added silently.

"If he doesn't matter to you, then it should be no problem."

She spread out her fingers and held her palm open, wishing he could see how little she felt for Jake compared to him. Why couldn't he let this go?

"Jake needs me, I can't just—"

"*I* need you. And I want to be the person that *you* need."

"You are," she whispered. "But I won't cut him out of my life just because you're back. You can't ask me that." Jake needed to learn boundaries. But it was her problem to manage, not Alex's. She'd grown up with an overprotective mother. No way was she going to submit to a domineering boyfriend.

Alex glared at her, his eyes hard and flat. She'd seen him jealous before, but never like this. Could he have changed so much in the past few months? Or did she just not know him as well as she'd thought?

"I'm sorry. I know it's not fair of me to ask that." He drew her close again, his heart beating fast against her shoulder. It took her a moment to lean into him.

"I just can't lose you," he said quietly. "You're the only one I still have."

He couldn't mean that—he had friends back in New York. He had his mom. And William would always be his brother. She brushed his hair back from his forehead. "I've been right here this whole time, waiting for you to come back."

"Let me stay here tonight," he murmured against her cheek. "I don't want to go to a hotel. And I *definitely* am not sleeping alone at Byrne House."

Vivian had welcomed him earlier. She might agree to it. "The couch is uncomfortable," Evelyn warned.

"Can't I curl up by the foot of your bed?" He kissed her ear, then the edge of her jawline. "I won't try anything. I swear." She heard the teasing smile in his voice, and knew he was himself again. The Alex she'd missed.

She pushed him away with a laugh. "You expect me to fall for that?"

"What? It worked on all the other girls."

It was a joke. Of course it was. But she felt a familiar prick of disquiet in her chest, all the same. Over the summer, Evelyn's classmate Caitlin Meyer had set her sights on Alex, even asking him to the school's kickoff dance. It had killed Evelyn to see them dancing with their arms around one another. Alex had never viewed Caitlin as anything but a friend, but the very thought of Caitlin and Alex together still made Evelyn's blood rise. Alex must have felt the same about seeing her with Jake.

In a few ways, Alex and Jake had similar flaws. It was a difference in scale, rather than kind. Both were a little possessive, moody when they didn't get their way, with tempers that simmered underneath the surface. Jake had veered toward extremes lately. But Alex—though he could never be cruel—was on edge, too. She had to keep them apart. If she didn't, one of them was bound to push the other over.

And that would not end well.

8

WHEN EVELYN CAME DOWN THE NEXT MORNING, the blanket and pillow were stacked neatly on the living room couch. Alex's suitcase was gone.

She was still looking around, bewildered, when Vivian came into the room sipping a cup of coffee. "Alex was up early," Viv said. "He made breakfast, by the way, if you want some scrambled eggs. That boy's really trying to run up the scoreboard, isn't he?"

"Where is he?"

Viv nodded her head toward the piano. A tented piece of paper sat in between family photos. Evelyn went to reach for the note, but her mother stopped her before she could read it.

"Evvy, you're being careful, aren't you?"

She looked up at her mom. Worry was pulsing off Vivian in waves, like heat shimmering off a desert road. Evelyn blinked, and the colors around her mother's head vanished.

Sometimes the flashes were like that—an aura around a person, revealing hints of their inner thoughts and emotions. It was distracting, and embarrassing too. She didn't want to invade other people's minds. It felt wrong.

"Um…" She tried to focus. "Careful, how?"

She didn't feel like having the birth control discussion again right now. She and Alex hadn't even slept together, though she had no objections to the idea. But she already knew that wasn't what her mom meant.

Vivian brought her coffee cup to her mouth, then lowered it again without taking a sip. "He went over to Byrne House this morning, all right? He wants you to meet him there. I read the note."

"*Mom.*"

"The last time you went to that place, you ended up with a broken leg. And when you were little, you got hurt much worse." Viv held up her hand before Evelyn could speak. "I'm not telling you how to run your life. Not anymore. But I need you to promise me you'll be careful."

Evelyn glanced at the window. The sun was shining, and the last few leaves were drifting down from the trees. Kids were flying a kite in the park. Even the mansion looked cheerful on a day like this.

"I promise to be careful. Can I go now?"

Viv didn't look reassured. "I don't want any other part of you to get broken because of that boy. Least of all your heart."

"I'll be fine," Evelyn said. But an ache—way down in her chest—said that she feared the same thing.

Viv nodded, then turned and left the room.

Evelyn snatched up the note and read it. Alex wanted her to meet him at Byrne House, just like her mom said. But it also told her to check her e-mail. When she did, she found a message with no subject and a single word in the body:

Mirror.

⁓⁕⁓

She rang the mansion's doorbell. Alex answered, opening the door wide. "Did you bring it?"

She patted her messenger bag. For the last four months, the mirror had been sitting in her keepsake box—which had relocated to her bedroom closet instead of the basement. In all that time, Evelyn hadn't been tempted to use it. And not just because of the flashes.

The mirror had once belonged to Ada—Walter Byrne's wife—who'd died tragically after Walter's brother Simon trapped her in the tunnels. For all its miraculous power, the mirror hadn't brought Ada or Evelyn anything but pain. She dreaded using it again. But Alex no doubt had a good reason for his request.

He led her inside. "I couldn't sleep. I was thinking about what you said last night. Daniella's letter? How she's trying to manipulate us? I say we get a step ahead of her. Find out everything we can about Daniella's motives, about this supposed invention she's after."

"What if that's exactly what she wants us to do?"

Alex stopped in the hallway and spun to face her. "Daniella thinks she's smarter than us, right? This is our chance to prove her wrong."

Evelyn understood what Alex had in mind: use the mirror to search Byrne House for memories of Daniella. The mirror showed events that happened in one particular place. Previously, Evelyn had been able to direct the mirror's visions to some extent, searching for individuals or images or strong emotions. But it wasn't like switching on a television and selecting a network. They might not find anything useful at all.

Yet Alex was right—they couldn't just sit here, waiting for Daniella's next move. They had to do something proactive.

Another invention, Daniella had claimed. *His greatest achievement, one that he never had the chance to show his wife.*

"There's something I'd like to check first." Evelyn went down the hall to a set of sliding double doors. Alex raised his eyebrows at her.

She went inside, inhaling deeply. The library smelled the same as she remembered—dust, leather, the perfume of beautiful old things. The shelf that held Walter Byrne's journals was in a quiet corner.

Alex hummed a sound of understanding. "But I don't remember anything about another invention when we read the journals before."

"We were focusing on other things." ·

She ran a finger across the leather-bound volumes. Then she reached a gap on the shelf, right where Walter's final journal should be.

The last time they'd been here in the summer, Evelyn had counted three missing journals. They had found two in a workroom on the third floor of the mansion; Darren, and possibly Daniella, had used Walter's writings in creating the new versions of the crystal serum. And Evelyn also knew the location of the third missing journal: clutched in the hands of Walter's skeleton, in the tomb beneath the labyrinth in the gardens.

But now, another journal was missing.

"There used to be a Volume Twenty-Five," Evelyn said, pointing at the new gap. "Walter's final journal." The very last one that Walter Byrne had written before he died. She was sure she'd glanced through it last summer, but she couldn't conjure up any details aside from messy handwriting and smudged ink.

"I think Daniella took it with her," Evelyn said.

Alex leaned against the bookcase. "I guess that fits with the letter she sent you. Think Daniella's actually telling the truth? She's out searching for this amazing invention?"

Evelyn wasn't quite ready to believe that. "I guess we'll have to use the mirror. Maybe that can tell us."

He nodded at the shelf of journals. "Should we start here?"

"Might as well." Evelyn lifted the flap on her bag and took out the mirror. She steeled herself to look through it. Would she feel sick, the way she did the first time she used it?

But then Alex held out his hand. "I think it should be me."

"You?"

Alex had used the mirror once, last summer, but after that it had always been her. Evelyn had been the one to find the mirror, and she'd had the deepest connection to Ada Byrne. So it had felt natural that she be the one to use it.

But though she'd gotten more accustomed to the physical effects of the mirror—nausea, fatigue—the experience had profound psychological effects as well. Stepping into the skin of another person, reliving their emotions…it could be extremely intense. Even traumatic. She was already living with that every day.

"You don't have to protect me," she said to Alex.

"I'm not. I'm trying to pull my own weight."

Again, Alex held out his hand. This time, she gave him the mirror. He pointed the glass at the bookcase and looked through. Evelyn moved aside, wary of being caught on his periphery. Right now, she had too much in her head that she preferred to keep to herself.

After about a minute, Alex lowered his arm and shook his head.

"I'm not getting anything. Just outlines of people, thoughts running together. No powerful emotions. Nothing really stood out."

"Should I try?" Evelyn asked, though she still wasn't eager.

"I have a better idea."

They went up the main staircase to the second floor. The hallway was long and narrow, capped by a window at the far end. Evelyn's feet sunk into the plush carpet runner.

They stopped in front of a closed door.

"Where are we?" she asked.

Alex pushed open the door, gesturing for Evelyn to go inside. "Daniella's bedroom."

The room was smaller than she'd expected, dominated by a span of windows. A sleigh bed stood against one wall beneath a tapestry of a flowering tree. White and pink blossoms spilled across the fabric like blots of paint. A rug with interlocking, maze-like patterns covered most of the floor, muffling the creaks of the wooden planks under their feet.

The armoire stood open, half the hangers empty, clothes dropped and forgotten on the floor. Daniella had packed in a hurry.

Alex held up the mirror. He positioned himself in front of Daniella's armoire. Then he squeezed his eyes shut and, once again, shook his head. Evelyn started toward him but he said, "Wait. Give me a chance, okay?"

He turned, this time facing the center of the room, and tried again. For several long minutes, Alex stared into the mirror. Then his knees buckled.

"Hey, easy!" Evelyn ran toward him, afraid he'd pass out.

"I'm all right," he said, "just…dizzy."

She set the mirror aside and helped him sit against the wall on the floor. "There was…so much," Alex struggled to say. "Almost all of it blended together."

He kept taking deep breaths. She squeezed his hand. After a few more minutes, he said, "I need to try again."

He reached for the mirror, but Evelyn stopped his hand. "You'd better rest. Did you see anything clearly at all?"

"There was one moment. But it was years ago, I think."

"Tell me," Evelyn said. The mirror worked in strange ways. It didn't always show you what you expected.

Alex rubbed his eyes. "Daniella was in bed. Her mom was standing over her. It was night. Her mom said, 'Dany, please come with me. It has to be now.' But Daniella shook her head and screamed at her mom to get out. She was furious at her mother for something. Hated her."

Her mother. Mrs. Byrne.

Evelyn assumed she had met Daniella and Darren's mother years ago, the same day that she met Alex as a child. But she had no memory of the woman. She'd never thought much about her before.

"Darren told me that their mother left them a long time ago," Evelyn said. "But I don't know what happened."

"I was trying to focus on the day Daniella left here in August. I even think I saw her throwing clothes into a suitcase, just for a second. But then the image shifted to her mother. Why?"

"That moment with her mother must have been a powerful one to Daniella," Evelyn said. "What if Daniella was thinking of her mother the day she ran in August? Remembering that conversation they'd had in the middle of the night, years before?"

Alex managed a smile. "So it's not that I'm just bad at this mirror thing? I saw something important?"

"Maybe." Though she wasn't sure what this knowledge could do for them. "If only we could find Daniella's mother and ask her."

His eyes brightened. "What if we can?"

9

"THAT'S HER, ISN'T IT?" ALEX ASKED, POINTING AT the picture on the wall.

They were in the tower bedroom on the third floor. The photo showed a smiling family of four. There were two children, obviously Darren and Daniella, still elementary age. The man wore a disheveled khaki suit: Reginald Byrne, who'd died in July. And beside him stood a much younger woman with curly dark hair. Her face looked just like Daniella's.

"I don't even know her first name," Evelyn said.

"It's Madeline."

Evelyn glanced up at him, surprised.

"I found some papers in there this morning." Alex pointed to the closet, which still had clothes in it. But unlike Daniella's armoire downstairs, this space was tidy. Men's clothing in dark colors hung neatly from the rod.

"Nothing all that interesting," Alex continued. "But there's an expired California driver's license for a Madeline Byrne. Says she was born in 1970. We could use the information to help find her."

"Seems worth a try."

Evelyn rotated slowly, looking around the circular room. It was decorated in the same style as the rest of Byrne House, with rich dark furniture and wood moldings that stretched up to the ceiling. Lace curtains hung on either side of a large, round window. An upholstered window seat stretched along the wall beneath it.

She'd been up here only once before—last summer, when she and Alex had come here to search for clues about who'd taken Milo. To her, that's what this room represented: those terrible days Milo had been missing. But people had lived here, too. Reginald Byrne, most recently. Madeline Byrne too, at some point in the past. Maybe even Walter and Ada long before them.

"Why were you up here this morning?" she asked Alex.

"As soon as it got light out, I came over here to see if Daniella had left anything behind." His eyes moved along the walls, then over the ceiling.

Evelyn ran a hand over the carved doors of another armoire. "There's so much history in this house. I don't know how long it would take to sort through it all."

She walked slowly to the window. Her house was visible on the other side of the block, across from the park. She couldn't help imagining Milo standing in this very spot, looking out. And Darren Byrne right behind him. She shivered. Her heart was beating like a fluttering bird trapped in a cage.

Alex wrapped his arms around her. "We can go if you want," he said.

"No." She tried to think of how to explain it—the way she felt about this house. What she'd seen all those times that she stared out her window at Byrne House, both frightened and drawn, yet unable to explain why.

"I should hate this place," she whispered. "But I can't." Even now, she found Byrne House fascinating. Beautiful. The way that even a tragic story was beautiful because it was so human and so real.

Alex knelt on the window seat. "I had this dream when I was home. I dreamed that we never fell from that tree in the gardens. You and I never got hurt. Daniella never made her brother go down in the mine, so he never got Walter's sickness. And if that were true, then Darren would never have kidnapped Milo or you or Jake. None of those terrible things would have happened."

His voice had gotten thick.

"But if we'd never fallen, if all those awful things had never happened, then I don't think you and I would be together now. And to me, that seemed worse. How messed up is that?"

Evelyn sat down to face him, resting her forehead against his. "You think I feel any differently?" She was glad that changing the past was impossible. Because she couldn't imagine having to make that kind of choice.

"We're together because of Byrne House," she said. "Maybe we're supposed to make happy memories here, enough to outweigh all the bad."

"I like that." He smiled and kissed her temple. "You know what? I have a surprise for you. I was saving it for later, but I think this is better. Don't move, I'll be back in two minutes." He dashed to the door and ran down the hall.

He was longer than two minutes. Evelyn got up to stretch her legs. She made a circuit of the room, glancing again at the photos of Madeline and Daniella and their family. But they showed only a brief moment in time. There were no pictures of Darren or Daniella growing older. None of the children and their father after Madeline had left. The frames were chipped and caked with old dust, as if they hadn't been moved or even touched in years.

She might've felt sorry for Daniella, if she didn't know better.

Evelyn went to the door and called out, "Alex?" There was no answer. She thought about going to look for him. But she settled on texting him instead. She pulled out her phone and turned back into the tower bedroom.

Something had shifted.

Blood. There was a lot of blood.

There was a thick white comforter on the bed. It hadn't been there before. A huge circle of blood was spreading out on the fabric. In the center of the red circle was a man. He had a halo-like ring of pale colors around his head—an aura—so faded she could hardly see it. As if the aura had almost evaporated away. But a few strands of green and yellow were still moving, twitching in little jumps, almost in time with the uneven dripping of the blood onto the rug. He was facing her, staring at her with a single greyish-blue eye.

The other eye was a ragged hole. Red tinged with black at the edges.

The vision tried to pull her in, take her over. She fought it. She didn't want to experience this. She couldn't.

Evelyn forced herself to blink, and the image was gone.

She pressed her hand over her mouth and ran for the bathroom. Slammed the door shut. She gagged a couple of times over the toilet, spitting out the few sips of coffee she'd had that morning. The water was ice cold when she splashed it onto her face. Then she sat on the basketweave tile, trying to slow down her breathing enough that she could think.

That man had been dead, but those little wisps of color —it was like he'd still been there a little, some part of him seeping away into the air of the room. Just enough that she could feel a deep sadness and loss, though she couldn't tell exactly what had happened to him or who did it. He'd looked young, and his ruined face had borne a look of shock at his fate.

There was a confusing hum of other emotions there too, maybe other long-ago memories somewhere close by. But the thick fog of despair coming from the man's body had blanketed the room, drowning out everything else.

The door closed in the bedroom. Alex.

"Evelyn? Where are you?"

She jumped up and turned on the faucet. "I'll be right out." She hoped the splashing of the water covered how choked her voice sounded.

She pressed her cold, wet hands over her eyes, avoiding herself in the mirror. What was she going to tell Alex? How would that go, exactly? *Oh, Alex, I just saw a murdered corpse lying on that bed there. And by the way, the only other person who knows about these flash things I've been having is Jake.*

There was no way she could tell Alex. Not now, right after they'd had their first real conversation in months. They'd opened up to one another. They'd definitely been having a moment. She'd tell him this afternoon—she just needed a chance to prepare.

Alex was holding her phone when she came out. "You dropped this."

"Oh. Right." She took the phone and pocketed it, careful to avoid looking at the bed. The bloody white comforter was gone, but just the thought of it made her bile rise again.

Alex sat on the window seat. He produced a little white box. "Sorry I took so long. Bottom of my suitcase."

Evelyn wanted to escape from that room, to go anywhere else. Alex stood partway up and gripped her wrist, pulling her onto the seat. "Come on. It's good. I promise."

He put the box into her hands. "Here. The top slides, like this."

He was smiling widely, fiddling with the hem of his shirt. He was nervous. Evelyn took a steadying breath and opened the box.

Inside lay a silver ring on a bed of white tissue paper.

"What is this?"

He laughed. "Don't worry. Not on my knees just yet." He picked the ring out of the box and held his palm open for her to see. It was a silver band, with tiny details of vines and flowers carved into the sides.

"It was Ada's," he said. "I thought you should have it."

Ada's. She took the ring from his hand and rubbed its surface between her fingers. It was silky smooth on one side, ridged with the carvings on the other. "It's gorgeous. Where did you find it?"

"My dad's cigar box. Remember the secret compartment I told you about last month, what I found? This was in there, but I wanted it to be a surprise."

Alex took the ring back and straightened out the fingers of Evelyn's right hand. He slipped the ring onto the finger next to her pinky. He looked up, his smile dazzling. "Fits you. You like it, right? I was worried it might be too morbid or something, because of what happened to Ada, or remind you too much of—"

"I love it." She did, truly. It reminded her of the good in Ada's life, the love. "But are you sure it's okay that I have it?"

He twisted the ring around her finger with his thumb. "My dad wanted me to give it to someone I loved more than anything."

Hot tears sprang into Evelyn's eyes and spilled onto her cheeks. Her lips started to tremble, wanting so much to tell Alex everything, while at the same time she swore to herself that she never could. She'd never spoil the beautiful memory of this moment. Not for Alex, at least.

"Is this one of those girl things, where crying hysterically means you're happy?"

She nodded, sniffling. "Thank you. I love it. And you. More than anything, you."

Don't think of what you saw. Don't don't don't

Alex slid down onto the floor, then pulled Evelyn into his lap. He cupped the back of her neck and kissed her. She put her hand on his cheek, kissing him back, but then her eyes flew open. They were on the carpet beside the bed.

Where the blood had been dripping onto the ground, spreading in a pool of red.

She pushed her hands against Alex's chest, but he didn't realize she was upset. He started nudging her shirt up along the side of her waist. She turned her head and his mouth slid onto her cheek.

"Alex, stop!"

He leaned back. "What's wrong?"

"Couldn't you tell I wasn't enjoying that?" She sounded harsher than she'd meant.

"Oh. I'm sorry. I didn't realize…"

She got up and crossed the room, holding her palm to her mouth.

"I feel awful about the things I said last night," he said softly, "but I've been trying to make up for it. I thought…"

She swallowed the bitter taste in her throat. "No, I'm sorry. You didn't do anything wrong. It's me." He was doing everything to be the perfect boyfriend, and she'd reacted like he was some kind of pervert.

Alex moved back to the window seat and leaned his head against the glass. Clearly he was waiting for her to say something else. At first, the words wouldn't come. And then she started to speak, hardly even thinking about what was coming out of her mouth.

"Everything's happening so fast." She was hiding the most immediate reason for her dismay, but different truths were bubbling up to the surface. "You only got back yesterday, and you wanted to spend the night and then you give me this ring and say everything I could want you to say, and—"

"And you thought I did that because I expected to get something? *Here?*" He gestured at the tower around them. "That's the guy you think I am?"

"I didn't say that."

They were both silent for an awkward minute. Then Alex stood up, his expression wracked with uncertainty. "No, you're right. I didn't mean to push you. Can we go back to your house? Start over?"

"I'll show my mom the ring," Evelyn offered.

He smiled, though his eyes were distant.

I'm the one who should feel guilty, she thought. And she did. She'd been lying to him since the moment he returned. Every second that passed, it got harder to finally tell him. But she'd meant what she said: Alex had been back in Castle Heights for less than twenty-four hours, yet he was already asking for so much. *I can't lose you*, he'd said. *You're the only one I still have.* Maybe what Alex needed was more than she could give.

They went into the hall and back down the stairs. The dead man's face—that despair—resurfaced in her mind. A tear slipped from her eye. She quickly wiped it away. She'd never met him, and yet somehow she knew him intimately. She'd shared the last moments of his life. As she and Alex left the mansion and walked toward her house, two questions burned within her. Each demanded an answer.

Who was that man?

And who had killed him?

10

THE NEXT MORNING, EVELYN OPENED THE FRONT door. Silvia and Milo stood on the porch. Their shoulders and hats were dusted with snow—the first snow of the season. Silvia lunged, pulling her into a hug.

"I'm so glad you texted," Silvia said into Evelyn's ear. "I've missed you."

Evelyn smiled at Milo over Silvia's shoulder. Milo gave her an awkward wave. In the summer, before she and Alex got together, Evelyn and Milo had been close. But they'd grown distant in the months since. Evelyn had gotten the sense that he simply wanted to forget everything that happened at Byrne House. For her, that wasn't an option.

Evelyn's mom appeared in the entryway, pointing her greasy spatula at them. "If anyone wants crepes, come and get them before they're cold."

Milo hung up his coat and headed for the kitchen, with Silvia close behind.

"Where's Alex?" Vivian asked. "Doesn't he want breakfast?"

She'd made crepes for *Alex*? *Now* who was trying to run up the scoreboard?

"He just left. He's picking up his mother from the airport." Evelyn had offered to go with him, but Alex declined. His mother probably didn't want her there.

After breakfast, Milo took dish duty. Silvia and Evelyn sat on the steps of the front porch, bundled in their coats and gloves against the cold. The sky was white, bristling with wind and sleet. "You should have told me Alex was coming back," Silvia said. "I've had the feeling lately that I'd be the last person you told if anything big happened to you."

"Oh Silvia, you know that's not true."

Silvia gave her the side-eye. "What about that ring you're wearing?"

Evelyn pulled off her glove. She described how Alex had given it to her yesterday—omitting the more uncomfortable moments. She spun the ring around her finger. Yesterday, Viv had given her a few pointed looks about the ring. She clearly didn't think her daughter was ready for such signs of commitment. But she was trying to welcome Alex, and that meant a lot.

"Okay," Silvia said, brushing snowflakes off her pants. "What's next on the list of things you haven't been telling me? 'Cause I'm not letting you off the hook that easy."

Evelyn gritted her teeth. "Jake and I talk sometimes. About what happened to us last summer."

Silvia nodded, her brows tight. "You can talk to me about that too. You know that, right? I'm a lot stronger than people give me credit for."

Evelyn smiled. "I just needed a little reminder. Now, you want to tell me what's up with you and Milo?"

Half an hour later, they shed their winter layers and went to the living room. Evelyn's mom passed by on her way out, saying she had some errands to run. Milo and Silvia sat together on the couch, while Evelyn took the easy chair beside the fireplace. Vivian had started a fire that morning, and it crackled and sparked, spilling warmth into the room.

Silvia put her hand on Milo's leg, which made Milo's eyebrows shoot up.

"She knows," Silvia said in a stage whisper.

"Oh. Okay, then. Good." Milo put his arm around Silvia, and they relaxed into one another, in the way of two people who share a comfortable intimacy. So they'd been pretending around Evelyn, too. It had taken this long for Silvia and Milo to share their happiness. How close had

Evelyn come to losing her two best friends without even realizing it?

Evelyn rubbed her hands against the knees of her jeans. "Silvia, I do need your help. Milo's too." She looked over at Milo. He smiled encouragingly.

"You both know about Ada Byrne's mirror," Evelyn continued. "How it can show you the past. But now, I'm having visions without the mirror, too."

They both sat back in surprise.

"I saw a dead man lying in the tower bedroom of the mansion. He'd been murdered." Evelyn's eyes stung with tears. "But I couldn't tell Alex. I don't want to mess things up with him again just when we've started to fix them."

"Wow," Silvia said. "This all makes so much more sense now."

"It does?" Evelyn asked. It still didn't make sense even to her.

Silvia smiled like she had this all figured out. "You saw a ghost. At first, you needed that mirror thing to see it, but lots of people can see ghosts without any help. Like Milo's great aunt—Mimi sees ghosts all the time."

"Mimi?"

Silvia waved her hand dismissively. "You'll meet her. Anyway, it's not that strange. I wish you'd told me before, but I get that you'd want to keep this a secret. Not everyone is a believer."

"I don't think ghost is the right word," Evelyn said. "It was an intense emotion. Emotions can leave impressions on a place, and the mirror—"

"Exactly," Silvia said, that same knowing smile on her face. "A ghost. So where do we start?"

"With what?" Evelyn asked.

"Solving the mystery!"

11

THEY STARTED IN HER MOM'S OFFICE.

"I'll Google old news articles about murders and suicides in Castle Heights," Milo said, already typing on the computer.

"And missing persons," Silvia added. "In case the killer disposed of the body and destroyed the evidence." She laughed at Evelyn's uneasy expression. "What? I've been streaming a lot of *NCIS* lately."

"What was the guy's clothing like?" Milo asked. "Any idea of the decade?"

Evelyn sat on her mom's desk. "Well, he had on jeans." She pictured the man sprawled out on the bed, trying to see the image clinically. Still, her stomach burned. "He had kind of long, blondish-brown hair." Matted with blood.

Milo turned around in his seat to face her. "What kind of shirt?"

After a slow, calming breath she said, "A white button down and a fraying tweed blazer. Sort of professory. But he wasn't that old—twenties, maybe?"

Blood had been inching up one of his cuffs. She could picture him so clearly, even the gold-colored stubble on his chin and the slight movement of a few strands of his hair. And that awful feeling of sadness, dissipating from around him into the air. She squeezed her eyes shut.

"Are you okay?" Silvia asked.

Evelyn nodded. "That's all I can remember. His clothes seemed pretty normal, so it couldn't have been that long ago. Maybe within the last few decades? I know it's not much to go on."

Her phone buzzed in her pocket. A text message. She pulled it out, hoping it was Alex.

Jake.

His text read, *Look out your front window.* She went to the living room and saw Jake leaning against the tree in her front yard.

She went back to her mom's office. "I'm going to take a break." Milo gave her a thumbs up. He and Silvia didn't look up from their screens.

Then she rushed out the front door, grabbed Jake by the arm and pulled him around the side of the house.

"What are you doing?" Evelyn hissed.

"Don't look at me like that."

"Like what?"

"I just wanted to talk to you. And maybe say hi to Milo. I saw him go inside."

"Since when are you and Milo friends again?" she asked.

Jake shrugged, avoiding her gaze. "We talk sometimes. He seems to care enough to check on me every once in a while. See if I'm still alive."

She rolled her eyes. It had only been two days since she last talked to Jake. "Fine, good to see you're alive. So what did you want to talk to me about?"

He shoved his hands in his pockets. "I was just worried about you. Those flashes you've been having, and the possibility of Daniella coming back." He shrugged, still turned away from her. "If you're too busy I can go. Obviously you feel well enough to bitch at me, so I guess you're okay."

She touched his shoulder. His muscles tensed under her palm, then relaxed. "I did have another flash, a really terrible one." She paused, unsure whether she should share this. But then the words spilled out. "I saw a dead man at

Byrne House, and it definitely freaked me out. I think he might've been murdered. Milo and Silvia are helping me figure out who it was."

She dropped her hand from his shoulder. Jake turned around.

"The Byrnes probably dumped the body down in the tunnels. Nobody would find it. Wouldn't be the first time, and certainly not the last, right?"

She kneaded her thumbs against her throbbing temples. "Not in the mood for black comedy right now."

"I wasn't kidding."

"Why don't we talk about how screwed up you are instead?" Evelyn asked. "I'm sure you had all sorts of scary dreams last night to tell me about. Did Darren catch up to you this time?"

"I'd rather talk about you."

She leaned against the side of the house. "Turning down the opportunity to talk about yourself? That's a first."

"Maybe I've changed." Jake's voice had dropped near a whisper. "You just haven't noticed yet."

"I'd better go back to help Silvia and Milo. They're going to come looking for me any minute."

He looked down at the ground, pouting. "Does Alex know about the dead body?" he asked.

"I haven't told him."

"But you've told me. Doesn't that say something?"

She turned around and headed back toward the house. She had no answer to Jake's question. Not that she would have given it to him, even if she did.

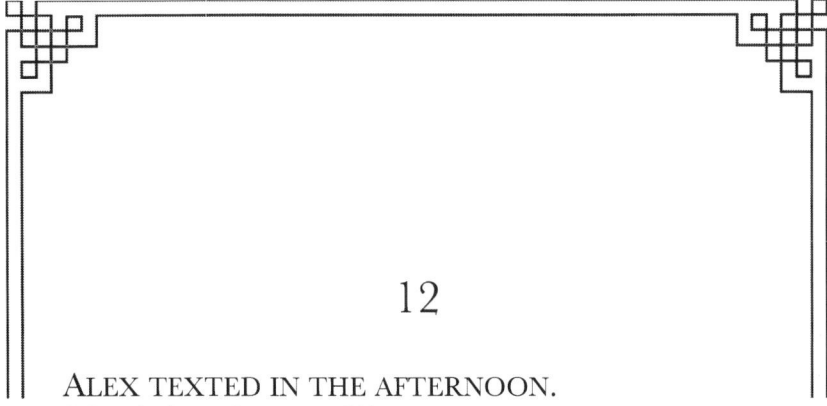

12

ALEX TEXTED IN THE AFTERNOON.

Mom is here. Come say hi?

She ignored the flurry of nervousness in her belly. "Mom, I'm going out for a while!" Evelyn grabbed her bag and keys, heading for the front door.

Footsteps came from the kitchen. "Evvy, wait. I wanted to talk to you."

Evelyn spun on her heel, sighing. "Mom, I told Alex I'd meet him. I haven't seen him all day." Silvia and Milo had only left an hour ago, after a long and fruitless span of internet searches.

Vivian took the keys out of Evelyn's hand and steered her to the living room couch. "I spoke to your dad last night," Viv said in a rush.

Not what she'd expected. "And...?"

Viv crossed one leg over the other, wiggling her red toenails. "I invited him to come stay with us for a couple of days. I know he misses you so much."

Does he? Evelyn thought. She was supposed to have visited him over Thanksgiving break. She'd booked a train to see Alex in New York during the trip. But then her dad cancelled; too busy with work. Different day, same old story.

"I have a lot going on," Evelyn said.

"You know your dad likes Alex."

"Yeah, I know." They'd met in the hospital after Evelyn broke her leg. Unlike Vivian, Evelyn's father had been almost too gracious to Alex. Playing the "cool dad" role, no doubt.

Viv reached back to arrange the pillows behind her. "I have some things I'd like to talk to him about."

"What kinds of things?"

She shrugged, lacing her fingers together in her lap. "Mom and Dad things."

Evelyn got up and went over to the fireplace, a million possibilities spinning through her head. What did Viv want to discuss with Evelyn's dad that she couldn't over the phone? Evelyn doubted it was about her. She and Viv hadn't even fought in ages.

"I've just been thinking that it could be time for a change," Viv said.

Evelyn stared at the family pictures on top of the piano, her chest tightening with emotions she couldn't describe. She'd felt almost no connection to her father in a very long time. But once, the three of them had been happy.

She spotted a photo of her parents dancing together. Smiling, laughing, their eyes locked. That kind of emotion didn't just disappear. The memories of their happiness probably permeated every surface in this house. Evelyn had worked hard to avoid having any flashes of her parents together—because seriously, gross—but she'd felt those old longings just the same. The way they once loved each other as intensely as she and Alex did now.

Was it my fault? Evelyn wondered. *Did my problems drive a wedge between them?*

"I don't remember this photo," she said, pointing at the image of her parents on the dance floor. And there were more over on the mantle, new ones that hadn't been here before. Her mom usually took the opposite tack, disposing of old photos and keepsakes without a thought. Especially photos of people who'd disappointed her.

Viv joined her. "I was going through old boxes. Reminiscing about the good times, I guess." She picked up the frames on the mantle and examined them one by one. "Do you remember your uncle?" she asked.

Evelyn looked up in surprise. She thought of her first flash, the one of Uncle Sammy as a child. "A little," she said.

Her mom scooped up a picture of the two of them, Viv and her brother, standing arm in arm. "Sammy was back from college here, looking so intellectual in that smelly tweed coat he bought at a thrift store. He would've loved your style, you know. All the vintage stuff...He was so handsome. I wonder what he's doing now." She put the frame back on the mantle, eyes wistful. "Probably skydiving in Cambodia or married to some fashion model. He could never turn down a thrill."

It had been a very long time since Vivian had mentioned her brother with anything but hostility. Sammy had been the one to bring Evelyn to Byrne House on the day she and Alex fell. Afterward, he and Vivian had such a falling out that Sammy had left Castle Heights. They'd never had a word from him since.

Apart from that flash of him as a child, Evelyn didn't remember him at all except for the photos. But that shaggy blond hair, that tweed coat...

No.

Evelyn's phone chirped with a text and she jumped, almost knocking the photo off the mantle.

"Is that Alex?" Vivian asked. "Weren't you going to meet him?"

Evelyn hadn't moved, her eyes still frozen to the picture. A sickening realization was spreading through her. The man who'd been murdered inside Byrne House, who'd died in the tower bedroom—

He was her uncle. Sammy Stanton.

13

"Evelyn! It's been far too long."

Ms. Foster beamed when she opened her front door.

"Sorry I haven't been by in a while."

Evelyn was still reeling from the revelation a few minutes ago—that her Uncle Sammy had been murdered inside Byrne House. It couldn't have been suicide. Otherwise, why wouldn't anyone have known? No, somebody had covered up his death. The same person who'd killed him.

She'd come straight here to Ms. Foster's, hoping to find answers.

"I'll get the kettle heating," Ms. Foster said. "I hope I can at least find some cookies in my pantry somewhere. I've been running low on provisions, as of late."

She cast an annoyed glance upward, just as thumping came from upstairs. "My sister."

Ah, Evelyn thought. The "Mimi" that Silvia and Milo had mentioned. More banging came from the second floor, along with a burst of classic rock that Evelyn identified as Stevie Nicks.

"She's driving me nuts," Ms. Foster whispered.

Ms. Foster was Milo's grandmother, and she knew pretty much everything that went on in Castle Heights. Aboveground, at least. She had no idea that tunnels connected to secret entrances in basements all over the neighborhood—including in her own house. But she might know something about Sam Stanton's connection with Byrne House.

They went into the living room, which looked very different from the last time Evelyn saw it: dreamcatchers hung in front of the windows and colored quartz crystals sat on every flat surface. The chairs and sofa were draped with southwestern woven blankets. A Christmas tree glinted with bright pink and blue tinsel. The scents of incense and herbs hit Evelyn's nose, quite a contrast to Ms. Foster's usual aroma of tea, whiskey and butter.

Despite the changes, Evelyn felt her shoulders begin to relax. She helped make the tea, humming *Rhiannon* under her breath. The chairs scraped the wood floor as they sat down at the table.

"Before anything else," Ms. Foster said, "I want to apologize for hiding things from you. I thought I was doing the right thing, based on what your mother had told me. I had to abide by her wishes. But I hate that I hurt you."

Evelyn lifted her teacup, then set it down again. The porcelain tinkled.

For years, Vivian had kept Evelyn's childhood accident at Byrne House a secret. She'd asked neighbors like Ms. Foster to never mention the incident. Evelyn was embarrassed that so many people knew the truth that she'd only recently learned herself. But she'd found peace with her mother in recent months. If she started thinking about her mom's mistakes, she'd end up angry again. And Evelyn had plenty of other things to be angry about.

"Actually, I wanted to ask you something about that day —when I fell at Byrne House. My unc—"

A woman wearing a rainbow-colored caftan and tight yoga pants swept into the kitchen. "You didn't tell me we had a guest among us, Joyce," the woman said.

Ms. Foster sighed. "Evelyn, this is my younger sister Mimi. She's visiting from Sedona. Mimi, this is Milo's friend Evelyn."

"Of course! Silvia's mentioned you." Mimi wore layers of wooden-beaded necklaces over her gauzy top, along with a pair of glasses straight out of a Warby Parker commercial. Her hair was flowing and auburn colored, with streaks of grey at the temples. She studied Evelyn intensely with sapphire blue eyes, the same color as her glasses. Her smile disappeared.

"Your aura is very unusual, Evelyn." The woman's bright blue eyes examined her. Then she flinched, taking a step back. "Are you feeling well? There's something…ill about you."

Ill? "I'm fine," Evelyn insisted. The tiny teacup started shaking in her hand, and she set it on the table.

Ms. Foster got up, waving her sister away. "That kind of talk upsets people, Mimi. Evelyn and I are right in the middle of something. Can you give her a reading another time?"

Mimi backed away, though she still looked concerned. She grabbed a cookie from the plate and left, her gauzy caftan trailing behind her.

"I'm sorry about that," Ms. Foster said under her breath. "Mimi takes her hobbies very seriously. Apparently I'm not attuned to the right vibrations."

There *was* a different hum here, something calming that Evelyn could feel beneath her skin. She wouldn't have noticed if Ms. Foster hadn't given a name to the sensation.

"She does mean well," the older woman added. "Mimi came to Castle Heights to cleanse my house of bad energy. Because of the break-in. It seems to be a lengthy process."

In August, Darren Byrne had broken into Ms. Foster's home through the tunnels. He'd been looking for Walter Byrne's missing journal. Of course, he didn't find anything.

Evelyn was still curious about Mimi and about that hum in the air, but she had a more pressing question. "Actually, I came to ask you about my Uncle Sammy. My mom's younger brother I mean, Sam Stanton."

Ms. Foster tilted her head warily. "Why do you ask, did you hear from him?"

Evelyn pushed away the image of Sam lying motionless in a pool of drying blood. "I saw a picture of him on our mantle, and it got me thinking. My mom doesn't like talking about why he left, but I couldn't help wondering what happened."

They're the reason he ran, Vivian had let slip once. *Those Byrne people. Anyone who gets involved with them regrets it in the end.*

"I know that my uncle was at Byrne House the day Alex and I had our accident," she said. "But I was wondering what connection Sammy had to the Byrnes in the first place. Were they just neighbors? Friends?"

"You mean you don't know?" Ms. Foster's tea almost spilled as she set it down. "Sam Stanton was Daniella and Darren's private tutor. He worked over at Byrne House for at least six months before he left town. He even lived at the guest house. He'd wanted to be close to you and your mom, or so I heard."

"I had no idea." Why hadn't Viv told her this? Why hadn't *Daniella*?

"According to the rumors, Sammy got fired for..." Ms. Foster glanced away uncomfortably. "Inappropriate behavior."

Evelyn recoiled, pushing away her tea. "What does that mean?" she asked, though she was afraid to hear the answer. Nausea rose in her throat.

"It may well have been unfounded. But the Byrnes drummed him out of town."

Sammy hadn't ever left Castle Heights. He'd died in that house, in that tower room. But why?

A memory came to her. A series of images, really. A man's golden head thrown back, the glint of sunlight on his white teeth as he smiled, twirling her in circles on the front lawn until she was so dizzy she couldn't stand up straight. She'd collapsed onto the grass and the world had kept spinning around her into a beautiful, mysterious haze of yellow and blue and laughter.

And then, he was just gone. Like a cloud had blotted out the light.

Had that been him? Her uncle?

"It's odd," Ms. Foster said. "Within a year after your and Alex's accident, the whole Byrne family was in tatters. Madeline had left, and Daniella and Darren were on their way to boarding school, not to return to Byrne House until after Reginald died."

Not long after the accident, Daniella had tricked her little brother into entering the same mine shaft where Alex and Evelyn fell. Darren had inhaled so much of the mineral dust, and had been so terrified, that he'd never been the same. Daniella had been horrified that Evelyn knew her deepest, darkest secret. Evelyn had learned all of this in the underground lab, when she'd seen into Daniella's mind.

And yet…Evelyn had also had the sense that there was more beneath the surface. More that Daniella didn't want her to see.

"What about Madeline Byrne?" Evelyn asked. "What was she like?"

Ms. Foster tapped a fingernail against the table. "Oh, let's see. She was beautiful. A bit aloof. I didn't know her well. She seemed distant from everyone, her husband and children included. I always had the sense that she wasn't happy, so I wasn't surprised when she left."

"Do you know where she went?"

Ms. Foster held her hands open. "I haven't a clue. It was very sudden, and very soon after Sammy was fired. That's why—well, there were rumors, as I've said. One of the rumors was that Sammy and Madeline got a little too close."

Uncle Sammy and Daniella's mother? "I can't believe all this." Evelyn scooted back in her chair. What else about her family did she not know?

"I think there was even an article in our local paper. It must've been terribly embarrassing for your mom, on top of already being so distraught that you were hurt."

"There was an *article*? Can I see it?"

Ms. Foster hesitated only briefly. Then she nodded. "Of course you can, if I have it. What's mine is yours."

They went upstairs and passed the guest room door. Stevie Nicks's smoky voice still crooned from inside. Ms. Foster went into her office and dug around until she found a box of *Castle Heights Register* issues from about a decade ago. The paper had only issued once a month, so luckily there weren't too many to sort through.

"I'll be on my laptop in the living room if you need anything." Ms. Foster retreated downstairs. She seemed to sense that Evelyn would rather do this alone.

Evelyn knelt on the office rug, lifted the lid off the box, and started to look. The papers at the bottom were oldest, so she started there, scanning until she found the issues from about twelve years ago.

Discarded papers started to pile up on the floor.

She couldn't find any mention of her uncle, though she saw plenty of old photos of Madeline Byrne: the same woman with curly dark hair that Evelyn had seen in the tower bedroom. She scanned one article after another, until the words started blending together. She was about to give up.

Then she found something. But it wasn't about Uncle Sammy.

It was about her and Alex. The day they fell.

May 27, 20—

Byrne House Grounds Safe?

After two children—a local resident and a young relative of the Byrnes—fell on the grounds of Byrne House this month, resulting in a brief hospitalization, neighbors are asking owner Reginald Byrne to order an extensive survey of his property to search for other structural weaknesses. According to a neighbor, who asked not to have her name revealed, the Byrnes may have been aware of such weaknesses on the grounds for years. "It was just a matter of time before somebody fell into a part of the old mine," the anonymous neighbor said. "Why aren't they allowing a thorough search? Makes me wonder what they're trying to hide."

Madeline Byrne responded to the Register's inquiries on the family's behalf. "We have children of our own, so we certainly understand the neighborhood's concerns," she said. "But this was just an unfortunate accident. We've looked into the problem, and there's no more cause for worry."

In response to the suggestion that the family has something to hide, Mrs. Byrne responded with laughter. "We certainly are not hiding anything underneath Byrne House," she told the Register. "The accident happened in a fragment of mine shaft, leftover from before the house was built. I've been down there myself, and I saw absolutely nothing but rusted mining equipment."

So far, the Byrnes have declined a search of their property. The topic is on the agenda for the next meeting of the Castle Heights Neighborhood Association, currently set for June 18.

It was surreal, finding a newspaper article about herself that she'd never known existed. Evelyn wondered if the anonymous neighbor might be her mother. She replaced the other newspaper articles in the box.

Ms. Foster was sitting on the living room sofa, typing away.

"Can I keep this one?" Evelyn asked.

"Take it," Ms. Foster said. "Let me know if there's anything else I can do to help."

Evelyn said goodbye and left, her thoughts occupied by all she'd learned.

Ms. Foster had said that Madeline and Sammy might've been involved romantically. And then both of them supposedly left town shortly thereafter. Evelyn knew that her uncle had never left Byrne House. What if the same was true of Daniella's mother?

What if Madeline Byrne was dead as well?

14

EVELYN DUCKED UNDER A LOW-HANGING BRANCH. The trees were dotted with flecks of snow.

She was in the Byrne House gardens. She'd felt drawn here after leaving Ms. Foster's. Somewhere, among these trees, was the place where she and Alex fell. Sammy and Madeline Byrne had been here as well. The answers were waiting if she could just find them.

The morning's brief storm had passed. A light breeze blew. Dead, wet leaves rustled underfoot.

Evelyn took the path around the edge, heading toward the taller trees. The brush was thicker here, the brick paths overgrown with weeds. One tree towered above the others.

The tallest evergreen, Alex had told her. *We decided to climb it.*

Maybe she should've brought the mirror—she could scan the gardens for some sign of her uncle. Or perhaps she didn't even need the mirror. She relaxed her eyes, concentrating. She pictured her uncle's face. Her head began to ache.

Sammy, she thought. *Where are you?*

Then, she saw something. The faint outlines of a figure. A person—the memory of a person—walking away from her. The figure had long, dark hair instead of her uncle's blond. A woman. Leading her even deeper into the gardens.

The figure disappeared into a thicket. Evelyn pushed into the dense wall of green. Thorns scraped her arms and scratched at her clothes. The figure was just ahead, dark hair swaying, pale clothes almost lost amid the branches.

Evelyn stepped into a clearing of clover and short grass. "Hello?" she whispered. But the figure she'd been chasing was gone.

Instead, she found herself staring at a thick block of stone. Its surface was smooth white, and it reached as high as Evelyn's head. She went closer. From here, Byrne House was out of sight. And so was she, at least from the perspective of anyone on the garden paths.

There were words etched into the marble. She read the inscription:

AD PERPETUAM REI MEMORIAM.

"Evelyn," someone yelled. "Evelyn?"

It took her a moment to understand—it was Alex's voice. He was out in the gardens somewhere, looking for her.

She pushed back out of the clearing and nearly plowed into him. "Hey!" He caught her by the elbows, his brow knitting together.

"I thought I saw you out here," Alex said. "What're you doing?"

She'd forgotten about Alex's text earlier. She was supposed to meet up with him and his mother. "Is your mom here?"

"She wants us to stay at Byrne House instead of a hotel. Which I would've told you if you'd texted me back."

"I'm sorry. I lost track of time."

"Okay then, what's up? What's so important?"

Evelyn glanced behind her. "I'll show you." She found the gap in the bushes again. She and Alex came out into the clearing. Alex turned in a circle, staring at the treetops above them.

"I think this is near where we fell." Alex pointed at the tallest evergreen, which seemed to stretch into the sky. "That's the tree."

"That's what I thought, too."

Alex reached for her hand. She squeezed back, knowing that he felt the same confusing mix of emotions that she did right now: fear of the dark place that was somewhere beneath their feet, yet also a sense of longing for that day that had bound them together.

Alex traced a finger over the inscription in the stone. "How'd you find this place?"

Evelyn thought of her conversation with Silvia that morning. *You saw a ghost*, Silvia had said. To tell the truth, Evelyn didn't know anymore what she'd seen. She'd thought it was another flash, some fragment of a memory like all the others. But she liked the ghost explanation better. It had nothing to do with Darren or his serum or the tunnels. Or, for that matter, Jake.

"I followed a woman with dark hair." She scratched her eyebrow, trying to act nonchalant. "I think maybe it was a ghost."

"A ghost? You're serious?"

Evelyn crossed her arms, shrugging. "Why not? Is a ghost really any stranger than a magic mirror that sees the past?"

He held up his hands, palms out. "Hey, I didn't say I don't believe you. I was just surprised. Actually…" He smiled sheepishly, pushing his hair back from his forehead. "I thought maybe I saw a ghost in my apartment in New York."

"*Really?* When?"

"I thought maybe it was my dad. Or at least, wished it was him. This happened around Thanksgiving."

Ah, Evelyn thought. The same time as the anniversary of his father's death.

Alex shook his head, smiling. "I don't know what it was, really. But we've both seen things we can't explain. When it comes to Byrne House especially, nothing should surprise us anymore."

He pulled her close and rested his chin on her head. Evelyn lay her cheek against his shoulder. He wore a flannel jacket that smelled of pine. For a moment she closed her eyes, relaxing into him.

"I missed you this morning," he said. "I finally got a call from William. I asked him, point blank, if Daniella bought my plane ticket."

Evelyn looked up at Alex. "What did he say?"

"He admitted that she orchestrated this 'reunion.' He claimed it's her early Christmas present to all of us, and he swore he was happy about it."

I knew it, Evelyn thought. "When do they arrive?"

"Soon. But they have to do something first. He wouldn't say what. I thought my mom would be pissed, but she's just excited to see William again. That's where Mom got the idea to stay at Byrne House instead of the hotel—because my brother asked."

More manipulation. Daniella wasn't doing much to hide it. *And we're all lining up for her, aren't we?* Evelyn thought. *Pawns moving around the board.*

The veins in Evelyn's temples were throbbing. "Do you think William knows what Daniella is really planning?"

Alex let go of her. "No. I don't. He sounded exhausted, actually." He leaned against the stone marker, like he was the one who felt tired.

"I went to talk to Ms. Foster," Evelyn said. "I learned more about Madeline Byrne. And I found this."

She stuck her hand in her pocket and felt the crinkle of old paper. The article.

"It's about us."

⁓⟍⟍⟋⟋⁓

They sat down on a sunny patch of grass. The morning's snow had melted here, and the ground was just slightly damp.

She waited for Alex to say something. He was quiet for a long while. Then he turned the newspaper clipping over, like he expected to see something more on the back. But it was just an advertisement.

"Why would Madeline Byrne say there was nothing down there but mining equipment?" Alex asked. "It's hard to remember exactly what I saw down there. But mining equipment? I don't think that was it."

Evelyn's memories were even fuzzier, more a series of feelings and sensations rather than clear pictures. "Tell me again what you saw," she asked. They hadn't discussed it in detail for months—not since the night of the kickoff dance.

Alex's face grew somber as he spoke. "When we first fell, I could hardly see. It seemed so dark, and I was confused and scared and in a lot of pain. I could hear your voice. Your hands found me. I couldn't really see you though. There was so much dust. And blood."

He cleared his throat. Then wiped his mouth with the back of his hand.

"The dust settled down. Pretty soon you started, you know—hearing voices that weren't there. Seeing things. But the space was so empty." Alex closed his eyes, as if he was visualizing the scene. "There was no equipment, no tools, nothing like that. The only sign that another person had ever been down there was a stone archway. I think it led somewhere else."

"A tunnel?" Evelyn asked. "Part of the mine?"

"I don't know." Alex screwed up his lips, his eyes still closed. "Sometimes, I imagine that we actually went into that passage, trying to find a way out. But I don't know if I just dreamed that part."

They'd both had strange dreams about Byrne House. Dreams that featured hidden doors, maze-like passages. It was hard to tell what was real and what wasn't.

Suddenly, Alex's eyes shot open. "There were *stairs*."

"Stairs? Where?"

Alex jabbed a finger at the ground. "Down there. That's something else I used to see in dreams sometimes, but just now the picture was so clear in my head. We tried to climb stairs in the dark, but they didn't lead anywhere. Just ran straight into the ceiling."

Stairs that lead nowhere. The thought made her cross her arms over her stomach. The shadows in the clearing shifted at the edge of her vision, but when she looked she saw only the wall of bushes. Closing them in.

"Are you sure?"

He sat forward, elbows on his bent knees. "What if Madeline Byrne was lying? I don't think it was a mine shaft at all, even though that's what we were all told. Either she'd never actually been down there, or she lied about what she saw."

"But my uncle was there that day," Evelyn said. "He helped get us out. If Madeline lied about what they found, then my uncle must've lied too—or at least agreed to go along with her story."

"Why would he do that?" Alex asked.

"There was a rumor that he and Madeline were involved."

Evelyn repeated what Ms. Foster had said about Sammy. How he'd been a tutor for Daniella and Darren. How he'd been fired for "inappropriate behavior." Alex's eyebrows rose as she spoke.

"Alex…" Evelyn folded her legs and hugged her knees to her chest. "What if my family never heard from Sammy again because he's dead?"

She felt him scrutinizing her. Waiting for her to explain. But the words were stuck in her throat.

"Why would you think he's dead?" Alex asked.

"I think I saw him at Byrne House," she blurted. "Yesterday. But he wasn't alive."

Alex stared at her for another long moment. "Wait, another ghost? Is that what you're saying?"

She nodded. In a way, it was the truth.

Alex exhaled. "If you did see him...Jeez, I'm sorry. That's awful. Why didn't you tell me?"

"I am now."

He pulled her into a hug. She held on tight, gripping his jacket with her fists, as if the ground was shifting underneath them and Alex was the only thing keeping her steady. As if he might be the one who'd decide to let go.

Their phones both buzzed at the same time. Alex reached his first. "It's from Silvia." His brows contracted. "She wants us both to come to Milo's."

Evelyn opened the message. *Something important*, Silvia had written. *Possibly life or death.*

15

Tealights flickered in tiny cups around Milo's dining room.

"What is all this?" Alex asked.

Milo's family lived a couple miles away from Castle Heights, so Evelyn and Alex had borrowed her mother's car. Along a sideboard, thick blue candles gave off wisps of smoke, filling the air with a spicy-sweet smell. The same scent she'd noted earlier at Ms. Foster's house.

Then she noticed the elongated, pink piece of rock on the table. A quartz crystal, like the ones Evelyn had seen in Ms. Foster's living room.

Milo glanced into the open doorway that led to the kitchen. "You remember Silvia mentioned my Aunt Mimi, right?" Milo looked uncomfortable. "She called Silvia this morning. They've been discussing your problem."

"My *problem*?"

There's something ill about you, Mimi had said that morning. What had Silvia told her?

They heard a throat clear. Ms. Foster's younger sister stood in the doorway to the kitchen. "Ah, that one must be Alex," the woman said, grinning knowingly. "You were right, Milo. A very dull aura."

"A what?" Alex shot an accusing glance at Milo, who was shuffling toward the back wall like somehow he might go unnoticed.

Silvia came out of the kitchen behind Mimi, cheeks glowing with excitement. "Good, you're here. Everyone sit down. You're going to thank me, I promise."

"I still have no idea what's going on," Alex said. No one gave an immediate answer, and he sat reluctantly in the chair beside Evelyn.

Mimi took her seat, the one directly in front of the pink crystal. "I can see it all in your aura, Evelyn. You're in pain." Her voice was kind, full of genuine concern. Mimi picked up the crystal from the center of the table, holding it reverently in cupped hands.

"The sight is a gift. But there's danger in it, too. The dead leave traces."

Evelyn gripped the sides of her chair. Tears flooded into her eyes. She shut them for a moment, not wanting the others to see, and her uncle's ruined face looked back at her from the darkness. Then Darren's lifeless body replaced him. She took a shaky breath.

"What's wrong?" Alex whispered. But she shook her head, unable to speak.

"How can I tell?" Evelyn asked. "If there are…traces on me?"

Mimi reached across the table, opening her palm. Evelyn offered her hand, and Mimi gently turned it over, closing her eyes as she moved her thumbs down the insides of Evelyn's fingers. Suddenly Mimi gasped, dropping the hand and pushing back from the table.

Evelyn trembled and held her hand to her chest, remembering Darren's blood. "What do I do?"

Mimi picked up the pink crystal again, holding it out in front of her like a talisman. "I just hope it'll be enough."

***

Silvia told them to go wait for her outside. Milo was already out on the front lawn. He crossed his arms when he saw Alex coming toward him.

"What the hell was that about?" Alex said. "Did you know she was going to say all that crap to Evelyn?"

"Not exactly. Silvia thought it was important. Why don't you ask her?"

"I'm asking *you*." Alex shoved a finger at Milo's chest. "This is your house. You know what Evelyn's been through."

Evelyn pulled Alex aside. "Stop," she whispered. "You don't have to sound so…"

"What, obnoxious? You managed to tolerate Jake for months, apparently, and I'm bugging you after a couple of days?"

Evelyn held up the pink crystal. The hazy inside of the rock glowed with trapped sunlight, as if the light was coming from inside it instead of out. It felt warm, and the jagged edges of the rock pressed gently into her palm. Maybe it was just her imagination, but her head did feel a bit clearer. Quieter.

Silvia came outside. "Are you mad, Evelyn? You're mad. I can tell."

"I'm not." She made a show of putting the crystal in her pocket. "Thank you."

"*I'm* mad," Alex cut in. "That was absurd."

Silvia looked over her shoulder, checking that no one else was listening. "I know you're grumpy at me Alex, but I can help you, too."

"By fixing my crappy, dull aura? I'm okay, thanks."

Silvia stepped in closer, putting her arms out to sweep the group into a tighter circle. "I know you have a lot on your mind, Alex. You're afraid that you won't be able to stay here in Castle Heights. You're worried about your brother, and whether you can make peace with him. Right?"

Alex didn't answer, but the anger had left his expression. He glanced down at the grass. She went on.

"It all has the same cause." Silvia gripped Evelyn's wrist along with Milo's. "There are probably some very messed up spirits hanging around the mansion."

"Evelyn told me she saw one yesterday," Alex said quietly. He linked fingers with her.

Two images appeared in Evelyn's head, one as bright as an overexposed photo—golden hair, his hands a comforting anchor as he spun her around the lawn. The other was in livid color, every sickening detail seared into her mind in red and black. She stuck a hand into her pocket, squeezing the pink quartz.

"My uncle," Evelyn said. "I need to know what happened to him."

Silvia nodded. "I think I can help. You just have to let me try the mirror at Byrne House."

16

"HOW DO I MAKE IT SHOW ME THE RIGHT THING?"
Silvia held the mirror in her hands.

They were in the guest house, where Uncle Sammy had lived when he'd been Darren and Daniella's tutor. It was a small cottage next to the garage; both were modern additions to the Byrne House property, their simple, functional design setting them apart from the ornate construction of the mansion itself. It was just as understated on the inside: beige carpets and walls, bare of furniture.

Alex had swiped the key from a hook in the kitchen. Then he'd offered to stay inside and distract his mother, which was a good thing—he was still fuming about the session with Mimi. Silvia wouldn't have been able to focus with him glaring at her.

"When you're looking into the mirror," Evelyn said, "think about a face, a date, a time of day, anything that helps you to imagine a scene in your head."

Evelyn positioned her so she was facing the door. She'd told Silvia all about the negative effects of using the mirror, but her friend was adamant. *I want to be a part of this.* And really, Evelyn was more than happy to let her do it. The flash of Uncle Sammy had been so awful. She was afraid to go back to that dark place again.

"But I don't know what—" Silvia hesitated. "What your uncle looked like."

Evelyn took out the picture she'd borrowed from the mantle. She'd gotten it when she ran home to pick up the mirror. Silvia took the photo, holding it gingerly.

"Then what?" Silvia asked.

"You just wait until it feels right, I guess. That's all I can really put into words."

Silvia held up the mirror.

"Milo, stand back," Evelyn said. "If you're in the way, the mirror will focus on you instead."

She stood behind Silvia. Milo hovered nearby with his hands a little out from his sides, like he wanted to be ready to catch her at a moment's notice.

Evelyn's eyes squinted against the glare from the mirror. Her gaze went out of focus. She was looking through the open doorway, and for a split second, she saw them standing just outside—her Uncle Sammy and Madeline Byrne. The air around them flexed and bowed, the way the air wavers at the base of the sky on a hot day—heavy with anger, confusion, distrust.

Evelyn flinched. They were gone. She was sweating, as if it were summer instead of December. She shed her coat and lay it over the back of the sofa.

"Oh—" Silvia fell to her knees, her shoulders slumping. Milo helped hold her up. He led Silvia over to a sunny corner, where they sat down on the carpet to rest. Her eyes were bloodshot.

"I saw them," Silvia murmured. "I really did."

Evelyn gently pulled the mirror from Silvia's fist. "You did really well," she said. "Rest a few minutes. We can try again in a while."

Milo and Silvia were whispering, heads bowed together in the sunlight. The gesture was so intimate that it made Evelyn's chest ache.

The door made no sound as she stepped outside.

Sammy and Madeline had been right here, years ago, on the gravel that separated the guest house area from the beginning of the gardens. It had been warm that day, the trees more pink than green with spring flowers erupting on the branches. She'd felt the tension between them, dense and thick, like air flowing out of a heated room.

Though she'd left her coat inside, she wasn't cold. The gravel crunched beneath her shoes as she pictured where Sammy and Madeline had been standing.

The mirror was still in her hand, heavy and solid. She looked down at it. It was the first time in months she'd had any desire to use it. She understood that Silvia wanted to help her. But Sammy was *her* uncle. This was her responsibility.

And I won't see him die again, she reassured herself. *Not here. There's no reason to be afraid.*

She found a spot with a good view of the guest house, but shadowed enough that she'd be hidden from anyone coming down the path. The air was crisp and clean as she inhaled. She sat down, concentrating on the brief scene she'd witnessed—Uncle Sammy and Madeline Byrne—and held up the mirror.

Madeline knocks on the guest house door. She's furious, her nerves crackling with adrenaline. Sam Stanton—the kids' new tutor, hired at outrageous expense from the best private academy—opens the door, eyebrows lifting in surprise.

"Mrs. Byrne."

Madeline pokes him in the collarbone with her index finger. "Just who do you think you are?"

Sam steps out onto the gravel. "I'm assuming that's a rhetorical question. What can I do for you?"

Sam's aura buzzes with curiosity, but also annoyance. Since day one, he's wondered if it was a mistake to take this job. He couldn't resist the challenge of it, not to mention the tidy salary and the free room and board. Plus, it's so close to the home he grew up in—where his sister Vivian and her little family live now. He's never spent much time with them and wants that to change.

But the Byrne siblings are impossible. Daniella is unnervingly smart for fourteen years old. Both are so wild they got kicked out of every private school in the Denver area—Darren because he can't keep his emotions in check, and Daniella because she won't listen to anyone she considers beneath her intellect. She's doing college level work, but emotionally she's still a child. She's struggling socially.

Yet Sam is fascinated by them, too. Their pride in the Byrne family history, Daniella's knowledge of unexpected subjects like mineralogy, homeopathy, organic chemistry. Darren's intense focus, when he quiets down. And their mother, Madeline—though she's almost a decade older than he is, Sam can't take his eyes off her when she's in view. Willowy limbs, wild curly hair, a gently upturned nose. Her lips pout sensuously when she's angry.

Actually, Daniella looks quite a lot like her mother.

"I walked into the library this afternoon and found my children on their hands and knees, scrubbing the floor," Madeline says. "I hired you to teach them, not turn them into janitors."

"They refused to do their assignments. There had to be some punishment. Most everything else I've tried has failed, so I thought I'd give manual labor a go."

"You can't be serious."

"And you can't be this deluded."

Madeline is taken aback. It's been a long time since anyone dared to speak to her that way, not since she married Reginald Byrne. Even the school administrators who'd turned Darren and Daniella out on their ears had been disgustingly ingratiating to her as they broke the news. As if they were saying, "Not interested in these two, thanks, but if you have other kids, we'd be more than happy to take your money."

But not Sam. He stands his ground without apology. "The only reason I'm still here is that I believe in Daniella and Darren. I see potential in them, rough as it is. But they need to learn compromise. Humility. Respect. Or they won't ever succeed."

"And they'll learn all that from scrubbing floors?"

Sam doesn't blink. "Yes."

Madeline laughs dismissively, though she's more than a little impressed. After all, this is why she hired Sam the same day he interviewed—his confidence. He shows it in the way he stands straight and tall, shoulders thrown back, his features as precise and elegant as a king's. Talking to him, she already feels calmer, hopeful like she hasn't felt in years. As if Sam has them all in his competent grasp, and maybe —this time—they won't fall.

Only now does she realize the miracle of what she saw in the library: her uncontrollable children, silent for once, as they diligently cleaned.

"Carry on then," Madeline says. "I'm sorry for doubting you."

They stand looking at each other another moment, before Madeline stretches out her hand. Sam takes it, shaking slowly, gaze unwavering. Both of them are warmed by the contact, eying each other curiously. Their touch lingers too long, begins to transform from politeness into something else.

They don't see a small white face peering out from between the trees. Daniella, hands chapped and sore from the cleaning fluid. She's brought a book to share with Sam—one of Walter's journals from the library. Sam sometimes meets her in the classroom after hours for private study sessions, so they can talk without Darren's energetic disruptions. But Sam has said to keep it just between them. She relishes the secret, this sign that Sam Stanton, handsome and worldly and intelligent, likes her best.

So why isn't he letting go of her mother's hand?

17

DANIELLA WAS GONE. EVELYN WAS STILL SITTING BY the guest house, staring into the trees. She tried to push up onto her knees and fell forward, pain searing across her temples.

"Evelyn!" Silvia cried.

Milo helped her sit back down, and Evelyn rested against the wall of the guest house, its wooden siding catching against her dress.

"I'm just a little dizzy." She closed her eyes, hoping her headache would fade soon.

Gravel scraped where Milo sat down beside her. "You were staring out into space, just like when you look into the mirror. But you weren't *holding* the mirror. It was behind you, on the ground."

"It seemed like you were in a trance or something," Silvia said.

"One of those flash things you mentioned?" Milo asked.

She'd definitely started out looking into the mirror, but somehow she'd dropped it and the vision kept going.

"I saw my uncle and Madeline Byrne. And Daniella was there too—spying on them."

Her upper lip itched just below her nose, and she scratched at it with her thumb. Then she saw the streak of red.

"You're bleeding," Silvia said. "I've got tissue in my purse."

Evelyn leaned her head back and pinched her nostrils closed with her fingers. Blood dripped into the back of her throat.

Silvia returned, holding out a packet of tissues. Evelyn pressed one to her nose. "Thanks."

"Do you want me to go get Alex?" Silvia asked.

Evelyn pulled back the tissue and saw a bright red splotch blooming at its center. She grabbed a fresh one from Silvia's pack and put it under her nose.

"I'd rather you not mention this to him. You heard how he reacted to the whole crystal thing. I don't want him to get upset about this too."

Silvia bit her lip and exchanged a glance with Milo.

"Seems like lately there's a lot of things you don't want to tell Alex," Milo said. "You sure that's a good idea?"

Evelyn forced herself up to standing and checked the tissue again. Only a few dots of red now. The bleeding had pretty much stopped. "Actually, can you tell Alex I went home? I'm not feeling so well. I'll see you guys later."

She retrieved her coat, which was heavy with the crystal in its pocket. Silvia handed her the mirror, and Evelyn felt them watching as she headed for the pathway around the house. She wobbled on the first few steps, but then recovered. Her head was still pounding.

She'd felt sick the first time she looked into the mirror. But she'd quickly grown accustomed to the sensations. And the last time she'd used it last August, before Alex left town —she hadn't experienced any negative effects at all. Maybe the flashes were different. Yet she'd never had this powerful of a reaction to one of the flashes before.

When she reached the street, she didn't feel like going home and explaining herself. So instead she went across to Walter Park and sat on a bench until she was sure the bleeding had stopped. Her phone buzzed. Alex, finally responding to her text.

But when she pulled out the device, she didn't see a message from Alex.

It was an unknown number.

The text read, *I take it your gift has arrived. I can make sure he stays. Are you ready to talk?*

Evelyn's cheeks flushed and her heart began to thump. She glanced up and down the street. "Where are you, Daniella?" she whispered.

She stared down at the phone in her hands.

Without even thinking, she tapped to write a response. The cursor blinked at her. Now was her chance. She could ask for the antidote. Fifteen minutes ago she'd been bleeding and disoriented after yet another flash. What if the antidote could help?

But she'd owe Daniella. And she'd be giving up a secret, something that even Alex didn't know—what would Daniella do with that information? It wasn't worth the risk. Especially for a cure that might not even work.

After another moment's hesitation, Evelyn tapped out, *Leave me alone.*

Then she shoved her phone into her pocket and headed home.

18

Evelyn opened her eyes. There were voices downstairs.

She checked the time on her phone: 5:30 a.m. Her mom never got up so early. And Alex had stayed overnight at Byrne House with his mom. So who could it be?

Cold air shocked her skin when she pushed her blankets away. But she felt better this morning. No more nosebleeds, her headache just a faraway pulse.

Gripping her phone in her hand, she snuck downstairs. Light shone from the kitchen. Her dad, Toby, was sitting at the table, hunched toward Evelyn's mom. Vivian cut off mid-sentence and looked up. Toby turned around.

"Hey sweetheart!" His chair scraped back, and he pulled her into a hug. "You're up early."

Her back stiffened until he let go. "So are you. When did you get here?"

"Late last night. I managed to get things sorted out at work yesterday. So here I am."

Vivian stood up. "What are you two in the mood for? Eggs?"

"Sure," Evelyn said. "What were you guys just talking about?"

Her father looked to her mom, but Viv had her head ducked into the fridge. "Just some things your mom wanted to discuss," he said.

Toby got out the skillet while Viv started breaking eggs into a bowl. Neither of them would meet Evelyn's eyes.

"Fine," she said, "I'll go and shower while you talk about whatever it is you need to talk about. But I'm going over to Byrne House as soon as Alex is up."

She went upstairs to clean up. She dressed in a pair of leggings, a white tee, and a chunky men's cardigan she'd found on a recent trip to her favorite thrift store. Outside the window was a world of white: snow filled the air, blotting out most of the view. The cars were already coated in a thick layer of snow.

She hadn't seen any suitcases downstairs. Did Toby bring clothes with him to stay? And for how long?

Where had he slept—in the upstairs den? Or in the master bedroom?

When she came back to her room, her mother was making her bed, like she used to when Evelyn was little.

"Breakfast is almost ready. Your dad's finishing things up."

"You didn't have to come all the way up here to tell me that." Evelyn sat in her desk chair and rested her feet on the edge of the bed. She picked up the quartz crystal for a moment, fiddling with it to keep her hands busy.

"I also wanted to have a chat, just you and me. When Alex got here last Friday, I told myself this could wait until after the holidays, but seeing your dad made me realize I should go ahead and tell you. While Alex is still here."

"This is about Alex?"

Viv stretched out her fingers, examining her nails. They looked chewed down to nothing. "Not really, no. But to you, I'm sure it will seem that way."

Evelyn set down the quartz crystal. She stared hard at her mom, wishing Vivian would stop hinting at whatever it was and just say it.

Vivian started to blur in Evelyn's eyes, first along her shoulders and arms and then around her face. Like the edges of her skin were smudging into the air around her, not separate anymore but one bleeding into the other.

Evelyn sensed her mother's emotions before they even made sense in words. Viv wanted more than anything to get away. Evelyn saw it just on the edges of her mom's thoughts. If she believed her daughter would agree, she would ask Evelyn to leave with her, right now, this morning. She wanted to escape the way her brother did years ago.

Then Evelyn's hand touched the crystal again, and the aura around her mother was instantly gone. She wondered briefly if there was some connection, but she could hardly think about that now. She tucked the rock into the pocket of her cardigan, came over to the bed, and sat down.

"I asked your dad to come to Denver so we could discuss him moving back here."

Evelyn gasped, her heart whirring like a hummingbird in her chest.

"Evvy, don't get the wrong idea. I didn't ask him to move back in with *me*." Her voice started to crack, and she cleared her throat and took several breaths before continuing.

"I've been offered a spot as principal at a high school in Seattle. The school is struggling, and I think I might be able to make a difference there."

What she was saying made no sense. "Seattle? What about your city council position?"

Vivian pressed Evelyn's hand between her palms. "I've decided to step down. I don't feel effective here. I need a different kind of challenge, without all the election and politics crap. But you've had such a difficult time since the summer, I didn't want to bring it up unless it was a sure thing, which it wasn't until a couple of weeks ago."

"You've known for *weeks*?"

Evelyn got up and went to the window, supporting herself against the sill. All the blood was rushing away from her head. The view outside was nothing but white, like she was inside a snow globe being shaken by some merciless hand.

Evelyn's mom sighed and got up from the bed. "I'm sure breakfast is ready by now. Dad's waiting for us."

She was trying to avoid the rest of this conversation. There was something else Viv hadn't revealed yet. She'd said something about Alex. Why did she think this had anything to do with him?

"I'm not going down until you tell me all of it."

Vivian started to leave the room, but then shook her head and turned around. "Your dad doesn't think he can move back to Denver. It's a lot to ask for him to pick up and leave his new life. Especially since I'll be heading to Seattle as soon as possible."

The picture was slowly coming together. Why Viv wanted her to enjoy this week with Alex, didn't want to tell her about all this. Evelyn sat down but didn't hit the chair right. She ended up sliding down to the floor.

"Sweetie." Vivian walked over and held out her hands to help her up. "I know the idea of spending the rest of your senior year in another place seems like the worst thing you can imagine, but it's only one semester. After that, if you want to, you can come back to Denver for college. We might not even have to sell the house. We'll see how our finances look, and—"

"Sell the house?!" Evelyn got up. "I can't deal with this right now."

Vivian held up her hands. "All right."

Evelyn kept her back turned until she heard her mom going down the stairs.

She picked up her phone from the nightstand and scrolled through her contacts. She went right past Alex's name at the top of the list and chose a different name instead.

19

J‍AKE OPENED THE FRONT DOOR AND USHERED HER in. She took off her coat and boots, brushing snow from her leggings. Voices and the clink of dishes came from the kitchen—his parents eating breakfast.

"My room's this way," he murmured.

She'd only been to Jake's new place once. Usually they preferred to meet in the park. But it was snowing too hard to stay outside today. Even the five minute walk between her house and Jake's had left her teeth chattering.

Jake led her through the living room and toward an open door. She hesitated. Until now, she'd only seen his room on FaceTime. This was a new level of intimacy, and she wondered if coming here was such a good idea. But she didn't want to go back home, either.

Jake put his hand on the small of her back and nudged her inside. "Come on," he said. "Unless you want to catch up with my mom and dad."

He closed the door behind them.

Jake had been inside her room just once, and she'd been uncomfortable at the way he examined all of her possessions. But now that she was here, she figured she should return the favor and snoop.

His room was smaller than Evelyn's. There was a twin bed against one wall and a short dresser covered in model sports cars. Jake didn't have a desk or any chairs. Evelyn kicked aside some dirty clothes and sat on the floor.

Jake pushed his pillow out of the way and flopped onto the bed. "You don't have to sit down there."

She said nothing. There was a poster on one wall of a classic silver Camaro—the same type of Camaro that Jake drove until the summer. She'd always thought that Jake didn't like the car, that he'd viewed it as a hand-me-down and wished for something newer. He'd seemed like such a shallow, spoiled brat.

Yet why would he hang a poster of the car unless he'd loved it?

"Fine, sit on the floor," Jake said. He scooted back against the wall. "Suit yourself. So, what's up? Have a fight with Evans?"

"This isn't about Alex."

"Then what is it?"

She decided to just spit it out. "Apparently my mother decided, without ever bothering to mention it to me until now, that we're moving to Seattle."

"*What?*"

Tears plopped onto her cheeks, and her chest started to heave up and down. "She doesn't want to be here anymore, and neither does my dad, and of course neither of them cares what I want. So I'm pretty much screwed."

She heard the hum of voices in the kitchen. She brought hers to a whisper. "My mom said I could move to Baltimore with my dad, as if that's any better. She's even talking about selling our house."

"Selling your house?" Jake crawled onto the floor beside her. "I don't get it. I thought your mom loved her job here."

"I thought so, too. But she's been acting weird, especially since Alex showed up, and I didn't get it until now. This is really happening."

She remembered those wisps of color coming off Vivian's skin, betraying the feelings she wanted to hide. "Mom hasn't been happy for a long time. She thought it was because of Dad, and after he left things would get better. But it didn't."

Evelyn lay her head back against the wall and cried, holding her sobs inside her chest so they were quiet. She didn't want Mr. or Mrs. Oshiro to hear. Jake looked like he felt sorry, or as close as Jake ever came to feeling empathy for someone else. Boredom mixed with pity, and discomfort showing in the way his mouth pinched in at the corners. Or was Evelyn being unfair? He'd comforted her plenty of times. Did Jake feel things more deeply, and he just had his own way of showing it?

"I'm such an idiot." Evelyn dried her face with the collar of her cardigan. "I actually thought she wanted to get back together with my dad. I thought she missed him and realized she still loved him. Can you believe that?"

"You're not an idiot. Well, not completely, there's still the whole Evans issue. But that's beside the point."

Evelyn shook her head, looking up at the Camaro poster. The car was parked in front of a city skyline. She wondered what city it was.

"Hey." Jake poked her knee with his finger. "Wherever you live, I'll come visit you."

"How are you supposed to get anywhere? You don't have a car anymore. All you have is that lame poster."

Jake laughed. "There's this great invention called an airplane? Seattle might not be so bad. It's got to be better than here, right? No more reminders of what happened."

"Maybe. I didn't really think about it that way."

He put his hand on top of her knee and squeezed. "Did your mom just tell you this morning?"

She wrapped her cardigan around her middle. "About two minutes before I called you."

"So I guess that means you called me first. Before him."

"Don't read too much into it. I just needed somebody to remind me how pathetic I'm being, so I'd stop crying. Alex is too nice for that."

"He's not too nice. He wants you to be weaker than he is, so he can take care of you. I know you don't need that."

Jake's hand was still on her leg. She knew she should push it away, but she was wondering, just a little bit, if Jake could be right.

"I know how strong you are. You don't need to hide it in front of me." His hand moved from her knee onto her thigh.

"Jake, stop. This can't happen."

"It already is. You called me first."

This time, she pushed his hand from her leg. "You're wrong." He had to be wrong.

"Ev, please. Look at me."

She tilted her head slightly, so that she could see him from the corner of her eye. He brushed her hair back. "You want this. I know you do."

He kissed the edge of her jawline, just under her ear.

When she felt Jake's lips on her, in that spot that Alex liked to kiss, she thought she might be sick. But she was relieved, too, to know for sure that despite the arguments and the months apart, she only wanted Alex. It was a mistake to have called Jake, and to let him almost convince her that she felt something for him. A huge, stupid mistake.

"Jake, don't—"

He put his hand on the back of Evelyn's neck and pulled her forward. Her mouth collided with his. Jake pushed his tongue past her lips and against her teeth. She opened her mouth to tell him to stop, but he seemed to take that as an invitation. He kissed her harder. Pushed her back onto the floor. She slapped at his shoulders and kicked her legs.

"What?"

"*Get off me.*"

Jake got up onto his hands and knees. She scrambled out from under him, threw open the door and ran through the living room. Near the front door, she collided with Jake's father, who'd just come out of the kitchen.

"What the heck? Jake, what's going on?"

Evelyn shoved her feet into her boots and grabbed her coat. She wrenched open the front door. Snowflakes whirled into the room. Jake and his father were arguing behind her, but she didn't stop. She didn't care how Jake explained this to his father, but she wanted nothing to do with it. How had she ever thought that Jake and Alex were the least bit alike?

Snow drove into her face, forcing her to squint. She managed to get her coat zipped up. Then she heard footsteps in the snow behind her.

"Hey!" Jake grabbed her arm, forcing her to stop. She tried to pull away, but he tightened his grip. "Don't you think you're overreacting?" He hadn't even put on a coat.

"I'm entitled to be a little upset when someone shoves his tongue halfway down my throat."

"I'm not *someone*."

"Oh, I'm so sorry." Her voice was shaking. "Am I supposed to be grateful that Jake Oshiro decided to come on to me? I needed to talk to you as a friend because I was upset, and you tried to take advantage of me. Crying might turn you on, but it doesn't really work for me."

"You've sent me plenty of signals the last few months. It's obvious what you want."

She shook her head, backing away. Was he right? Had she led him on? She'd kept on seeing him, even though she knew how he felt.

No. She'd told him *no*. That was what mattered.

Jake's lashes were coated with snow, but his eyes burned. "When are you going to stop lying to yourself and admit that you're better off with me? What do I have to do?"

"Stay away from me. You and I aren't friends. We're nothing."

He let go of her arm. She turned and faced into the storm, heading home.

"Are you going to tell him?" Jake called after her. "So he can protect you from me?"

She didn't answer. But no, she wasn't going to tell Alex. Because he'd probably do something really stupid. She wouldn't waste another moment of time on Jake.

20

EVELYN RAN TO HER STREET, HER HOOD UP, HOT tears pooling in her eyes. She wanted to see Alex, touch him. Rid herself of the residue of Jake's kiss. But she couldn't go to the mansion's door so upset. She certainly didn't want to explain to Alex or—God forbid, his mother— all that had happened that morning. She needed to collect herself first.

She went through the Byrne House gate and into the gardens. The trees and paths all lay beneath several inches of white. Large snowflakes drifted from the colorless sky. Everything was quiet, and she could smell woodsmoke from nearby fireplaces. Did it snow in Seattle and Baltimore? Of course it did. Maybe more than it snowed in Denver. But she refused to imagine herself living in one of those other places. She planned to go to college in a different town, maybe even a different state. But Castle Heights was always supposed to be home.

She thought of the quartz crystal that Mimi gave her, how the aura around her mother had seemed to disappear at the same instant that she held it. She dug inside her coat, trying to find the rock in her cardigan pocket. She was sure she'd put it there earlier and hadn't taken it out.

Her phone was in her pocket. But the quartz crystal wasn't there.

She cursed. She must have lost it at Jake's house. And she certainly wasn't going back for it.

While she was still having these thoughts, a blur of movement caught her eye.

Someone else was out here in the snow. A figure with long dark hair, no coat despite the frigid temperature. The same figure she'd followed in the gardens yesterday, though this time she seemed younger.

"Hey!" Evelyn called out, and ran after her.

She saw the girl duck into a gap in the bushes. Evelyn followed and found herself once again in the clearing with the stone memorial.

The dark-haired girl was gone.

The storm was far calmer here, the trees and bushes too thick to allow much through. A few snowflakes fluttered down from the sky.

Had she seen a ghost? Or just a flash of some long-gone memory? She didn't know the difference anymore, if there ever was one. But this clearing was as good a hiding place as any. And right now, all she wanted was to hide: from Jake, from her parents, from Alex too. From the many truths that she'd been avoiding.

She sat and leaned her shoulder against the stone. It was like a block of ice, freezing even through the layers of her sweater and down coat. But she was grateful for its solid weight. She wondered who had created this marker and why. The stone had cracks running through it, with mildewy-looking plants growing in them. It looked old, at least as old as the other statues on the Byrne House grounds. The word "MEMORIUM" in the inscription made it sound like a reminder. But for what, or whom? Walter had already created a statue in honor of his beloved Ada. Perhaps it was for some other member of the Byrne family.

Maybe Walter's brother Simon had built the marker. Yet Evelyn couldn't imagine Simon Byrne mourning anyone so intensely. In her letters, Ada Byrne had described Simon's cruelty. Evelyn herself had seen the terrible things that Simon did to Ada in the underground lab; the way he taunted her, made her believe that Walter was a monster. Simon had trapped Ada in the pitch-dark tunnels, and she'd lost her will to live. She'd only survived a few more weeks afterward. Because of Darren's serum, Evelyn had been forced to live through Ada's torment with no way to escape or to change what had happened.

Last summer, Evelyn had been so sure that Byrne House was trying to tell her something. Perhaps it had been Ada Byrne herself, calling out for someone to witness her suffering.

Was someone else reaching out to her now? Her uncle?

That girl she'd seen twice now, who'd led her here to this hidden clearing?

Evelyn closed her eyes and concentrated on the reassuring pressure of the stone against her shoulder. She tried to open her mind and listen. There were memories of Walter Byrne somewhere nearby, simmering like a low fire —his despair at losing Ada, his rage—but still indistinct. She felt nothing of Simon.

She sensed someone else, someone kind and reassuring. Her Uncle Sammy appeared right in front of her, so solid it was hard to believe he wasn't alive. Then a woman walked into view—an older version of the girl in the snow.

Madeline Byrne.

Sam turns when he hears her coming through the bushes. "Mrs. Byrne. Thank you for meeting me."

Madeline adjusts her dress, brushing prickers from her sleeves. "Your note was very mysterious."

"I'm sorry, I didn't want to be overheard." He sweeps his eyes over the clearing, looking for any sign that they're not alone. Daniella and Darren can be quiet when they choose. Sam wants their mother on his side before the siblings interfere.

"The kids turned in their research papers today," Sam says. "And they're both about Walter and Simon Byrne."

Madeline groans. She's so sick of those names. No wonder Sam wanted to meet somewhere clandestine—Reginald would not appreciate Sam, an outsider, questioning the importance of the Byrne family history. "My husband encourages it," she says, trying to navigate this conversation delicately. "He's not someone who reads much, I guess you could say. But he likes the idea of descending from genius. Makes him feel important."

Talking about her husband has upset her, the aura around her head clotting like spoiled milk.

Her discomfort is obvious to Sam, and his thoughts reach out toward hers in sympathy. "That's understandable. But no one outside this house will ever take Daniella and Darren seriously if…" He stops when he sees the tears in Madeline's eyes.

"I'll try to talk to them," Madeline says. "Or if I have to, I'll get rid of those journals." She cringes as she imagines the reactions of Reginald and the kids.

To her family, she's as much an outsider as Sam.

Madeline wipes at her eyes. "I thought they were making progress."

"I thought so too. Daniella especially." Sam thinks of Daniella— her sharp eyes when she's listening, her knowing smiles—and the colors seeping from his skin turn to pink.

"They have cousins visiting next week for a memorial service," Madeline says. "It could be a nice distraction for them." Though it will be miserable otherwise. Reginald hates that branch of the family— the Evanses, who own half of the Byrne estate, including half of the mansion. They've never wanted to live here, never asked for anything, but Reginald still complains about them.

"The older cousin just started college," she says. "William, I think. Maybe he can tell the kids what it's really like, or… something." She lifts her hand, a throwaway gesture, and she accidentally brushes against Sam's coat.

Madeline's fingers hover beside his elbow, like a bird searching for a place to land.

She drops her hand to her side, but then says the first thing that jumps into her mind. "Would you like to come? I mean, the funeral will be dull I'm sure, but there will be a wake after. Too much Byrne family in one place. I could use an ally."

Sam doesn't react for a moment, and Madeline's aura shrinks, turning pale and yellow. What was she thinking? That they were friends?

Then Sam smiles. "I'll be there." He ignores the warning voices in his head—his aunt's voice and his grandmother's—telling him that he *should stay out of Byrne family affairs. That soon he'll be too deep to be able to come up for air.*

But he's always loved a challenge. That's why he paraglides in the mountains on his days off, why he took a job at Byrne House in the first place; that little thrill of knowing he might fail. The whisper of danger.

Sam reaches out and squeezes Madeline's hand, just briefly, before letting go.

For her, it's enough. Joy ignites the air around her, bright as the sun.

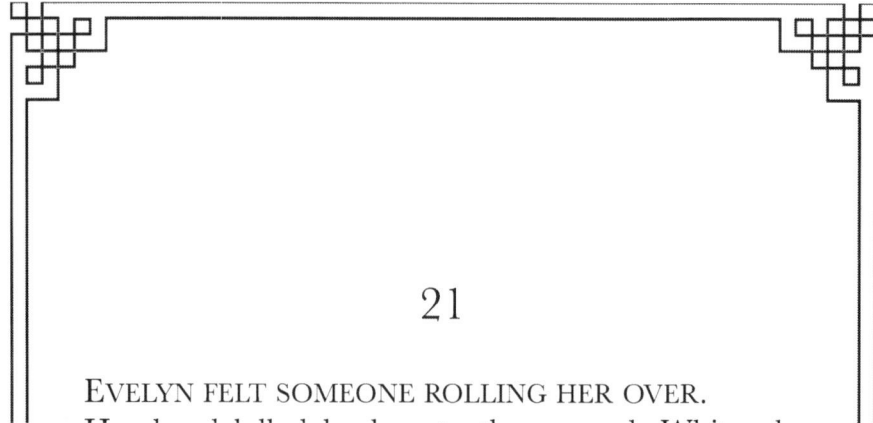

21

EVELYN FELT SOMEONE ROLLING HER OVER.

Her head lolled back onto the ground. White glare assailed her eyes.

"What are you doing?" she murmured, though her lips didn't want to move.

"What am *I* doing?"

She opened one eye and saw Alex bent over her. "What are you doing taking a nap in the snow?" he asked. "You could die out here."

"Don't be dramatic." Her words slurred. All of her felt slow and stiff. She sat up, cradling her head. She glanced up at the sky, squinting. It had stopped snowing, and the sun glowed faintly behind the clouds.

The headache from yesterday was back, but now it was more like a migraine. "My mom and I had a fight before breakfast, and I needed some time to think by myself. I... thought I saw someone out here."

The flashes had been stronger, more overpowering, since yesterday—when she'd started using the mirror again. As if the two together had a multiplying effect. Did that explain these blinding headaches?

"How'd you know I was here?" she asked. She was starting to shiver. Alex rubbed her arms through her coat.

"I texted a bunch of times, and when I went to your house your mom said you'd left. Something told me I should check the gardens, and then I saw your footprints." He shook his head. "Let's go inside. Get you warmed up."

They went into Byrne House through the back door. The kitchen smelled of takeout food and cleaning solution. Alex poured Evelyn a cup of coffee. A pot had already been brewing.

"My mom's an all-day caffeine fiend these days," Alex explained.

"Talking about me?" Mrs. Evans—Lila—came into the kitchen, holding an empty mug. She was a petite, pretty woman with shoulder length blond hair. She looked nothing like either of her sons.

"Hello, Evelyn," Lila said, and then did a double take. Her eyes swept over Evelyn's wet coat, her bedraggled hair. Then Lila managed a polite smile, apparently deciding not to comment on the obvious. Evelyn returned the greeting with a nod.

At least Lila had never been out-and-out rude. Lila's indifference was better than the way Vivian had treated Alex last summer—like he was a dangerous criminal with evil designs on her daughter. Like Viv, Lila probably had some very bad memories of the day Evelyn and Alex fell when they were six. But Evelyn had no idea how to prove herself worthy of Alex to his mother. Any time Mrs. Evans was around, Evelyn couldn't think of a single intelligent thing to say.

"Have you heard from your brother today?" Lila asked Alex.

He filled his mother's coffee mug. "No updates since last night, Mom. We'll see him before Christmas. That's all he said."

She inhaled and stood taller, as if stoically accepting this news. "Then we'd better get moving on that decorating, hadn't we? I'll go pick up some supplies." Lila turned on her heel and walked out into the hallway.

"Don't forget to check Google maps for traffic, Mom," Alex called after her.

Evelyn sat at the table and sipped her coffee, letting the heat of the cup thaw her fingers. Now that Alex's mother had gone, the room was decidedly warmer.

Alex pulled up a chair beside her. "She's not used to driving," he explained. "But she wanted to rent a car. She's got '*so many errands*' getting ready for Will." He leaned his elbows on the table, his bangs falling across his forehead. Evelyn slipped her fingers into his hair, watching the strands change from dark brown to golden in the light.

"I haven't told her yet that I'm staying in Castle Heights after the holidays are over," Alex murmured. "She won't like it, but I'll just have to figure out a way to make this work. Maybe she'll want to stay here, too. Unless she really does have a boyfriend back home."

Evelyn tapped her fingers against her mug. *You have to tell him*, she thought. Especially after the things Jake had said that morning—which she didn't want to think about.

"My dad showed up last night," she said. "And my mom finally told me why she's been acting so weird lately."

He smiled a little. "Yeah?"

She had to do it quick. She might not be able to get the words out otherwise. "She's taking a new job in Seattle. And I'll probably have to move next semester, to live with her or with my dad in Baltimore."

Alex didn't move. He blinked his eyes, his mouth set in a line.

"It's not for sure," Evelyn said. "It's possible my dad will move back here. But it's really not likely. One of us is getting screwed in this, and I'm guessing it'll be me instead of him."

Alex sat up and smoothed the back of his hair with his open palm. "This complicates things."

Evelyn tried to laugh but it came out as a sob instead.

"Come here." He scooted his chair closer. His arms surrounded her. "It's going to work out."

He was just saying that to make her feel better. "How? There's nothing I can do. They get to make all the decisions, and I just have to go along with it."

"There's always my back-up plan."

She lay her head against his shoulder. "You have a back-up plan?"

"We could get married." His chest moved as he laughed, but his laugh sounded strange. Almost nervous.

"Don't joke," she said.

Alex tightened his arms around her. "I'm not joking. I mean it."

She lifted her head, looking at him. "No, you don't."

"Yes, I *do*. I love you, Evelyn Ashwood. Marry me."

"Stop." She pushed back, the legs of her chair scraping. "You know we can't get married."

"Why not? We love each other, and we want to be together. We want to be able to make our own decisions, without our parents making them for us." He picked up her hand and slid Ada's ring off her finger, then held it out.

"We've already got a ring. You just have to say yes."

"*No.*" She couldn't believe he was serious about this. There were about a thousand reasons this was a terrible idea. "We're still in high school. Where would we even live?"

"Your house. Your parents did the same thing, right? Moved in there after they got married? But your parents wouldn't even be there. It would be just us."

"We don't have jobs. Or money." Evelyn stood up. She couldn't breathe. This room was too tight. Why did old houses have such small kitchens?

"I own part of Byrne House," Alex said. "I talked to one of my dad's friends—he said I could force a sale, if it really came to that. The money would get us started, and we could work too while we finished school." He caught hold of her hand, trying to pull her close again. "We'd be together, all the time. Our own life. Just us."

"You talk about it like getting married will make everything perfect. It won't. Look at my mom and dad, they were completely in love, got engaged at eighteen, and it all fell apart." She pointed to the ring in Alex's hand. "Or Walter and Ada Byrne. Loving each other isn't any guarantee."

"You're seriously comparing us to Walter and Ada? A mad scientist and his dead wife?"

"You know what I mean. We haven't even been together that long. How do you know you'll feel the same a year from now?"

"You think I'll wake up one day and decide I don't love you anymore? Or want someone else? You have that little faith in me?"

He was being sarcastic, but that was exactly what Evelyn was afraid of. That he would get tired of her and leave again. What if, deep down, he was worried about the same thing, and this whole marriage idea was a way to avoid admitting it to himself? Already things were different between them, after so much time apart. What if he just wanted to hold on tighter to something he already felt slipping away?

"I won't change my mind," Alex said. "Maybe the problem is that you don't feel the same way I do."

"Of course I do. I love you."

He dug his heels into the ground, pushed his chair back, and stood. "Forget I asked. Let's get something to eat, I'm sure you're hungry."

"Alex, come on. I do want to marry you. Someday."

"It's okay. You said no, I got it." He held out Ada's ring without looking at her. "Here. I shouldn't have taken it."

She hesitated. After what he'd said, she didn't know anymore what the ring was supposed to represent. "Maybe you should keep it for now."

"Put it back on. *Please*."

Alex grabbed her hand and set the ring on her palm. She slid the band back onto her finger.

22

ALEX HADN'T SAID A WORD IN TWENTY MINUTES. He'd been staring out the window. Byrne House's rose garden was a dark tangle of thorns. The sun was out, and the snow was already beginning to soften. The sound of dripping water pinged in the gutters.

Evelyn spun Ada's ring around her finger. She picked up her sandwich, then set it down again, remembering the look on Alex's face when she'd tried to give back the ring. Maybe if he'd asked her to marry him a few months from now, or even a few weeks, she could have said what he'd wanted to hear. But just days after showing up in Castle Heights again?

"I didn't say what I really meant earlier," Evelyn said. "It sounded all wrong."

"We're pretending that didn't happen, remember?"

"Alex…"

"It was just one of those stupid things that comes out of my mouth sometimes." He smiled easily, though his eyes were distant. Closed off. "I was really thinking about the wedding night, anyway."

The joke fell flat. Neither of them laughed. Evelyn took a bite of her sandwich, but she could hardly taste it.

"You said you saw someone in the gardens," he reminded her. "That's why you were out in the snow?"

She swallowed. It took her brain a moment to switch gears. "I thought I saw a girl—or maybe a woman, I'm not sure—with dark hair. I saw her yesterday, too. She keeps leading me back to the stone marker in that clearing."

"What do you think she wants?" he asked.

Evelyn took a slow breath. "I think she has something to do with my Uncle Sammy. She might even be Madeline Byrne."

"Wait, you're saying Madeline is *dead*?"

That twist in her chest again, as if her heart kept winding tighter. But it was too late to tell him about the flashes. Things had gone much too far.

She rubbed her forehead. "Maybe it wasn't her. I don't *know*."

Alex sighed. "Okay. We need to find out more about Madeline Byrne, and we need to find out what really happened to your uncle. So let's get the mirror. Let's figure out what your ghost wants us to see."

They brought the mirror to the gardens. She'd told Alex an edited version of what she'd seen the day before by the guest house: Madeline and Sammy discussing Daniella and Darren, and the beginnings of a flirtation between them. She also added that Sammy and Madeline planned to see one another the day of the funeral—the day that Evelyn and Alex would end up falling.

"I think that's where we should focus," Evelyn said. "We need to know what happened between Madeline and Sammy that day." Her boots sunk into the damp ground as they walked.

Alex's face darkened. "Do you think we might see *us*, that day when we were kids? See us falling from the tree?"

She hadn't thought of that. Her mom had kept the accident a secret for so many years because Viv feared that Evelyn's mind couldn't take the truth. Now, Evelyn knew those fears were unfounded. She'd remembered, in vague terms at least, what had happened. But it would be another thing altogether to see those events play out in the mirror. She'd be reliving the experience. Feeling the same terror that, at six years old, had left her unable to speak.

She wasn't a little girl anymore. But still, the thought was unnerving. And besides, after what happened yesterday when she used the mirror, she had no idea how she'd react. She'd already had a powerful flash that morning. Her headache was only just letting up.

"Would you mind being the one to do it?" Evelyn asked. "I just don't know if…"

Alex's expression melted. He cupped the side of her neck with his hand, his thumb brushing her cheek. "I'd do anything for you if you ask, you know that right?"

He kissed her—just a gentle, fleeting touch—but longing flared at Evelyn's center. She wished they could go back to some earlier time, when everything had been easier between them. If such a perfect moment even existed.

He took the mirror from her outstretched hand. Alex exhaled and relaxed his shoulders. Evelyn watched for the familiar expression of deep concentration and the glazing of his eyes. He was absorbed in a vision.

Did he see Uncle Sammy and Madeline? Or did he see himself, on that day years ago that he and Evelyn met—those brief hours when they were kids, still innocent of all the pain that Byrne House had in store for them? She couldn't watch anymore. She turned away from Alex, just for a moment.

In that instant, she saw a flicker of something by another tree, not far from where Alex was sitting.

The dark-haired girl again. But this time, Evelyn recognized Daniella Byrne. It was definitely her, though about a decade younger than the Daniella that Evelyn knew.

Evelyn watched her come closer. She could sense a little of Daniella's emotions—sadness, jealousy—but they were muffled, as if cotton filled the space around her. Daniella was translucent, disappearing and then reappearing a few steps away from where she'd been before, like an old TV cut through with static and interference. Like she was working very hard to keep her emotions in check.

Daniella stopped and looked up at the tallest evergreen tree—the one that Evelyn and Alex had climbed as children. Anger swelled inside Daniella as she looked at the tree, and then her eyes moved down to the ground.

She hadn't meant for them to fall. It was all Darren's fault that her parents blamed her. They said she shouldn't have been alone with William, her older cousin, which was ridiculous. She'd only been talking to him.

But Darren and her parents didn't know that she slipped away from William, too. She'd gone to look for her teacher. Mr. Stanton. He'd disappeared, and she'd had a sickening suspicion of where he'd gone.

Now, Daniella was the only one who knew the truth:

The true fault lay with her mother.

Evelyn watched Daniella walk into a dense mass of trees and brush. She was going somewhere, a hidden place that filled Daniella's aura with dread.

Daniella vanished behind another tree, this one thin and straight with pale bark. She stepped around it and pushed her way through the thick bushes just beyond it.

Evelyn followed, as if pulled along by the strength of Daniella's memories, and found herself in the secluded clearing with the block of stone at the center.

She was on the back side of the stone marker, the side without the inscription.

Daniella walked up to the stone face and ran her hands over the grooved surface. It had three narrow channels, like seams, running down along its length. Daniella stuck her index finger into one of the channels and wiggled it around.

Suddenly the entire back face of the stone swung back, revealing thick, tarnished hinges set along the inside. They were completely hidden from view when the door was closed. Without hesitating, Daniella stepped forward, leaning into the dark. Listening.

She blinked and Daniella was gone. The stone was closed up again, as if she'd imagined the whole thing.

"Evelyn?"

Alex was calling for her. She cursed under her breath. She'd left him alone.

She ran back—it wasn't more than a few steps, really, skirting a few trees—and found Alex looking around himself, the mirror dangling from his hand by his side.

"I'm right here, sorry!"

He hugged her. "Where were you?"

Alex was holding on so tightly she could hardly breathe. "I thought I saw…something. How was it?"

He held onto her for another moment before letting go. He sat down in the wet grass, oblivious to the melting snow. "I saw your uncle. But only for a minute. Then I saw you and me. I knew I might, but…It was worse than I expected." He looked up into the tree branches and down at the ground, like he was picturing the fall.

"I felt us down there," he said. "Underground. Almost right below where we're standing."

He started shaking. Evelyn wrapped her arms around his shoulders. "I'm sorry. Should we go inside for a while?"

They both stood. "I'm going to try again later," Alex said, insistent. "I did see your uncle. I can find him again."

"You don't have to." She meant that they could find some other means of investigating what happened to her uncle. But Alex reacted strongly. He stuck the mirror into his coat pocket.

"No," he said. "You're *not* using the mirror here."

"Okay," she said slowly. She hadn't even been suggesting that. But she bristled at the command in his tone. Since when did Alex get to decide how and when she used the mirror?

"Evelyn, I'm not being overprotective. I just don't want you to have to feel what I'm feeling right now." He took her hand and squeezed it. Then he turned to walk back to the pathway.

She was about to follow him, but she still felt the pull of what she'd just seen. How Daniella had opened the back of that stone marker. She had to know.

She tugged on his hand. "Alex, wait. There's something I want to look at. It's not far from here."

"It's cold, and I'm tired of being out here. This can wait until later."

"It won't take long."

Suddenly, Alex stepped in closer and held her by her upper arms. "I have an idea. Let's get away from Byrne House for a while. Take my mom's rental and drive up to the mountains."

"But—" She started to point.

"Ev, please. I know this thing with your uncle is important to you. But I'm sick of Byrne House mysteries. We need time together away from here, just us." His eyes pleaded with her.

She couldn't just leave. Whatever was happening to her —these flashes—there was a reason behind it. She felt it. Something she was supposed to understand. About Uncle Sammy and Madeline and Daniella, yes, but not just them. Something more.

And Alex had no right to tell her where she could and couldn't go.

"The mountains will still be there later." She pulled away from his grasp and spun, winding her way through the trees. She reached the back of the stone marker and traced each of the channels in the ice-cold stone with her finger. Two on the sides, and one in the middle. The latch was somewhere inside the channel on the right. She stuck her finger inside, as Daniella had done, and wiggled it around, dislodging dirt and particles of crumbling stone mixed with snow.

The bushes rustled behind her. "This is what you wanted to look at?" Alex asked. "We were just here, like, an hour ago."

She moved her finger up and down the channel, searching for the latch. Her finger slipped into a gap, just out of sight under the face of the stone. When she tried to pull her finger back, it caught on something hard. A loop.

"What are you doing?"

She pulled and felt a snap as the loop moved. Cracking and popping noises rang out as the face of the stone began to swing outward on its hidden hinges.

Alex jumped back. "How did you do that?"

She let go of the loop and pulled her finger out of the channel. She pushed open the stone door the rest of the way. The sun had started to sink into the sky, shedding beams of light directly into the gloom inside the stone marker.

It was hollow, a tiny space that even Evelyn would have to crouch to get inside. Planks of warped wood covered the floor, held down by another, narrower set of hinges. There was a metal catch on one side of the wood.

A trap door.

23

"Ev, HOW DID YOU KNOW ABOUT THIS?"

"I thought I saw someone, and I followed her. The same way I found this place the other day."

"The ghost thing? Again? How often has that been happening?" He scrutinized her warily, like he was searching for the girl he knew and couldn't find her.

"Right," she said, though this wasn't an answer to his last question. She bent over and reached for the catch on the trap door.

"What are you doing?"

She turned back to look at him. "I'm going to open it."

Alex's eyes slowly moved over the mildew-streaked inner surface of the stone and finally rested again on the trap door at its base. "Let me do it. I don't want you to fall into wherever this goes."

He crouched down and grabbed the catch. The hinges and the wood groaned, the door first swinging up and then down flat, leaving a square hole in the ground. Sunlight hit the top few steps of a staircase.

The stairs descended underground into darkness.

"We need a flashlight," Alex said. "Wait here. *Don't* go down without me."

He stepped out, then twisted around to her again. "Evelyn. Please, I'm asking you. Wait for me, okay?"

"Alright, I will." Apparently he thought she was going to run down a dark staircase she'd never seen before, without a flashlight. But considering the bizarre way she'd been acting lately, maybe she couldn't really blame him.

A couple of minutes later he came back with a high-beam flashlight. "You're still here."

"I told you I would be."

"Yeah, well…" He pointed the flashlight at the staircase and started down. "Stay behind me."

She rolled her eyes, but hung back to let him go first. Then she started down.

The stairs were slippery with layers of dust, and crumbling in spots where old bricks showed through beneath the rotting wood. Alex held out his hand and helped her to the bottom, though of course she could've done it herself.

They slowly rotated in a circle, aiming the flashlight into the corners of the room.

"I know this place," Alex said, his voice low and hoarse. "We both do."

Evelyn looked up. There was a discolored area on the ceiling, like another material had been used to patch up a large hole. She already knew what he was going to say.

"This is where we fell."

Alex let go of her hand and pressed his palm flat against his scar, as if it hurt him. "It's just the same as I remember. Except over here." He turned the flashlight to the brick archway across from them, which had caved in with debris. "That passage used to be clear."

Evelyn walked to the wall and followed the perimeter of the room. She could sense so much here. Rage, despair, overwhelming love, so many familiar voices among others she didn't know. Madeline and Sammy were here. Walter.

Darren Byrne, sobbing alone in the corner.

And a terrified little girl and bleeding little boy. Their fear made her heart clench.

All these memories, these voices, were grasping for her at once, desperate to be heard. Her shoulders shook with the effort of holding them back. Maybe Silvia was right about the ghosts—they were more than just imprints, echoes of dead things. The memories here felt *alive*.

Alex turned the flashlight on her. "Evelyn, how did you know about the door in the back of that statue? How could you possibly have known that was there?"

She almost gave up and told him about the flashes. Everything. But explaining it—that would take more effort than she could manage. Especially down here.

He stepped into her path. "Did you already come here with the mirror? Is that how you knew?"

"Sure."

"That's not an answer!"

She couldn't stand that light in her eyes. She tried to go around him, but he blocked the way. She was working so hard to hold back all the memories around her. A hot trickle of salt and metal ran down her throat and tickled the inside of her nose. She turned away, hoping Alex couldn't see it.

"Alex, *please*. I'll tell you. Just not now. I can't take it right now."

"Fine." He stepped aside and let her pass.

She started toward the cave-in, stepping over scattered rocks and brick and thick, dead roots. The air coming through the archway vibrated and glinted with tiny particles, reflecting light from some unseen source.

"Do you feel that?" she asked. Now the ground had a subtle vibration as well, moving up through her feet, buzzing in her joints.

"I don't feel anything." Alex's voice was flat, distant. As if she were already on the other side of the archway, and he was far behind.

"I need to go over there." Evelyn edged as close to the archway as she could manage and started pulling rocks from the top of the pile. She needed to clear enough space to crawl through to the other side.

"Talk to me," Alex said. "Why do you want to go over there? Does this have something to do with the tunnels, when Darren was chasing you last summer? I'm here with you, you're safe, you don't have to escape from anything."

She threw handfuls of crumbled brick behind her onto the ground. "It's not about that. Why don't you help me instead of asking questions I can't answer? You want to know what's back there as much as I do."

She could already see it around him, underneath the confusion and worry, licking at the surface of his skin like flames. The desire to finally know where that archway led.

Alex watched her for another moment. Then he wedged the flashlight in between some rocks, at an angle so they could see what they were doing, and started to help her clear the passage. He took over the bulk of the effort of moving the heavier rocks out of the way.

After they'd cleared a space in the debris, they both stepped back. Alex bent down for the flashlight, handed it to her, and stepped through the archway. Without a word, he reached over and picked her up. He lifted her through the gap and set her down on the other side.

"What now?" he asked.

Evelyn aimed the flashlight into the passage before them. It had a low, rounded ceiling and narrow walls. It was a straight shot ahead for a few yards until it curved away out of sight.

"Do you think it connects to the tunnels?" Alex asked.

"I don't know."

He grumbled under his breath. He didn't believe her.

"I really don't, I swear."

"I'm surprised you haven't already run ahead yet."

It was probably because he still had his arms locked around her waist from carrying her.

Alex kept one arm around her as they walked forward, following the passageway. There were no gas lamps in the walls down here, no wooden support beams. In some places, roots had worked their way through cracks in the ceiling, trailing down water stains along the uneven walls. There were brushstrokes in the plaster, bulges where the mortar poked out too far from between the bricks. Sloppy, nothing like the careful construction they'd seen in the other tunnels that Walter masterminded under Castle Heights.

But Evelyn felt Walter down here, stronger than anything else. A low boil of anger that made her flinch every time her mind touched it, like something hot.

Her nose tickled again. She wiped it with the back of her hand. They hadn't walked for very long when a dead-end appeared up ahead.

The passageway ended in a riveted metal door.

"My God," Alex said. "I dreamed of this place. It's real."

He pulled on the handle. It didn't budge.

Evelyn brought the flashlight up to the keyhole. It wasn't right—it didn't have the triangular top of the tunnel locks she remembered.

"This lock isn't like the others," she said. "My key won't work."

"We should go back, anyway. This place makes me nervous."

He let go of her waist and turned to go. Evelyn pointed the flashlight to light his way, but at the same time she glanced back toward the locked door.

She just wanted to touch it for a moment before going back. Her rational mind told her it would be cool to the touch, like the other metal doors beneath Byrne House. But suddenly she felt convinced it would be warm. Like there was something burning, silent and without smoke, on the other side of the door.

She pressed her hand flat against the middle of its surface.

Blinding light rocketed up her arm, starbursting in her eyes. Images flashed into her brain, hundreds and thousands at once, a blur that spread out in her head like a bottle of ink emptied into water.

Gold.

The bright metal was everywhere. The entire inner surface of that door was gold.

Then the images vanished, and all she could comprehend was searing, overwhelming *pain*.

PART 2
REFRACTION

24

THE FLASHLIGHT FELL FROM EVELYN'S HANDS.

She heard it thud, and her cheek hit something solid a split second later. Her ears registered a high-pitched vibration, coming from everywhere at once, ringing through her head. She felt it in her throat.

She was screaming.

Alex swam in her vision amid echoes of light, as if she'd been staring at the sun. A golden sun, split and multiplied into a thousand glittering discs of burning heat. He put his hands on Evelyn's cheeks, his face inches from hers. His mouth was moving.

"Alex, we have to get away from here." She could barely hear her own voice, but she kept talking. They didn't have much time. "Something awful is down here, something's happening, we have to get out!"

He picked her up and ran. The pain receded, like Evelyn's brain was surrounding it and locking it away, protecting the rest of her from whatever it was. By the time Alex got to the stairs, she was confused and disoriented. But the images were fading.

Aboveground, Alex lay her in the grass and crouched at her side. There were smears of blood on his neck and shoulder. Her blood. He panted and stared down at her with an expression of pure shock, his scar purple against the white of his skin. Then he scooped her up again into his arms.

"I'm taking you to the hospital."

"It's just a nosebleed."

He stood up, cradling her against him. Evelyn kicked her legs. "Put me down, I'm fine!"

Alex lost his grip, and she fell onto the grass. He took a few steps backward and collapsed against the stone marker, sliding down to its base. "What. Is. Going. On."

She'd seen something down there. A flash of Walter Byrne—that seemed right. But now she couldn't remember what it was. She pressed her hands against her temples. The trees kept moving in her vision, though she was sitting still.

"Not right now."

"*Yes* right now. Is it the dust from the crystals? Like when we were kids?"

His voice was too loud. She couldn't think. "No. Just let it go, please."

"Let it *go*? Do you have any idea what you look like right now?"

Alex pulled the mirror from his coat pocket. "Do you see yourself? Your face is covered in blood. You were screaming down there like you were on fire and shouting about something awful that was going to get us. I'm supposed to let that *go*?"

She pushed herself up and doubled over, hanging her head. Her hair stuck to the sides of her face.

"I just can't right now. I can't."

He gripped the mirror in his fist. "Can't what, exactly? Trust me enough to tell me what the hell is going on with you? You've suddenly been seeing ghosts everywhere, then this morning I find you passed out in the snow, and then all this. You're obviously hiding something, and it's been going on for days. It's making you sick."

Evelyn was tired, more tired than she'd been since the tunnels last August, and she didn't want to lie to him anymore. Right now, she couldn't remember why she'd hidden any of it from Alex. She could hardly remember where she was or how she got here. She needed Alex to help her home, to her room, so she could rest. Then she'd tell him everything. All he wanted to know.

She dragged her gaze upward.

"I'd rather hear it from you," he said. "But I'll find out for myself if that's how you want it to be."

He stood over her, holding the mirror in front of him.

"Alex," she whispered. "No."

He wasn't serious. Alex would never do that to her, just take her thoughts and feelings that way. Not deliberately. Last summer, he'd sensed her emotions after he'd been injected with Darren's drug. But back then, Alex had no choice.

"I know something's wrong," he said. "Something's messed up in your head so you can't think straight. I have to know what it is."

Evelyn sat up, her stomach rolling with nausea. "I'll tell you later. Just give me a chance. *Please.*"

"I don't believe you. This is the only way I'm going to get the truth."

He pointed the mirror at her.

She wondered if she'd feel something as the mirror forced open her mind. Some sense of invasion. But as she watched Alex stare at her through the mirror, his eyes dull and unfocused, she felt only exhaustion. A headache continued to pound between her eyes. She didn't have the energy to control her stream of thoughts.

Images and memories flipped through her mind. All the things she'd been trying to hide. The flashes, the murder, Madeline and Uncle Sammy. Jake. The kiss. God, the kiss. Alex would know. He'd be furious. The more she tried to shove it all down, the more it bubbled up where he was sure to see.

After a minute or two she stopped fighting it. If this was what Alex wanted—every doubt she'd had, every feeling of jealousy and anger at him—he'd get it.

She was a little tempted to focus in on him, to see if she could pry her way into his head in turn. Bring on one of the flashes. But she wasn't that cruel. Besides, she was too exhausted to do anything but sit and wait for it to be over.

Finally, Alex closed his eyes and covered them with his hand. He sat down hard on the grass and lay the mirror in front of him between his feet.

"Happy now?" Evelyn's voice was hoarse. "Get what you wanted?"

He rubbed his hand against his forehead. "You know I'm not happy."

"How would I? I can't see inside your head. I wouldn't do that to you."

Alex looked up, a cruel smile on his face. "You wouldn't? You don't care about hurting me. You let Jake kiss you, and you were more worried about protecting him from what I might do than you were about how I'd feel."

She pushed herself away from Alex, resting her back against the stone marker. "Of course. That's what matters most to you, out of everything. That some other boy kissed me."

He slammed his palm into a tree trunk. Half-melted snow rained down, "I'm supposed to act like that doesn't hurt?"

She had to close her eyes. She couldn't take the way he was looking at her, with his mouth pinched up under his nose. Like she was some foreign, repulsive thing.

"You have no faith in me at all," he said. "You wouldn't tell me you were having visions that were making you sick, or that you saw your uncle *dead* covered in *blood* in the tower, because you thought I was too weak to handle it. All your lies about 'ghost sightings.' You never even gave me a chance."

Evelyn stood up, bracing herself against the stone. Every part of her ached, but she couldn't sit there while

Alex distorted everything, made it sound like this was all her fault.

"I tried to tell you how hard it was, how I couldn't stop thinking about what happened in the tunnels, but every time I did, you got so quiet and sad on the phone that I couldn't take it anymore. You were glad I stopped talking about it."

He walked from one end of the clearing to the other, fingers scratching through his hair. "I worried about you all the time while I was away. But you kept insisting you were fine. You claim you needed me, but within a month you'd already replaced me."

"That is not true."

Alex turned his face up to the sky. "Why did it have to be him? Maybe this wouldn't hurt so bad if it were anyone else, but him...have you wanted him since last summer? Since the tunnels? He understood you so well, right? He knew what you needed, and I didn't."

"That is so unfair. Nothing happened between me and Jake until this morning, and you know exactly how I reacted. I told him to stay away from me. You're jealous because I had a friend."

He spun to face her, his eyes aflame. "A friend who you go to every time something's wrong, instead of me? Even when I'm here, living two minutes away from you? Yeah, that does make me pretty freaking jealous. I think I have a right to be."

"Everything's about what *you* expect, what *you* need. That's exactly why I didn't go to you. I didn't want you to be upset. I wanted you to be *happy*. I've been trying so hard, but I can't keep up. You expect me to be ready for everything just because you are, ready to jump in the car and drive to the mountains if you decide you feel like it."

He threw back his head and laughed. "Yeah, I'm such a bully, aren't I?"

"Then you ask me to marry you because the idea just pops into your head, and I'm horrible for not jumping up and down and screaming yes."

Alex's chest heaved a few times as he glared at her. Then he walked away to the edge of the clearing, seeming to study the trees. A few brown leaves still clung to the branches, curled around themselves. Alex plucked a leaf and crushed it between his fingers.

"You must have been laughing at me this morning," he said. "Practically begging you to marry me, thinking that you actually loved me the way I thought you did, when I had no idea you were with Jake just a few minutes before. I probably sounded like such a pathetic loser to you."

Her legs wouldn't hold her anymore. She slid against the stone marker till she reached the ground, clutching her knees to her chest.

"When I found the ring in my dad's cigar box, there was a letter from him, too. He wrote me that letter right before he died, saying he knew I'd find the right person to wear that ring someday. And I knew it was you."

He rubbed the toe of his shoe against the tree, and brittle pieces of bark flaked down onto the grass. "But if I knew what I know now, I would have never come back to Castle Heights. This was all a huge mistake."

Evelyn took off the ring and threw it at him. It landed in the grass, next to the mirror where he'd dropped it.

"Then why don't you leave? Go back home to New York. It's what you were going to do eventually, anyway."

Alex ducked between the bushes, out of sight, without picking up the ring. She rolled over, facedown in a patch of wet dying grass, and cried.

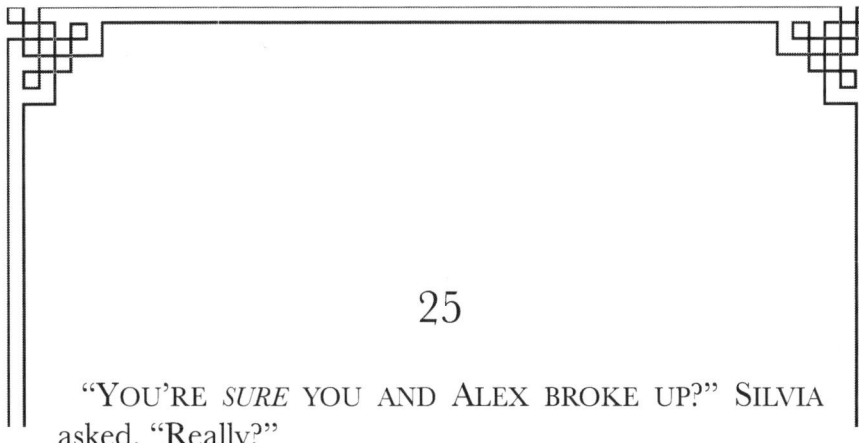

25

"YOU'RE *SURE* YOU AND ALEX BROKE UP?" SILVIA asked. "Really?"

They were sitting on Evelyn's bed. Silvia had one leg drawn up beneath her, the other stretched out. Evelyn was tucked into the tightest ball she could manage, with her head resting against her knees.

"He said he wished he hadn't come back to Castle Heights," Evelyn replied in a monotone. *And I threw Ada's ring at him.* She regretted so many things about yesterday, but throwing the ring was a top contender. It had been childish. She hadn't been thinking straight.

"I just can't believe it." Silvia exhaled. She rubbed Evelyn's shoulder. "No matter what happens, you're going to be okay. You know that right?"

A jolt hit Evelyn's stomach. Fresh tears sprang into her eyes. Losing Alex hurt worse than anything she'd ever experienced—even the pain of breaking her leg and escaping Darren in the tunnels. Because that day, no matter how terrifying some of those moments were, her thoughts of Alex had kept her going. She'd known to her core that he loved her. That he'd find her.

Now she was back in the dark. But Alex wasn't coming.

There was a knock at her bedroom door. "Mom, go away," she said. She'd been avoiding her parents since she got home yesterday. They only knew that she and Alex had argued; thankfully they hadn't seen the blood on her clothes.

The door cracked. "I'm not Mom," Milo said. "Is it safe to come in?"

Silvia jumped up and opened the door wide. Milo stood in the hall holding a paper bag.

"I brought bagels," he said.

"Of course you did." Silvia plopped back onto the bed. "Carbs are Milo's answer to everything," she said in a stage whisper. The bag crinkled as Milo opened it, passing bagels around. He sat at the desk chair.

Evelyn took a couple of bites, though she couldn't taste it. "Thank you both," she said. "I'm sorry I'm such a disaster." Her eyes were swollen from crying. She'd hardly slept, and she certainly hadn't showered.

"You're not." Milo had always been too nice.

"Hey, in this room we're practicing radical honesty." Silvia grinned. "And, actually, it *does* kinda reek in here."

"More than kinda," Milo mumbled.

"Hey!" Evelyn said.

"What? Radical honesty!" Milo stuffed half his bagel in his mouth.

Evelyn felt the smile on her face. Then she thought of Alex and the pain returned to her insides. But it was less this time. She took another bite of her bagel.

Silvia was right about the radical honesty. She'd told Silvia everything—including the stuff about Jake. Evelyn had also given Silvia permission to tell Milo the awful details, even though she was ashamed of the things she'd said to Alex, and of all the things he'd said back.

You don't care about hurting me. You have no faith in me at all.

He was wrong. She hated herself for hurting him, though she was still furious with him too. It wasn't that she'd lost faith in Alex. Her faith in love itself had been shaken.

"What're you going to do?" Milo asked gently.

"I really think Alex is going to realize what a mistake he's made and apologize," Silvia cut in. "The real question is, will Ev take him back?"

Evelyn was sure that Silvia was wrong. Alex's last words to her had such finality. But if somehow a miracle happened, and he did take it all back?

Yes, she'd made stupid mistakes that she'd regret forever. She shouldn't have called Jake instead of him. She should've tried again to explain about the flashes, even though the first time he hadn't wanted to listen. She'd gotten obsessed with solving Byrne House's endless mysteries, and she had nothing to show for it except a broken heart.

But she couldn't forget what Alex had done, either. The way he'd used the mirror against her. All the cruel, unfair accusations.

Milo swiveled back and forth on the chair. "What if, maybe, it's Alex who most deserves the apology?"

Silvia leveled a glare at him.

Milo held up his hands. "Fine, I'll stay out of it."

"No, please," Evelyn said. "Tell me what you were going to say."

"Just that you might've been wrong." Milo pushed up his glasses. "No," he said more confidently, "you *were* wrong. You should've told Alex the truth from the start. You know I'm not that crazy about him—he can be arrogant at times —but Alex clearly loves you. He deserved better."

Every word rang true. Alex did love her, she believed that. At least, he used to. "He deserved my trust, you mean?" *He deserved my honesty, even if it wasn't what he wanted to hear.*

"Yeah, I can hardly believe I'm saying it, but..." Milo nodded. "I think he did."

Silvia scooted closer and wrapped her arm around Evelyn's shoulders.

"I'm really sorry if that hurts," Milo said.

Evelyn wiped tears from her cheek. "It's the truth. It's supposed to."

⁓⁓⁓⁓⁓

That afternoon Evelyn's dad came up from the basement, a dusty cardboard box in his hands. "Look what I found," he said.

She followed him into the living room. He'd already set up the tree, fresh from the nearby parking lot-turned-Santa's village. The room smelled of evergreen. It reminded her of Alex—whatever pine-scented product he'd been using lately. She inhaled deeply. The pain in her chest intensified.

Vivian had gone off somewhere, leaving Evelyn and her father alone. It was supposed to be some dad-daughter bonding time. All she could think about was Alex. Every moment, she was on the verge of tears. Her dad had been sneaking worried glances at her, but he hadn't asked. She ground her teeth together. He had better *not* ask. He'd lost the right.

Toby opened the box and held up a little bundle wrapped in tissue paper. It was a hand-painted ornament that Evelyn had made as a child, something with messy neon fingerprints all over it.

"I remember this one," he said. "Fourth grade?"

"First."

"Right." He hung the ornament on the tree. Instead of the business casual attire he'd arrived in, he was wearing cargo shorts. His t-shirt bore a logo for *Dirty Water IPA*, which Evelyn hoped was a joke.

"It's been really great seeing you everyday," he said. "I've missed that. I can't believe how much you've grown up."

"Yeah, two years will do that," Evelyn said dully. She jabbed a hook into a pinecone ornament.

Her phone pinged with a text. Her heart began to race as she unlocked it. But, as usual, the message was just from Jake.

It said, *I'm sorry. I need professional help. Please forgive me.*

She typed back, *Screw you.*

"Is that Alex?" Toby asked.

She didn't respond. Instead she kept stringing hooks onto stray ornaments.

Her dad tried to catch her eye. "So, I have some news. I'll have to take off in the morning. I got a call about a work emergency this afternoon, and believe me, I tried everything to get this off my plate. But they need me in person." Toby laughed, a braying sound that made her cringe. "More qualifying airline miles, right?"

Evelyn shrugged one shoulder. "Whatever."

"I'll be back by Christmas itself. I promise."

He'd promised she could come visit for Thanksgiving, too. And look how *that* had turned out.

Her phone buzzed again. Jake wasn't giving up. This one said, *Thank you, Sir, may I please have another.*

She nearly threw the phone across the room. Jake could be charming when it suited him. But it was unconscionable to think she'd make up with Jake and not Alex.

"I've been trying to fix up my condo." Toby was still trimming the tree, oblivious to her distraction. "But it doesn't feel like home without you there."

"That's because Castle Heights is my home."

"But couldn't you make a new home? Maybe even one with me?"

She put down the ornament she'd just picked up. "You seriously want me to come live with you?"

"It would be part time, of course. I know your mom wants to see you, too."

She opened her mouth. No sound came out. She imagined screaming that she hated him, that he didn't deserve her forgiveness, but what good would that do?

What would it be like, starting over? Leaving Castle Heights and Byrne House behind?

"You won't really be a minor too much longer, but I'd like to work out a joint parenting arrangement with your mom. One of us would be the primary. I'm just leaving open the option: it could be me."

Evelyn sat on the couch, all the fight going out of her at once. She missed Alex. What did it matter where she lived, or what she did, if he didn't want her anymore?

"I don't know, Dad. I'll think about it."

She didn't want to choose between her mother and her father. She wanted to choose *herself*. And even now, the only place she could imagine herself was with Alex.

More than anything, she wanted to rewind to last Friday and start over. She'd tell Alex everything she'd been holding back, even the parts that would make him upset, and stop herself from worrying so much about him leaving that she couldn't be happy when he was here.

She took out her phone and pulled up Alex's name in the contacts. Her thumb hovered over the message icon. But she couldn't undo what had happened.

Now, it was too late.

26

EVELYN'S PHONE WOKE HER. THE ROOM WAS DARK.
She sat up in bed. Light from the street lamps outside bounced against the thick layer of clouds and filtered in through her window. Her phone rang again, piercing the silence of the house. Hopefully her dad wouldn't hear it next door in the den. She had no clue what time it was.

She leaned over the side of the bed, grabbed her jeans from the floor, and pulled her phone out of her pocket.

Caitlin Meyer was calling.

She hadn't spoken to Caitlin since last August—the night of the kickoff dance, when Alex had gone as Caitlin's date but ended up kissing Evelyn instead. She'd seen Caitlin plenty of times in the halls at school, but after receiving nothing but hostility, she'd never expected to speak to Caitlin again.

"Hello?" she asked hesitantly.

"I'm going to say this very quickly," Caitlin said, "and then I'm going to hang up."

Evelyn pushed back her comforter and swung her legs off the side of the bed.

"Okay…"

"I'm at Brian Monroe's house. Alex is here. He's completely drunk and making an ass of himself."

Evelyn covered the phone with her hand and cursed. Then she said, "Why are you telling me this?"

"Because he asked me to call you, and he's too messed up to call you himself. You need to come get him."

"Come get him?" She held the phone out, checking the time on the screen. 2:47 a.m. Great. "How? I don't have a car. You know that."

"Call an Uber or something like a normal human."

Caitlin hung up.

Evelyn lurched out of bed. First, she had to get herself dressed. Then, she had to find a car. And the directions to Brian Monroe's house. He was a senior, wasn't he? On the varsity baseball team. Caitlin hadn't bothered to give her an address, and she'd never been to his house before. She barely even knew the guy. How on earth had Alex ended up there?

Had he gone to the party to meet *Caitlin*?

He asked me to call you.

Evelyn closed her eyes a moment, pushing the jealousy away. She couldn't think any more about Caitlin right now. If Alex needed her, then of course she'd go.

After pulling on her clothes, she tiptoed downstairs to the kitchen to get her mom's keys. Vivian always left them on a table by the back door. She stuck out her hand, feeling in the dark for the thick bundle of her mother's keyring. But all she found was a pile of old receipts.

She couldn't find the keys anywhere. Nor could she locate her mom's purse or jacket. After searching the entryway and the hall closet, she started to wonder. She went to her mom's bedroom; the bed didn't look slept in. Then she went to the living room and peered through the window onto the street.

Viv's car wasn't out there.

Evelyn tried to remember what time her mom had returned last night, but she couldn't. She'd finished decorating the tree with her father, said goodnight, and gone to her room.

Had Vivian not come home?

She pressed her fingers against her eyes. She had no time to think—let alone worry—about her mother right now. Maybe Viv just needed some space.

That left her dad's rental car, but then she'd have to find *his* keys. Probably buried inside a suitcase or stuck under the den couch, knowing her dad.

She tried calling Milo and Silvia, but they didn't answer. No doubt asleep.

Fine, she thought. *Lyft it is.* But she couldn't get the app to work. The credit card was out of date, and she couldn't handle yet another search of the house for her wallet, and she was on the verge of tears.

She had one option left. Several minutes of agony later, she gave in and sent the text.

Jake pulled up in his mom's minivan.

Evelyn got in. "Did you find the address?" she asked.

"Yeah." He was grinning, his teeth flashing in the street lamps as they drove down the block. "So we're going to Brian Monroe's party? Together?"

"Not exactly." She'd told Jake she wanted him to take her to Monroe's house. She hadn't explained why. She'd thought it would be easier that way to get him to agree. "We're picking someone up."

"Really. Let me guess."

She watched the streets morph from tree-lined to neon-blasted as they left Castle Heights and hit the main boulevard that stretched across town.

"Alex usually just calls a Lyft to get around, right? He's a self-sufficient guy. So that must mean he's misbehaving and you're going to force him to come home. Didn't think that was your style, Ev."

"Just drive, Jake. Please. You kind of owe me."

He settled back in his seat, one hand on the steering wheel. "After this I think we'll be even. You pulled me away from a binge watch of *Westworld* to run this errand for you. Although—the look on Evans's face when he sees me pull up with you next to me—that'll almost be payment enough."

Cars sped past them. Jake was driving slow, probably five under the speed limit. She drummed her fingers against the passenger door, resisting the urge to tell Jake to hurry up. He'd probably just slow down even more. The light changed to red and they crawled to a stop.

"You left a pink rock in my room," Jake said. "Come to my house after this and I'll give it back."

She rested her elbow against the passenger door, gazing out the window. "Keep it. My gift to you." He needed the positive energy at least as badly as she did.

"So did you tell him?" Jake asked.

"Tell him what?"

"You know." Jake was tapping his thumb against the steering wheel in time with the song on the radio. Like he was having fun.

She kept her eyes on the street, but she knew he had a smirk painted across his face. She could hear it in his voice, teasing her, daring her to react. "He knows about what you did a couple days ago, if that's what you mean."

"Hmm, guess I'd better watch out, then. Did you fight about it?"

An impossible question, however she answered it. Jake would have something obnoxious to say about Alex no matter what.

"Ah, a really bad fight," Jake finished for her. "Bad enough you don't even want to talk about it. Bad enough Alex runs off to Brian Monroe's party and you need me to drag him back at three in the morning."

She sighed and let her head fall back against the headrest. "Yeah. Bad."

They turned onto Brian Monroe's street. Evelyn knew which house it was by the lights blazing in every window and the constant stream of people in and out of the front door. There were a lot more heading out than in. Maybe the party was dying down.

"Wait here," she told Jake. "I'll go in and get Alex, and then we can leave."

She got out and slammed the door, then knocked on the driver's side window until Jake buzzed it down. "Don't provoke Alex, okay? Please? I just want to take him home with as little arguing as possible."

Jake waved his hand, dismissing her. "Whatever you say. Go get him."

Evelyn started up the sidewalk to Brian's front door, dodging discarded plastic cups. A girl on five inch heels wobbled past her.

"Hey," Jake called after her, "he gives you trouble just come get me. I'll take care of him."

27

THE FRONT DOOR OPENED ONTO A SMALL LIVING room and a kitchen, with a low wall separating one room from the other. She didn't see Alex, so she headed into the kitchen. The keg looked abandoned, with hoses sprouting out of it filled with half-dried foam. There were empty plastic tequila and rum bottles on the counter surrounded by cups and open beer bottles.

Next she wandered into a hallway. Voices and light came from somewhere deeper in the house. She kept going.

The hallway turned, and she came into a large, wood-paneled den with brown shag carpeting. *Godzilla* played in black and white on the big screen TV on one wall, but nobody seemed to be watching it. Everyone was focused on a table in the center of the room with three guys and a girl on folding chairs, playing a drinking game. She recognized Brian Monroe, but she didn't know the others. Brian launched a quarter across the table. It bounced once and splashed into one of the glasses.

She spotted Alex. He was slouching on a huge sectional sofa in the corner, drinking from a clear liquor bottle. She started towards him.

Then someone leaned into him on the couch. Caitlin. Her red hair was in a high ponytail. She looked up, and her eyes met Evelyn's.

Then she casually held Alex's shirt by the collar, pulled him forward, and kissed him. He did nothing to resist.

Time seemed to stop. Alex and Caitlin. Here. Together.

She couldn't breathe. Cobwebs inched across her vision until all she could see was Alex kissing Caitlin on the couch. She felt a tug on her arm and heard someone laughing, and she wanted more than anything to get out of there and go someplace that had air to breathe but her feet were stuck in place. Like that shag carpet had sprouted and woven itself around her shoes.

Everything had gone quiet in the room except the tinny-sounding screams from the monster movie on the TV. Then she heard murmurs, and saw elbows nudging, heads nodding in her direction.

Alex pulled back from Caitlin and looked over.

His eyes narrowed at first, then got wide as his jaw went slack. He pushed Caitlin away. She bounced onto the couch cushion next to him. He dropped the bottle on the floor as he stood up and it toppled over, sloshing clear liquid all over the carpet and the base of the couch.

Evelyn turned and ran down the hall.

"Wait!"

She sped through the kitchen and into the living room, where she smacked into another partygoer.

"Hey, are you okay?"

She tried to push the boy out of the way so she could get to the door, but Alex caught up with her. He held Evelyn by the shoulders. "Ev, stop, wait a second. Please."

She looked back at him. His lips were red from Caitlin's lipstick. Evelyn slapped him on the cheek. It didn't seem to faze him. He grabbed the hand she'd used to slap him and held her arms as she struggled to get away.

"I have no idea how that happened."

"Her tongue in your mouth? That didn't look like an accident." She heard a chorus of "Oooo" coming from the kitchen.

His eyes clouded over. "Kind of like you and Jake the other morning, when you let him put his hands all over you? That wasn't an accident either."

The kitchen erupted with laughter and shouts.

"Is that why you asked Caitlin to call me?" she said. "Some kind of revenge?"

He looked confused. "I didn't ask her to call you."

Her face was burning. She dropped her voice. "Please let me leave before I start crying. This is already humiliating enough."

Alex let go of her hands. Evelyn turned and left the house.

Jake was sitting on the hood of his mom's car when she came out. He watched her approach, his eyes taking in the scene behind her as the crowd from the kitchen poured out onto Brian's front lawn.

"What the hell is he doing here?" Alex yelled.

Jake smirked at Evelyn.

"He gave me a ride," she said. "We came here to pick you up, because I thought that's what you wanted."

She wrenched open the car door.

Alex reached past her and slammed the door closed. "You're not going anywhere with him."

She spun to face him. "You have no right to tell me who I can be with. We broke up, remember?"

"Really?" Jake hopped down from the car hood. "Broke up? This I didn't know."

"Shut your mouth." Alex put himself between Evelyn and Jake. "You're lucky I don't shut it for you, after what you did to her. You're sick, pushing around a girl half your size."

"Yes, you're so big and strong, and Evelyn's so weak." Jake laughed and looked over Alex's shoulder at her, lifting his eyebrows as if to say, *I told you so.* "I can't imagine how she survived the last few months without you."

Alex took a step closer to Jake, wobbling on his feet. He put out a hand to brace himself against the car. "I'm happy to kick your ass if that's what it takes to make you listen. I told you to stay away from her." Alex's voice was starting to slur, so it sounded more like *I tuld you ta staway frumer.*

Jake leaned back. "Could you exhale in some other direction while you threaten me? Your breath is practically flammable."

Then Alex shoved Jake against the car, and Jake jumped up and pushed Alex, sending him stumbling back onto the lawn. He lost his balance and sat down with a hard thump in the grass.

"You're both being idiots." Evelyn pointed back at the house. "They're all staring at us. Someone's probably recording all this on his phone right now."

"Good!" Alex said. "I want everyone to see him with the...with him down in the..."

"Alex, stop it. You're smashed." He was up on his knees, trying to stand as he kept pointing at Jake. Evelyn couldn't leave him there like that, and she definitely did not want to hang around in Brian Monroe's front yard for another second. She hooked an arm around Alex's elbow to help him get up, and so he'd stop waving his finger around at Jake.

"I'm taking you home."

"I'll only go if he apologizes to you."

Jake smiled. "Evelyn, I'm very sorry for kissing you. Although right now I'd guess you're realizing it wasn't so bad. At least I didn't smell like paint thinner."

Alex lunged at Jake again as the crowd hooted behind them. She could barely hold onto him. "Get in the car," she said through her teeth.

Jake walked around to the driver's side, and she held open the door to the backseat. "Only if you sit back there with me," Alex said. "I don't want you near him."

"Fine. Just get in."

Alex ducked into the back, and she slid in behind him. Once they were in the car, he tried to take her hand, but she pulled away and scooted as far toward the window as she could.

"Don't think that because I'm letting you ride with us that I've forgotten what I just saw."

Jake started the car and drove away from the curb. "What did she see, Evans? It must have been good."

"Shut up. Shut *up*." Alex closed his eyes. "How'd you know I was there?"

"Caitlin. She called me, and I was stupid enough to fall for it. Why were you there with her?"

"She texted me a while back. I decided to respond."

Evelyn rested her forehead against the window. The glass was bracingly cold.

Caitlin had wanted to see Evelyn humiliated in front of everyone at that party. The perfect revenge, apparently—Caitlin thought Evelyn had done the same to her last summer. Evelyn's stomach lurched as she thought of Alex's mouth on Caitlin's. She curled herself into a ball on the backseat and pressed her eye sockets against her knees.

"Ev, I'm sorry. I'm really, really sorry. You have no idea."

"Sorry you got caught doing whatever you were doing?" Jake asked. "I'm sure that was frustrating for you. Sucks when someone just shows up, with no warning, when nobody wants him there, anyway…"

"I had no clue she was going to kiss me," Alex said.

Jake whistled. "Wow."

"Both of you just be quiet," Evelyn snapped. "Don't talk to me. Or to each other."

Jake snickered, but he didn't say anything else. She focused on the movement of the car and the swishing noise it made as they drove. She tried to ignore the sound of Alex breathing and his shifting around on the seat beside her. He whispered something to her, and his fingers brushed her arm, but she smacked them away. She just wanted this night to be over. She wanted to go back to sleep and not get out of bed for a month.

The brakes whined as Jake came to a stop. "Byrne House," he announced.

"Come on, Evelyn." Alex scooted toward her, like he expected them both to exit from her door.

"I'm not going anywhere. Especially not with you."

"I'm walking you home. I'm not leaving you here with him."

"No offense," Jake said, "okay maybe I do mean offense, but you aren't the best person to be walking around the neighborhood right now. You'll probably get lost crossing the street."

Alex got out on his side and walked around the bumper of the car. He opened Evelyn's door. "Get out."

"No."

He bent down into the backseat and hoisted her out of the car, then slung her over his shoulder.

"Put me down!"

She kicked her legs and punched Alex's back with her fists. The driver's side door opened as Jake got out.

"This has been hilarious," Jake said. "Definitely way better than what I'd otherwise be doing. But you should put her down now."

"Don't come near me." Alex clamped one arm around Evelyn's thighs and opened the gate.

"Just go away Jake," she said upside-down. "I can handle this."

She heard Jake say, "Doesn't look like it," but he sounded far away.

Alex took the path around the side of the house. All the blood was rushing into her brain, making her face feel swollen and achy. "This is ridiculous."

He pulled on her legs, sliding her down his front until she was eye level with him. He was still holding her off the ground. "You have to give me a chance to explain."

"I'm not doing anything except going home, alone. Put me down *now!*" She pushed her hands against his shoulders.

"Alex, I think she wants you to put her down. You should probably do that before one of you gets hurt."

Evelyn craned her neck around, even though she already recognized the voice.

Alex's older brother stood in the back doorway of Byrne House.

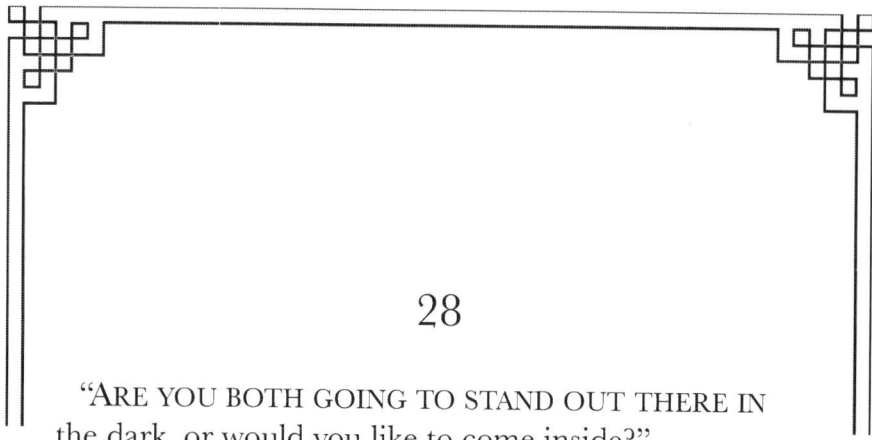

28

"ARE YOU BOTH GOING TO STAND OUT THERE IN the dark, or would you like to come inside?"

William took off his coat and laid it over one arm. A pile of suitcases sat just inside the door on the tile floor of the kitchen.

Alex set her down. "Will. You're back. I didn't...I mean I wasn't trying to..."

William aimed an exasperated look at Alex. Then he turned to Evelyn. "I can see my brother doesn't have much more sense now than the last time I saw him."

Alex glanced at her, apologetic and uncertain, before he walked into the house behind William. Evelyn followed them in. Alex slumped his shoulders so much he looked shorter than his older brother, even though he was a couple of inches taller.

"Where's Mom?" Alex asked.

William picked up a suitcase and walked from the kitchen into the main hall. "She's asleep, I assume. In case you didn't notice, it's four in the morning. I just got in from the airport. My flight was delayed. Where've you been?"

"Where have *I* been? Are you kidding?"

"Is Daniella here?" Evelyn scanned up and down the hallway. The stairs and all the doorways were dark. But she could be here somewhere, watching and waiting.

William didn't answer her. He set his suitcase by the stairs and said, "Alex, we need to talk before Mom gets up. If you're sober enough to carry on a conversation."

"You can't send Alex away," Evelyn said. She was still angry, but in this moment her fiercest instinct was to defend the boy she loved.

"I agreed that Alex could come back to Castle Heights because I thought he'd behave himself. Clearly I was wrong." He was so damned calm. As immovable as the statue in Walter Park.

"This isn't Alex's fault. It's mine."

William returned Evelyn's gaze for a moment, then finally said, "Daniella won't be here for another few days, which is a good thing. She's had enough to worry about."

Like hiding the Byrne family's many secrets? Sending harassing letters and texts? Evelyn doubted that Daniella had told William even a fraction of the truth.

Or was Daniella still waiting for Evelyn to "beg" her to come back? That wasn't going to happen. *Unless she can talk some sense into William,* Evelyn thought. Daniella had talked him into this holiday family reunion in the first place. *Daniella is the only one he'll listen to.*

"I want everything sorted out before Dany arrives," William finished. "And *that's* why Alex and I need to talk. Alone."

"Can't this wait until tomorrow?" she asked.

Alex dropped his eyes to the floor. "Evelyn, you should go."

She put her hand on Alex's forearm. A faint glow began to rise from his skin. An aura. He was so sad and ashamed and exhausted. There'd been a small flicker of hope when she'd come for him at the party, but now his hope was dying. If William sent him back to New York—even forbade him from Castle Heights altogether—Alex wasn't going to fight it. Their mom wouldn't either. Ever since Alex's father had died, Lila Evans had relied on William to manage things for their family. Of her two sons, she'd always preferred the elder.

I can't lose you, Alex had said to Evelyn the night he arrived. *You're the only one I still have.*

Evelyn remembered the fear she'd sensed a couple days ago in the underground shaft—the place where they'd fallen as children. A little boy, terrified of what might be coming. But that little boy had someone else with him, a girl he was determined to protect, and that role had given him strength.

The same fear emanated from Alex now. He feared what William was going to say—because he was afraid that it would be true. Alex had always wished for his brother's approval. But he rarely received it. As he got older, Alex had learned to protect himself by professing to hate William. But right now, Alex hated himself even more.

She couldn't leave him here alone. "I'll stay with you," she whispered. "I love you."

"I need to do this by myself." He wouldn't look at her. "I'm so sorry. For everything. Please go."

William gestured for Alex to follow. She stood there in the hallway, watching Alex trudge upstairs. Finally he glanced back at her, the dim light of the hall pooling in his eyes.

Outside, Jake was still waiting in the minivan. He leaned across the cabin and shoved open the passenger door. "Hey, you okay?"

She kept walking. "I told you to go away."

Jake started the car and drove slowly alongside her. "Don't be like that. Get in. Let's get breakfast."

"Go to hell, Jake."

"Seriously? After everything that just happened, you're still mad at me?"

She stopped and stared straight at him through the open car window. She knew she was taking out her anger on the easiest target, but she didn't care. "After everything that happened I still would take Alex back a million times before I'd even consider forgiving you."

Jake accelerated past her and turned the corner. Then the street was quiet. The barest slip of breeze whispered on its way to the park, carrying the first pricks of sleet. The tips of her nose and ears were turning numb. She crossed to her house and started up the walkway, digging into her pocket for her keys.

A car turned onto the street, its headlights swinging across the front of the house. It stopped, and the lights went dark. Vivian got out. At the same moment, she saw Evelyn.

They both froze in place. Like they were each hoping that, if she stood still enough, the other wouldn't see her.

Viv blinked first. She locked her car and strode up the sidewalk. She had on jeans and an old Nirvana t-shirt that Evelyn had stolen long ago and thought was in the laundry. Viv's hair was up in a messy ponytail.

"What are you doing out at this time of night?" Viv asked.

"Technically it's morning. What are *you* doing out?"

"Don't even. I see it was a mistake to hope I could trust you. You're grounded young lady."

Evelyn flung her arms wide. "Why don't you just ground me until you're ready to move to your new job? Then you can pack me up in a box and ship me with the rest of your stuff. I'm sure that would be a lot easier for you."

"Don't tempt me." Viv shook her head. "I leave your dad to watch out for you one night, and this is what happens."

Evelyn trudged up the porch steps to the house. "I'm too tired for this. And you know what mom? I'm too old for this. I'm going to bed."

"*You're* too old?" her mom muttered.

They went inside. Evelyn was halfway up the stairs when her mom said, "Evvy, wait."

She turned around.

Viv paused, examining her fingernails. "I was driving. For hours. I needed some time away to think."

Evelyn came down a couple of steps. "Think about what?"

Viv crossed her arms and bit the inside of her cheek. "I want you to know you can choose your Dad. All right? You'll be a lot closer to Alex in Baltimore than Seattle. If that's what you want, I'm okay with it. It's your choice entirely. Whatever you decide, I'm behind you one hundred percent."

Evelyn nodded, though she was shocked. She'd never expected her mother to utter those words: *This is your choice entirely.* But she didn't feel better. What was the point of having a choice when she couldn't bear any of the options?

"As for you sneaking out tonight," her mom added, "we'll discuss consequences tomorrow."

Up in her room, she tossed her phone on the desk and sat down. She was too wired to go to bed. She stared at the lights in the windows at Byrne House, wondering what was happening with Alex. She did want him back. And Alex obviously wanted that, too. But for so long, his brother had been telling him he was too selfish. Too reckless. Unworthy. Alex had started to believe it.

There had to be something she could do. In the past, when she'd had no good options available, she'd chosen to go her own way—like stealing Detective Penn's notebook last summer during the search for Milo. Going to Byrne House to search for clues. There'd been costs to those choices. But in the end, she'd fallen in love with Alex and filled in the holes in her memory. She'd stopped Darren from hurting anyone else. Every risk had been worth it.

She got out her phone and thumbed through the screens until she'd pulled up the message from the unknown number. The text was already sent before she could change her mind.

Daniella, I'm willing to talk.

29

WET SNOW STREAKED ACROSS EVELYN'S WINDOW. All day, she watched Byrne House for some sign. A break in the weather. A light in the second floor window that was serving as Alex's room.

Nothing.

The darkened skies of the day blurred into night, though still she hardly slept. She tossed and turned, replaying every mistake she'd made the past few days, every wrong turn. Her phone buzzed with messages, but none from the two people she might've responded to. Her dad called, saying he'd made it home to Baltimore. Eventually, Viv forced Evelyn out of her room. She ate, showered, managed to sleep. Her mom hadn't mentioned punishment again. Apparently she thought Evelyn's self-imposed exile was punishment enough.

Two days passed in a blur.

Up in her room again, she went back to her post by the window. The snow had let up, and a few meager rays of sun found their way through the clouds. She wanted to charge over to Byrne House demanding answers from anyone and everyone she met. But she was afraid of what she'd find when she got there.

What if Alex was already gone?

She checked her phone again. Daniella still hadn't written back. Evelyn hadn't texted again, but inside, she was begging to see Daniella turn up at her door. *I don't care anymore what she wants,* Evelyn thought. *Just as long as she can bring him back.*

New clouds were rolling in, thick and grey, from the west. It looked like it would snow again soon, unless the wind decided to change and carry the storm around them. Either way, it didn't matter. All she could do was wait and hope.

Day shifted into night again, and still she waited by the window, stiff and cold. Her forehead was resting against the frigid glass. Her breath made circles that grew and receded. Vivian had long since said goodnight. Evelyn was about to give up and try to sleep.

Then she saw movement. Someone was coming out of the mansion.

The figure crossed the lawn. Opened the Byrne House gate. His heavy coat obscured his outline, and a duffle bag dangled by the straps from one hand. He passed through a circle of snow-filled light under a street lamp, and his profile emerged.

Her heart danced. It was him.

As he walked along the sidewalk, he looked up at Evelyn's window. She watched him approach like she'd watched him cross the park a few days earlier—when he'd unexpectedly returned to Castle Heights and she'd thought he was only a vision—and he seemed as far away as he did then. She couldn't quite make herself believe he was really almost here, coming back to her.

Alex kept walking straight on until he reached the intersection. Then he crossed the street diagonally, toward Evelyn's house.

Quickly, she pushed up the sash of her window. Snowflakes blew into her room. She leaned out onto the small porch roof that extended beneath her window.

He stopped beneath the tree, staring up at her.

"Wait," she said, raising her voice only as much as she dared. "I'm coming."

She went back into her room and closed the window. On the second floor landing, she stopped. Everything was dark. She listened for the television or the faint clicking of her mother's laptop keyboard. But she heard nothing.

She snuck downstairs, slipped on the nearest shoes she could find, and unlocked the front door. Alex was still standing out on the lawn, his coat dusted with white.

Evelyn stepped out onto the porch and pulled the front door almost shut behind her. The world felt deserted, the snow muffling all the usual sounds.

"You came down," Alex said, setting his bag on the ground. "I was thinking about climbing your tree, like I used to, but that seemed a little extreme in a snowstorm."

She was wearing a pair of leggings and her oversized, thrifted cardigan. She tugged the sweater closed, already shivering. The sky and the snow around them glowed an eerie pink. She pointed at the duffle he'd brought.

"Are you going somewhere?" She held her breath, waiting for his answer.

Alex shrugged. "Anywhere that doesn't have my brother in it. The specifics depend on how this conversation goes."

"I've been really worried about you."

He rubbed his hands over his face. "After everything, you were worried about me?"

"I didn't say I'm not mad."

"That's good. 'Cause all the speeches I prepared assume that you're really pissed."

She walked down her porch steps onto the lawn. Snowflakes tingled on her cheeks as they melted. Alex's cheeks were red. His eyes were red, too. She leaned forward, almost touching him, but then she placed her hand against the rough bark of the tree instead.

"I wasn't sure how much you'd hate me," Alex continued, "so I prepared some different rhetorical options. I'd say groveling is the way to go. Equal amounts of explanation and apology, with some crying thrown in to keep it interesting."

He snuck a glance at her. "You're not smiling."

"Would you just come here?"

Immediately, he reached for her. His arms held her tightly, the compression soothing.

"Are you feeling okay?" he asked. "I was worried about you, too."

"I'm fine. Physically, anyway. Alex, I'm sorry. I really am."

His chest started moving up and down, gulping air. He pressed his face into her neck. "I hate myself," he whispered. "I've done everything wrong."

"It's my fault. I shouldn't have kept anything from you. I don't even really know why I did."

"I do." He lifted his head to look at her. Despite the late hour, the snow-filled sky was bright enough that Evelyn could see every detail of his face. The fine lines of his scar. His irises, a thousand shades of green. "It's because I left you here, and you didn't feel like you could count on me."

"That's not really it. I've been..." Even now, after he'd already seen into her head, this was hard to say. Hard to even admit to herself. "I've been so scared that I'm broken inside. That there's something wrong with me that can't be fixed. Not by you or me or anyone."

His palms were warm on either side of her face. "You've always been the girl in my dreams. But that's not who I want —I want the real Evelyn, no matter how messed up or broken you feel. I want to help you get better. But if we can't fix it, that won't change how I see you. That just means you're scarred like me."

She stood up on her toes. His lips were cold when she kissed him.

"I thought you'd left," she said. "I felt like I was breaking apart."

He brushed snow from her hair. "I did think about leaving, mostly to punish myself for what I did. I felt so guilty about using the mirror against you. The awful things I said. I only went to that party to get wasted. I swear, I had no idea what Caitlin was going to do. I didn't kiss her back."

Evelyn didn't want to hear anything else about Caitlin Meyer. "Could we just agree that we both did and said some really horrible things that we didn't mean, and leave it at that?"

"I'll shut up. But I am sorry."

She looked over her shoulder at the house. The lights were still off. If Viv had heard the talking, she would have come to check on them.

Evelyn took Alex's hand. "Let's go inside," she said. "I'm freezing."

In the entryway, she put a finger to her lips. He nodded. He started toward the living room, but Evelyn led him up the stairs instead.

30

On their way up the stairs, Evelyn cringed at every creak the house made. Once Alex was in her room, she silently closed her door and pressed the lock.

She sat on the edge of her bed. Alex took off his coat and laid it on the floor to dry.

"Do you want to talk about what happened with your brother?"

He sat in the desk chair, his knees touching hers. "Not so much."

"But *something's* been going on. William arrived days ago." Alex had been in that house with his brother for all that time. She'd always believed that, deep down, William loved Alex. But she didn't really know. William hadn't acted much like it.

Alex took her hand and stroked the back of it, as if she was the one who needed comfort.

"He told me all about how I'm a liability to the family—I lied about Daniella being part of Darren's schemes last year, I can't be trusted. I'm incapable of loving anybody but myself." Alex pressed his lips into a hard line and looked away. "He threatened to send me to some military boarding school, which he's said before, but I think he was really serious this time."

"He couldn't do that, could he?"

"Nah." Alex ran his fingers through his hair. "He thinks so, anyway. And my mom probably wasn't going to stop him. But yesterday, suddenly...William changed his mind."

Daniella. Evelyn's gaze sought out her phone on the nightstand. She still hadn't received a reply to her text. But perhaps Alex's words were reply enough. Daniella had gotten the message, and she'd done what Evelyn wanted without Evelyn needing to specifically ask. It was unnerving. But nonetheless—despite everything—Evelyn couldn't help feeling grateful.

"So William's not mad anymore?" Evelyn asked. But then why had Alex brought a bag with him, like he'd moved out?

"He said he's giving me a second—or maybe by now it's a hundredth?—chance. As soon as Daniella arrives, we're going to have a nice Christmas together as a family, just like we were supposed to. But I'm not going to pretend for them. I'm done. I've tried and I've tried, but I finally had to admit to myself that I can't fix things with him."

He leaned forward, resting his elbows on his knees.

"Evelyn, I need you to believe that Will's wrong about me. I love you. So much. You could see that if you used the mirror. I want you to."

The mirror. She could turn it on him, the way Alex had used it against her. She could find out everything she needed to know. To be absolutely sure that she could trust him again.

"Or maybe you don't even need the mirror anymore," he said. "Can you just focus on me, and see it in my head? If you concentrate hard enough?"

She'd been getting better at it. If she wanted to, maybe she could reach into his mind. Just enough to feel what he was feeling, to know everything he'd said was true. Like skimming the tips of her fingers barely under the surface of a pond, testing the coolness of the water.

She got up onto her knees, put her hands on either side of his face. Stubble pricked at the centers of her palms. He sat up straight and lifted his chin and held her gaze.

He would really let her do it.

She still wasn't happy that Alex had used the mirror to get the truth out of her. But she understood. And she knew that if she demanded proof from Alex now, instead of choosing to trust him, that cycle would never stop.

"I believe you," she said. "That's all I need."

"You're sure?" She nodded, and he relaxed. "You'll tell me if you start having doubts again?" he asked.

"I promise to be honest with you, even if you won't like it."

He grinned, capturing her hand and kissing the middle of her palm.

"But Alex, you have to promise something in return. I don't want to be told what to do. My mother has been controlling and overprotective for as long as I can remember, and I refuse to take the same from you."

"I promise," he said quietly. He touched her finger where Ada's ring had been before their fight. But he didn't mention the ring, and Evelyn didn't either.

"If you're not going back to Byrne House, do you want to stay here?"

"I was hoping. There's your couch, if your mom's still feeling generous. Or if not, I guess I could sleep on Jake's floor. He owes me for not murdering him. Yet."

Evelyn didn't want to think about Jake. She didn't want to think about anyone, or anything, but Alex.

"Stay here." She touched her index finger to his lower lip, and let it slip down to his chin. "With me."

"Hmm," he said. "Let's see, crash at Jake's place, or sleep here. Are we talking the floor or the bed?" His throat moved, swallowing. She was pretty sure he was holding his breath.

She leaned over and kissed the corner of his mouth. "You could ask Jake what he's offering and get back to me."

Evelyn switched off the light, but left the curtains open. They still had the street lamps and the moon to see by.

Shadows of tree branches swayed on the wall above her bed.

"It's probably just for tonight though," she said. "I don't think my mother's going to let you move into my room."

Alex got up from the desk chair and sat on the edge of her bed. "I didn't think so."

She opened a drawer and pulled out the t-shirt she liked to sleep in. Evelyn took off her cardigan, draping it over her desk chair. Then she turned to face the wall and started to peel off her shirt.

Alex inhaled sharply. "Should I...go?"

"I told you that you could stay here."

He laughed quietly, a breathy sound. "Yeah, but you didn't say I could stay while you were undressing. I didn't want to make any assumptions."

"You don't have to look if you don't want to."

She took off her leggings next. The room was chilly, and goosebumps rose all over her skin. Her sleep shirt made a whooshing sound as she pulled it on. She looked back at Alex. Moonlight reflected in his eyes like they were aflame. Her skin began to flush with warmth.

"I've been thinking a lot the past few days," she said. "My parents, my plans for next year, whether I could figure out a way to stay in Castle Heights. And then I thought about you and me. A lot about you and me."

She'd edged closer until she was standing right in front of him. "We have no idea what's going to happen," she said. "After the holidays, we might be apart for the next semester. Maybe even longer. I don't want to waste any more of our time together."

He slowly exhaled. "What does that mean, exactly?"

"It means I don't want you to sleep on the floor."

He gripped the fabric of her shirt and pulled her nearer, until his knees were snug around her thighs. Evelyn grabbed the edge of his long-sleeved t-shirt, and Alex lifted his arms as she pulled it over his head. She ran her cold hands down his back. His skin was smooth and impossibly warm. He sucked air into his chest.

She kissed him. He responded tentatively, though she felt his heart thumping wildly against her.

"I want to be with you," Evelyn said. "The way I haven't been with anyone else."

"We don't have to rush. If you're not sure."

"I know *exactly* what I want. I don't need protecting."

Alex pulled her into his lap and kissed her, no longer holding back. Evelyn discarded her shirt on the floor. Alex lifted her slightly in his arms, pressing her against his stomach and chest. The heat of his skin added to hers. His aura appeared, though she hadn't sought it out. She could see his emotions shifting around him, shimmering along his shoulders and down his arms, in so many colors they blended together into a silvery, liquid light. Nervous and exhilarated and a little bit scared, like her.

And blindingly, hopelessly in love.

They crawled onto the bed and under the sheets, and he pulled the blankets up around them. The shadows of the tree branches moving against the wall above them disappeared, along with the rest of the world.

31

"DID YOU KNOW THAT ALEX IS ASLEEP ON OUR couch downstairs?"

Evelyn's mother loomed over her. Vivian's eyes blazed with the midday sun shining from the window.

Evelyn pulled her blankets up. "I know he's down there. I have no way to know if he's sleeping or not."

"Don't get smart with me. You need to explain this situation."

"He needed a place to sleep. It was fine last week, why not now?"

For obvious reasons, she and Alex had decided that it was actually a bad idea for him to sleep in her room. So around four in the morning, she'd grabbed an extra pillow and blanket from the linen closet and snuck him downstairs to the living room. Then she went back upstairs to her bed and tried to sleep, but it had taken forever. Every few minutes, she rolled over and smelled his shampoo on her pillow, and her heart had started beating so hard it shook her entire body.

Vivian glanced over at the view of Byrne House. She wrapped her arms over her stomach. "That was before his mother got to town. Mrs. Evans is going to wonder where he is, and I'm not looking forward to telling her that he spent the night at our house. It's already almost lunchtime."

"Alex can tell her whatever he wants. He came here last night and said he couldn't stay at the mansion with his brother there. William treats Alex like he hates him. Alex isn't going to take it anymore."

"So we're in the middle of a fight between Alex and his brother? Fantastic." Viv sighed and rubbed her eyes. "I've completely lost control around here, haven't I?" she muttered.

"You aren't going to make Alex leave are you? Please let him stay. He doesn't have anywhere else to go."

"He has a place to go. It's called Byrne House. Where he can live with his creepy family, who I'd managed to avoid all these years until *you* dragged me into this. I'm not going to kick Alex off the couch while he's asleep, but beyond that, it's really out of the question."

The wood floor creaked downstairs.

"He's up." Evelyn jumped out of bed.

Viv blocked the doorway. "You're not going down like that. You're in pajamas. Get dressed."

"Mom, you're being—"

"Get. Dressed."

Evelyn took a lightning fast shower and set out some fresh towels for Alex to use. Then she threw on one of her favorite Bohemian skirts and a turtleneck and raced down the stairs. As she'd expected, Viv was holding Alex hostage in the living room, making him answer all kinds of questions about what had happened with William.

Alex stood up when she walked in. He still had on the pajamas that he'd brought with him last night, plaid pants and a sweatshirt with matching plaid trim around the collar and cuffs. Insanely cute. His hair was a mess, like he'd been tossing and turning all night, rubbing his head against the pillow. She wanted to run her fingers through it. But she'd probably end up making it messier.

He grinned at her, eyes traveling over her from head to foot.

Vivian looked from Evelyn to Alex, her eyes narrowing. "Alex, you're not allowed in Evelyn's room, is that clear?"

"*Mom*! That's ridiculous!"

"If you both can follow that rule, I'll consider letting Alex stay on the couch again." She retreated to her office, closing the door with a thud behind her. Discussion over.

"You have to tell her," Alex said.

"God. *No*. Do you have a death wish?"

He turned his back to the office door, lowering his voice even further. "Not about last night. I mean your uncle."

Her eyes moved automatically to the fireplace, where Uncle Sammy's pictures sat on the mantle. There was one with Viv and Sammy arm in arm in footie pajamas, some Christmas morning decades ago.

Viv needed to know. But Evelyn had no idea how to tell her. And she still didn't know what really happened to him. Their investigation—such as it was—had stalled.

"You could tell her about the mirror," Alex said.

"Next option?"

The corner of Alex's mouth hitched up. "I'll work on it. Sit down? I need to talk to you about something."

She sat beside him on the couch. "That sounds very official. Is my mother rubbing off on you?"

His eyes were pained. "Evelyn, my mom texted me. She's pissed that Will and I are fighting again. She's going to stay a couple more days for Christmas, but then she's going home. And she expects me to come with her."

All Evelyn could do was shake her head. Her lungs felt like they were turning to stone. He grabbed her hand.

"Hey, I'm not going. But there's more. Daniella will be here tomorrow."

Evelyn swallowed. Daniella had already fulfilled her part of the deal—she'd helped manage William. Now, she'd want payback from Evelyn.

"Apparently," Alex went on, "Will confessed that he and Daniella got married while they were gone. My mom is hurt. I'm guessing that's a big reason she's so eager to get home. According to my brother, this was the whole reason Daniella and Will left town last fall: to elope."

Evelyn kept her voice at a whisper. "That's a total lie."

"We know that. Before, he blamed me for them having to leave. Now he's completely changed his story. But my mother believes whatever Will says."

Daniella had run because the police came knocking at Byrne House. But that was just the most immediate reason. She'd also taken Walter Byrne's last journal. And, based on Alex's mirror vision in Daniella's bedroom, Daniella had needed something from her mother Madeline. But what, they still had no guess.

Where did the elopement fit in? Was it just a distraction? Evelyn knew that Daniella did care for William. But she doubted that Daniella would do anything without some strategic value in mind.

An eerie feeling crept up Evelyn's spine and settled at the base of her skull. It was a memory—maybe something she'd experienced, or maybe something she'd seen in a flash. She couldn't get a tight enough hold of it to turn it over and get a good look. All she had was a sense of foreboding. Not unlike the feeling of intuition she'd had a few days ago in the hidden room beneath the gardens—just before she put her palm against the metal door she couldn't unlock.

"What is it?" Alex asked. "Your mind is going at light speed right now, I can see it."

She'd been staring out the window at the weeds in her front yard, trying to remember. But it was like running in place, and she was getting nowhere.

"I was just thinking about the room under the gardens, where we fell. And that door we found. For some reason, thinking about Daniella and Walter's journal made me think of it. Like there's a connection. I just can't figure out exactly why."

A crease formed between Alex's eyebrows. "We still don't know what happened to you down there. I know it was one of those flashes in your mind—I saw that in the mirror when I aimed it at you." He grimaced, still guilty.

"What did you see?" she asked.

"In your memory, it was all one color, really bright. Like staring at the sun. I couldn't see past it."

Molten metal. A boiling, devastating heat.

"Bright like metal," she said. "Like gold." But nothing more came.

Alex nodded thoughtfully. He leaned forward to make sure Vivian's office door was still closed. "When we were down there, in that passage, it seemed like we were still under the gardens. But it went a long way from the room where we started, and I'm pretty sure it went back toward the mansion, instead of another part of the gardens, or toward the street where it would link up with the other tunnels. I think it ended up back under Byrne House itself."

"But we've already seen the metal doors in the Byrne House basement. We know where they lead—the tunnels and Ada's tomb. Unless there's another door down there that we've never found before."

"That wasn't my theory, exactly."

"Then what's your theory?"

Alex smiled sheepishly, as if he didn't really believe this himself. But he seemed uneasy, all the same. "That it's some secret room that Walter built, directly under Byrne House, hidden away from the rest of the basement."

32

THERE WAS A KNOCK AT EVELYN'S FRONT DOOR.

Alex had just gone out for groceries with Vivian. Clearly a goodwill gesture, to smooth over the fact that he'd stayed last night and had nowhere else to go. He'd even offered to pay. Vivian had refused the offer, but she'd seemed all too happy to take Alex shopping with her. Evelyn had seen the calculating glint in her mother's eye. Alex was in for some uncomfortable questioning. But he'd asked for it.

The knock came again. "Just a sec," Evelyn said, shuffling in her sock feet through the entryway. She was about to open it. Then she looked through the glass and saw who was out there.

Daniella Byrne was standing on her front porch.

She had her head down, inky hair falling past her face. Evelyn could only see her profile through the frosted patterns of the glass. Daniella knocked again, a quick tap-tap against the wood. Evelyn tried to keep her face calm and expressionless, while her stomach wrung itself like hands around a wet dishtowel.

I texted her, she thought. *This is my house. I'm the one in control.*

Evelyn opened the door. "I thought you were due back tomorrow."

"Hello to you, too." Daniella tilted her head, appraising. As if she'd heard the fear crouching in Evelyn's throat. "Don't worry, I come in peace." Her lips curved in a smile.

Daniella had her chin dipped, looking through her lashes. No doubt the submissive expression was very effective with men. But Evelyn wasn't tall enough for the full effect. She wondered how she'd missed noticing it before—how carefully Daniella controlled everything about her face and the placement of her body. Her arms hung straight at her sides, her long fingers spaced evenly apart, palms slightly turned outward.

"May I come in?" Daniella asked.

"If you want to talk, we can talk here. You could've just texted. Or dropped off a letter, like last time."

She sighed and smiled, showing a glimpse of a pointed incisor at the corner of her mouth. "A courier brought the letter, but only because I couldn't be here myself. You know, if we're going to work together, we'll have to get used to being civil."

Work together? Evelyn wanted to say. *You can go to hell. Your brother's already there.*

But she didn't dare.

She showed Daniella to the living room.

"This is lovely," Daniella said as she sat down on the couch. "Did you know Ada Byrne worked closely with the architect on the design of these houses?" Her eyes moved over the room again, then settled on Evelyn.

"What do you want from me?"

Daniella smoothed her skirt over her lap, and then looked down at her hands where they cupped her knees. "Believe it or not, Evelyn, I'm nervous. I was making conversation. There's such an awful misunderstanding between us, and I don't know exactly how to fix it."

"A *misunderstanding*?" Evelyn clenched her fists against the tremors that threatened to overwhelm her. "That's what you're calling it?"

"I told you in my letter. I forgave you for anything that might've happened last summer. And I hoped you'd forgiven me." She shifted her weight, sinking into the couch cushion. "It must have been terrible, what you went through. But

Darren's gone now. And wherever he is, I doubt we need to worry about him coming back."

Evelyn wondered if this was a subtle attempt to bait her. Daniella knew well enough that her brother was dead. Of course, Darren's body was still sealed up in the underground lab, with the door welded shut. So unless Daniella cut her way into that room, she couldn't know with absolute certainty.

"We can put that behind us," Daniella said. "I'd prefer to talk about something that could benefit us both, if you'll hear me out."

"This 'amazing invention' of Walter Byrne's."

"You sound skeptical." She moved forward to the edge of the couch. "We've both studied Walter's work. Different sides of it, anyway."

Evelyn stood up, crossing her arms over her chest. "How about this? You take Ada's mirror and you leave me alone. I think one of Walter's inventions should be plenty."

Daniella shook her head. "I'm not so interested in the past. You keep the mirror for now, as a gesture of my good will. I know this must be hard to believe, given what you've already seen of Walter's discoveries. But we can find something even greater than the mirror. You and me."

You and me. The idea made Evelyn cringe. "Why do you want this invention, anyway? How do you know it'll be worth anything?"

"You think I want to *sell* it? I'd thought you, of all people, would understand that some things are worth more than money. This is my family's heritage. Our legacy." She pushed her long hair past her shoulder. "And based on what I've read in Walter's journal, it'll be useful in other ways."

Evelyn had to admit, she was curious. But that was Daniella's intention. "What makes you think I could help? You already know more than I ever could about Walter's research."

Daniella closed her eyes and bowed her head, a picture of humility. "Evelyn, you understand the emotional side to Walter's work. Walter described it in his writings—the way emotions imprint on a place—but I'd never been able to grasp it. You have such deep empathy. I know that's one of my weaknesses, the reason I could never fully decipher Walter's meaning. It's why I dismissed the value of his work for so long."

Her honesty took Evelyn by surprise. But then she realized Daniella was just trying out different tactics. She wanted to see which buttons she had to push to open Evelyn up.

"The truth," Evelyn said, "since we're being honest, is that I don't want to help you."

"If we're being *really* honest, the truth is that you owe me." Daniella's smile turned vicious.

"I never agreed to anything."

Yet just yesterday, she'd been thinking that she'd give Daniella whatever she wanted if it meant holding on to Alex.

Daniella's gaze was unflinching.

Evelyn walked across the living room, trying to think. Daniella was responsible for bringing Alex back to Castle Heights. She'd somehow forced William to back off. Though Alex was angry with his family right now, he still needed them in his life. Daniella could turn Alex's mother and William against him forever. Maybe she could do even worse things that Evelyn hadn't even thought of yet.

"How about this," Daniella offered. "Don't think of it as helping me. Think of what you'll get out of it."

Neither of them had spoken Alex's name. But the subtext of this conversation was clear: Alex's well-being was at stake. Evelyn needed to take him out of the equation.

Her eyes rested on the mantle. All those Stanton family pictures.

"Did you know my uncle?" she asked. "Sam Stanton?"

Daniella didn't move, but her eyes went out of focus. Like it was taking a while to process what Evelyn had said.

"Sam?"

She heard something in Daniella's voice. Not just recognition. Emotion.

Evelyn turned around and concentrated. An ache settled in between her eyes. Colors began to flicker around Daniella, like flames just starting to ignite. Daniella had been truthful so far—even about Walter Byrne's invention. At least, she believed it to be true. But her aura was shifting. At the mention of Sam Stanton, her confidence had started to crack.

"Mr. Stanton, of course," Daniella said. "He was our tutor when Darren and I were kids. I didn't realize he was your uncle. Why are you asking?"

True, except the part about not realizing. Daniella had known all about Evelyn's family ties. But there was more. She wanted to hide something.

"Why are you staring at me that way?" Daniella asked.

Evelyn glanced away, blinking her dry eyes. When she looked back, Daniella's aura was gone.

"He disappeared eleven years ago," Evelyn said. "Never contacted my mom or the rest of our family again. And Byrne House was the last place anyone saw him."

Daniella brushed a tiny piece of lint from her skirt. "Afraid I can't help you there."

Again, Evelyn concentrated. She tried to bring back the aura. But though her head pounded, she couldn't read the truth in Daniella's mind. She had one option left.

"Tell me what really happened to my uncle," Evelyn said. "And I'll help you find Walter's invention."

Please don't let me regret this, she thought.

Daniella smiled. Not a false smile this time, but a thin curve of closed lips, repeating the satisfaction that Evelyn saw now in her eyes.

"Come to Byrne House tonight," she said, standing. "We'll discuss it. And while you're there, I can show you Walter Byrne's final journal. I'll make you a believer yet."

Evelyn dug through her bedroom closet until she found her keepsake box. Carefully, she removed the lid. On the very top sat the mirror. She picked it up, staring at the mirror's intricate gold handle. She'd been ready to give it to Daniella without a second thought. Now she wasn't sure. The Byrne family history was as much a part of Evelyn's past as it was Daniella's.

She set the mirror on the floor and sought deeper inside the box. She kept all sorts of mementos here: newspaper clippings about Castle Heights, old family photos. Finally, she found the bundle of Ada Byrne's letters. She'd discovered them over the summer, and they'd described not only Walter's increasing madness, but Ada's unfailing devotion to him. No matter how much Ada doubted her husband, she'd loved him until the end.

Evelyn opened the bundle and carefully smoothed out the papers, bending them the opposite way to try to flatten them. She skimmed through them, looking for any sort of clue that Walter was working on another invention. As she read, she thought of the happy times Ada had shared with Walter in their brief life together before she died. And her many regrets—that they didn't have more time. That she didn't try harder to break him from his obsession with his research. But she never regretted marrying Walter. Not for a second.

Alex had slid Ada's ring onto Evelyn's finger. *Marry me.* The words had seemed ridiculous in that moment, words from a fairytale. But Alex's voice hadn't wavered. He'd sounded so sure. Did he feel the same today?

Before she could complete the thought, her phone rang. Silvia was calling on FaceTime. Her smiling face appeared, hair sprouting from a bun on the top of her head. "Hey, Evelyn. Any progress on your murder mystery?"

"I haven't been thinking about it much," Evelyn lied. But it was a white lie. Now that Daniella was involved, Evelyn didn't want Silvia mixed up in this. "Maybe Mimi's crystal is helping." Although the crystal was still in Jake's room somewhere.

"You're not blowing me off, are you? I thought you wanted my help."

"Silvia, I do. But things are just too crazy. William and Daniella are back, and Alex is staying at my house. We'll talk about it after Christmas, okay?"

She was quiet for a long moment. "Promise you won't use the mirror without me? I don't want you getting sick again, like in front of the guest house."

"I promise."

They said goodbye. A moment later Evelyn wanted to call her back and tell her everything. She didn't want to repeat all the mistakes she'd made with Alex. But Silvia was the closest that Evelyn would ever get to a sister, and she didn't want Silvia to have anything to do with Daniella Byrne.

While she was still looking at her phone, an e-mail notification flashed across the screen.

She didn't check her e-mail often. Most of her friends used text or other apps, anyway. She opened her mailbox and saw how many unread e-mails were waiting.

Fifty. All from Jake.

The first few had variations on the subject line, *You left your rock here*. The rest had no subject at all. Evelyn deleted the messages without reading a single one. She wasn't interested in sarcastic comments about Alex or rehashing the same nightmares about Darren again. Jake would just have to learn to deal with himself alone.

Silvia, Milo, Jake—she couldn't turn to any of them right now. She had Alex, but for how long? Her mom wouldn't let him stay here forever. And what about after the new year, when her mother took off to Seattle for that new job?

There was no use worrying about all that now. Vivian and Alex would be home any minute. She picked up the keepsake box to return the contents and put it back into her closet.

But something nagged at her. Something she should've seen in the box, but didn't.

She sorted through the contents, stacking each precious photo and piece of paper on her desk. She found her key to the tunnel doors. It was old and tarnished, made of iron, with a triangular shape at the top. Ada's ring was here too; she'd stored it after the fight with Alex, and she still wasn't quite ready to put it back onto her finger. Everything seemed to be here. Maybe she was mistaken.

But then she remembered. Darren had a copy of the tunnel door key, too.

Darren's copy of the key was gone.

It wasn't possible. She sorted through the contents of the box again, then felt around on the closet floor to see if it somehow fell out. She searched through her drawers, tore through her laundry, throwing things aside until her room was in shambles. She felt Darren's cold, stiff fingers reaching out toward her from underground. *You'll never be free of me. Never feel safe.*

She hadn't touched Darren's key for months. She hated touching it. She'd even thought about throwing it away, but she felt safer knowing she had it and no one else did. So she'd kept it shut up inside that black box and hidden in her closet. No one besides her knew it was there.

Yet somehow, it had disappeared.

33

DANIELLA ANSWERED BYRNE HOUSE'S DOOR.

"Oh. You brought Alex."

He pushed past her, then turned to block the way to the hall. "You may have Will fooled, but not me," he said. "I don't really care what crap you spend your time on over here, but when you try to drag Evelyn into it, I have a problem."

"And yet you're both here," Daniella said lightly.

Alex had been livid when Evelyn told him about Daniella's visit. He couldn't believe Evelyn wanted to come here tonight. He thought the idea that Daniella could exert some nefarious control over him was absurd. *You owe her nothing*, Alex had said.

But Evelyn felt that she had no choice—Daniella knew something about her uncle. Evelyn had to play along if she wanted to find out. She'd listened to Alex's opinion, but he wasn't going to stop her.

"I thought you'd told William that you were never coming back to Byrne House."

"I'm just here for Evelyn." Alex glanced anxiously around the hall.

"Will and your mother are out, anyway. So you can relax." Daniella shrugged, like she didn't care either way.

They followed her down the hall. Daniella passed the library and entered a room filled with musical instruments— a golden harp in one corner, a violin hanging from pegs on the wall. The thick folds of the curtains gave the space a feeling of backstage, hidden from view before the start of a performance.

Daniella stood off to the side beside a baby grand piano. "Walter's journal is there," she said, pointing at a small table. "I'm hoping you'll be able to help me decipher it."

It was a leather-bound journal marked with the fading numerals XXV on the binding. Evelyn picked it up and flipped open the cover. Tight handwriting had marked the dates: October 3 to December 30, 1900. She'd seen it before in the Byrne House library. But she hadn't paid it close attention back then.

The pages were thicker than she remembered. Sturdy, crinkling like an unfolding road map as she turned them, which was a good thing given the volume of ink on both sides of most of the pages. Tiny scrawl filled them, line after line of dense text with almost no space between. At the bottom, the text curved up onto the margins and stretched in misshapen loops around the page, framing the writing in the center. Evelyn brought the journal up and bent her head, trying to read it. She could make out letters and numbers, a word here and there, but the writing was so small it made the space between her eyes ache.

Other pages were nearly blank save single words —"pendulum" on one, "escapement" on another—or equations with more symbols than numbers, dotted with smudged, inky fingerprints. She lifted the cover and let the pages fall in rapid succession. On some, the text was so dense the page was almost black.

None of it made the least bit of sense to her.

Daniella was going to be disappointed.

The journal fell open to a page about a quarter from the end, and Evelyn's thumb moved to hold the place before she lost it. There was a drawing of a labyrinth with a blot of ink in the middle. She followed the pathways along the edges of the maze with her finger. She was fairly sure that it was *the* labyrinth—the one in the Byrne House gardens, with the same layout as the tunnels under Castle Heights.

At first, the labyrinth on the page looked like a carefully sketched drawing, but as she looked closer, she realized that tiny writing formed its walls. Long stretches of formulas, packed with so many symbols it looked like another language. She recognized a few things from her chemistry and physics classes: alpha, beta, gamma, omega. There were lots of other symbols she'd never seen before, strangely curving in on themselves in intricate patterns. She couldn't imagine how Walter had managed to draw them so small.

At the top of the labyrinth page were the words: AD PERPETUAM REI MEMORIAM.

Just like the inscription on the stone marker in the gardens.

It was beautiful in a strange way. Or it would have been, if not for a huge splotch of ink, as big as Evelyn's palm, that blacked out the center of the labyrinth. Like someone had up-ended a bottle of ink right onto the page.

Alex touched the tip of his index finger to the ink blot. "Is that supposed to be there?"

"It's been like that since the first time I saw it as a child," Daniella said. "And my father said the same. As far as I know it's been there since Walter's time. Whether he or someone else did it, and whether by accident or not, I can't say."

Evelyn relaxed her mind. A flash might tell her more about Walter's emotions when he'd written the journal. But she felt nothing. Just the dry paper in her hands. Her flashes had only illuminated people and places; maybe it didn't work on a single inanimate object.

"What do you see?" Daniella asked, peering at Evelyn a little too closely.

"Nothing you haven't already seen yourself." Evelyn flipped through the remaining pages in the journal. Except for that same ink stain—which had bled through the center

of each page, diminishing to a tiny dark spot on the last—
they were blank. The back cover fell into place over the last
page with a dry thump.

"I don't get what you wanted me to see," Evelyn said.
"It all looked like gibberish, or might as well be because I
didn't understand any of it."

Daniella walked around the sofa and leaned over. She
opened the journal, shuffled through the pages, and stopped
on a page Evelyn had missed before.

"Here. What about this."

She pointed at two blocks of text on either side of the
binding. On the lefthand page, Walter had written the word
"Reflection" at the top, above the rest of the text. Like a
title. On the right he wrote, "Refraction."

Alex shifted closer to Evelyn and murmured the words
aloud under his breath.

REFLECTION

Bending, folding, shaping asymmetry into symmetry
Visible the invisible, knowable the unknown
Undying the already long dead
All becomes present, as clear as a pane of glass
Events folded flat, fixed into place
Frozen in the window of my creation

REFRACTION

The path changes, deflected
The image shifts, death comes now before birth
Angles intersected infinitely resolve into a single point, and reverse
Distortion filtered regains proportionality
The mechanism loosed will then unwind
Revealing what is yet to be revealed

"This first part," Alex whispered to Evelyn, pointing at
the lefthand page, "it almost sounds like he's describing…"

She met his eyes and nodded. *All becomes present, as clear as a pane of glass.*

The mirror.

Daniella sat down in a chair beside the piano. "As a girl I would read this journal, imagining it held the greatest of secrets, if I could only solve the puzzle of how to unlock them. I gave it up years ago. But something last August recalled these passages to me, and suddenly I saw the potential of what they could mean."

"When Darren showed you the mirror," Evelyn said. That moment had changed everything. For both of them.

Daniella's gaze didn't waver. No trace of guilt or shame. "Exactly. I realized that the device you call 'the mirror' is a means of revealing the same things that Walter's drug allows the user to see. A window into the past."

"*Undying the already long dead,*" Evelyn murmured.

"You can imagine my shock when I made the connection and recalled these passages. For the first time in years, I believed that Walter's final journal had meaning. These pages aren't just the ravings of a lost mind."

Alex stood. "So you left Evelyn to die in the tunnels so you could do more research on this stupid journal? Maybe Walter wasn't insane, but you—"

"Alex, please," Evelyn said. "That isn't going to help."

She looked down at the open pages in front of her again. *Reflection. Refraction.* Two pages facing each other, two sides of the same thing…

Alex pointed an accusing finger at Daniella. "The only reason Evelyn is alive right now is that Darren is dead. You realize that, right?"

Daniella's eyes shifted down. "I've had a lot of conflicted feelings about that. But Darren was dangerous. Out of control. He suffered for so long. In a way, it's a relief."

"So Evelyn did you a favor. Seems to me like you're the one that owes her, not the other way around. Why don't you tell us what this is really about? We already know about the mirror. Why is Evelyn here? What is she supposed to be getting from reading this?"

"I think she already knows that," Daniella said, her voice reasonable and calm. "She knows what I'm offering her, how it will repay everything."

Once again, Daniella crossed the room toward Evelyn. "Reflection," she said, touching her pink fingernail to the word. "The mirror. The past." Her finger moved to the other page, hovering just above the writing. "And refraction. I can see it in your eyes, Evelyn. You know as well as I do what this means."

Alex threw up his hands. "What?"

Evelyn squeezed her eyes shut and opened them again, taking a breath. It was impossible. Even for Walter. But if the mirror existed, why not something even more astounding?

"It's another invention," she said. "The counterpart to the mirror. The other side of the same thing, in Walter's mind at least. If 'reflection' is about seeing into the past, then 'refraction' is…"

Daniella nodded, waiting for her to finish.

"The future," Evelyn said quickly. Before she could reason herself out of it. "It's an invention that sees into the future."

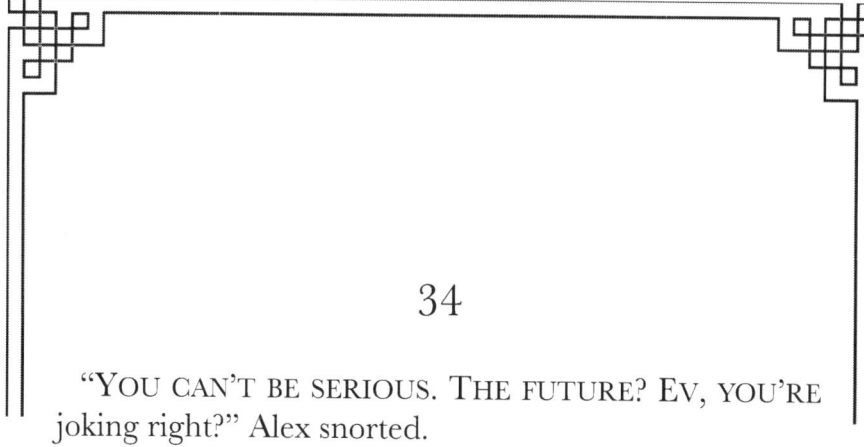

34

"YOU CAN'T BE SERIOUS. THE FUTURE? EV, YOU'RE joking right?" Alex snorted.

Evelyn set Walter's journal back on the table. "I'll consider helping you," she said to Daniella, ignoring Alex's shocked stare. "But only if you share what you know about my uncle. I told you before; that's the only deal I'll agree to."

Daniella turned to the piano and pushed one of the keys with her finger. A sharp note rang out. "He's gone. There's nothing else to say."

"I knew Sam," a new voice said.

They all turned. A woman stood in the doorway. Her hair was no longer the rich brown Evelyn had seen in visions, and her face was deeply lined. But her delicate nose was the same. Her eyes, though—they'd lost the sharpness that Evelyn remembered. Her gaze was hesitant. Haunted.

Evelyn opened her mouth, unable to hide her shock. This was the woman she'd been hoping to find, whom she'd feared was dead—right here at Byrne House like she'd never left.

"Alex, Evelyn," Daniella said, playing another piercing note on the piano. "This is my mother. Madeline Byrne."

"I remember you both, of course," Madeline said. She came closer. "That terrible day. Sam was there. He helped get you out."

Daniella slammed down the cover over the piano keys. "Mother, that's enough. We're not discussing it."

"You're right, I'm sorry." Madeline gestured at the journal on the table. "Walter Byrne? You're dragging more people into your obsession?"

"They're here willingly," Daniella said.

"Like I am?" Madeline smiled sadly at Evelyn. "I hadn't heard from Daniella in years when she showed up at my door, looking for an old journal I'd taken with me when I left Byrne House over a decade ago."

Alex glanced quickly in Evelyn's direction. "What journal? Another one of Walter's?"

"No," Daniella said. "This one belonged to Simon."

It took a moment for her words to sink in. "Simon Byrne had a journal too?" Evelyn asked.

Simon had been cruel, sadistic. What could Daniella possibly want with a journal written by him?

"I never paid much attention to Simon's writing when I was growing up," Daniella said. "But in August, I wondered if Simon might have recorded something about Walter's last invention. Maybe Walter told him about it. Unfortunately, I realized that my mother had taken it."

So that was why Daniella had been thinking of her mother the day she left.

Madeline picked up Walter Byrne's final journal and flipped open its cover for a brief moment. Then she put it back on the table, facedown.

"It started with my husband," Madeline said. "This obsession with Walter and Simon Byrne. Then it spread to my children. Simon's writings were more colorful, to say the least. I couldn't have them reading that filth. And some of the entries were paranoid, disturbing—Simon was terrified of his own brother. I saw no reason to give Darren and Daniella more nightmares."

Madeline brushed a wayward curl from her cheek. "Or ideas," she added quietly.

"Mother, enough."

"Simon said he was afraid of Walter?" Evelyn asked.

Madeline nodded. "Simon thought Walter blamed him for his wife Ada's death, and he often worried that Walter was losing his mind. Plotting revenge. Sometimes I wonder if it was the influence of this house, more than anything. On the both of them."

Madeline's eyes swept over the room before settling on a frayed spot on the rug. "I've seen it myself, the way it eats away at you. Old thoughts like the ones in these journals—they're hungry. They take something from you. I'm sure it sounds absurd but it's true. I wish I could make Daniella see that. Some things are better left alone."

"Not that you gave me a choice in the matter," Daniella said. "You never did."

"I've tried to do what's best for you, that's all."

"What happened to the journal?" Alex asked.

"Tell them what you did, Mother."

Madeline fingered a strand of her colorless hair. "I burned it."

35

EVELYN WOKE EARLY AND WENT DOWNSTAIRS. SHE paused in the living room and watched Alex as he slept.

He was all arms and legs, almost too big for the couch. Hair sticking out all over the place. She wished she could crawl under the blanket with him. But she didn't want to wake him.

They'd been up late after they got back from Byrne House, debating the page from Walter's journal. Alex definitely didn't believe that Walter had invented another mirror that could see the future. He didn't want Evelyn to continue working with Daniella at all. But he had also agreed to respect her decision, whatever that might be.

Evelyn still wasn't sure what to do.

Daniella had given up nothing about Uncle Sammy's fate, and Evelyn couldn't tell if Daniella was lying. She thought back to that day in the underground lab last August, when she'd peered into Daniella's mind and seen the guilt over what Darren had become. With the crystal serum coursing through her veins, Evelyn had read this truth so easily. Yet she hadn't sensed a single thought or image of her uncle, though Evelyn now understood—because of the flashes—that Sammy had meant a great deal to Daniella.

What if Daniella had given up the truth about Darren so that she could hide something else? Something important about Evelyn's uncle?

If that were true, then Daniella probably had no intention of *ever* revealing what she knew about Sammy's disappearance. Evelyn had no reason to trust her or to help her...Unless Walter's mysterious invention was reason enough.

And that was the catch in her thoughts, the reason she couldn't sleep. The possibility that Evelyn couldn't ignore. What if she could really see the future? Then the current mess of her life would become clear. She'd know exactly what to do.

Evelyn went into the kitchen. She filled the electric kettle with water, pondering all these things. She had plenty of time. The microwave clock read five-thirty, so it would be a while before Alex or even her mother woke.

Then she heard a tapping sound and looked up.

Jake stood outside her kitchen window.

Evelyn shook her head and said, "Go away," moving her lips slowly so he could read them through the glass.

Jake left the window and reappeared at the back door. He started knocking again, louder this time. Evelyn was afraid he'd wake Alex, so she unlocked the bolt and opened the door a crack.

"What the hell are you doing?" she whispered.

"I thought maybe you'd forgiven me by now."

"You thought wrong. I appreciated the ride the other night, but the ten thousand e-mails didn't really encourage me to talk to you."

"You wouldn't respond. What was I supposed to do?"

"I don't know. Get that professional help you were talking about?" She glanced over her shoulder.

"You're afraid I'll wake him."

How did he know Alex was here? "Have you been spying on us?"

Jake leaned into the gap in the doorway, his nose inches from hers. His eyes kept moving around her face, like he was reading something in it. His pupils were dilated, so large they almost swallowed the brown of his irises. Something was definitely wrong with him.

"Are you *high*? At five in the morning?"

"Is it five? I didn't go to sleep."

He pushed on the door. Evelyn braced it against her shoulder to hold it in place. "If my mom sees you like this she'll call your parents. And then the police. Don't doubt that for a second."

"Thanks for caring."

"I don't have time for this." She had too many important things to puzzle out. She started to shut the door. Then Jake pulled something from his pocket and held it out.

It was the pink quartz crystal that Mimi had given her.

"I brought this back." Jake spoke hopefully, like a little boy eager for approval.

She sighed and took the crystal. Maybe if she gave him a little bit of attention, he'd leave her alone the rest of the holidays.

"What do you really want, Jake?"

"For you to talk to me. I'm going crazy, Ev, I swear. I'm going to do something. I can feel it. I just need you to talk to me for a few minutes, so I'll calm down."

She hated Jake for doing this. He wanted her to think he'd hurt himself, and it would be all her fault because she wouldn't do what he wanted.

"Hate me if you want to," he said. "I'm not bluffing."

He was giving her the creeps. But she'd feel terrible if he really hurt himself. "We can talk for five minutes. But I have to go upstairs to change first."

She shut the door and locked it. She went upstairs and got dressed, not bothering to keep quiet. If Vivian or Alex woke up by the time she went back downstairs, then she wouldn't go. Instead she'd call Jake's parents to let them know he was threatening to do…something. He'd been pretty vague.

But Viv and Alex didn't wake up.

She and Jake walked to the park. The sky was cloudless and blue. Nearly every trace of snow was gone, and it was warm enough that Evelyn probably didn't need the heavy jacket she'd put on.

"Didn't take you long to forgive him," Jake said.

He *had* been spying. "It's none of your business. Why don't you start talking about this crisis you're having? I don't want to talk about Alex."

They reached the center of the park. Evelyn stood in the open, halfway between a fir tree and the statue of Walter. Jake walked from tree to tree, scratching the back of his neck and pinching the skin between his eyes with his fingers.

"I can't sleep," he said. "I haven't slept in days." He waved his hand in front of his face. "I'm starting to see these weird spots."

"You should go to a doctor."

"I tried a sleeping pill yesterday. It didn't work."

She had no idea how to make him listen to reason. "What do you expect me to do about it, sing you a lullaby?"

He smiled. Something was off about it. Too much teeth. "That could be nice."

"Jake, seriously. This has to stop. I'm not your girlfriend. I'm barely even your friend. Whatever we were doing before, it's over now. Alex is back and he's not leaving."

"I just want to be able to talk, like we used to. Why does that have to change?"

He knew why. Because he'd been a jerk and he'd kissed her and practically acted like a stalker. His problems were too big for her to solve.

But she did understand why he couldn't sleep. She understood why he'd installed a deadbolt in the door that led to the basement in his new house, even though the basement walls were uniformly blank. No metal, no rivets.

"Okay. Fine. Tell me about the weird spots."

"It started yesterday. Like tiny dots in different colors. But they're getting bigger. Sometimes they look almost like shapes. And once, one of the dots spread out around my mom's head. What if I'm having flashes of the drug Darren gave us? Like you?"

His eyes got brighter when he mentioned the flashes, not scared at all, as if he hoped it were true.

"Believe me, you'd know," Evelyn said. "I don't know why I get them and you don't. Maybe the drug affected me differently. Or I was exposed to the crystal more often, and it had a cumulative effect."

Jake sat down on the grass and draped his arms over his knees. "It's because you're special."

She couldn't tell if he was being sarcastic. It didn't seem like it. "I'd rather not be. I hate feeling so out of control."

"But you're starting to control it, right? You could do it, if you wanted to. You could look at me and…you could see into me."

"I don't know. Maybe. But I won't." She thought of the glow on Alex's bare skin the other night. How calming it was, how beautiful. She doubted she wanted to see whatever was floating around Jake right now.

Jake breathed faster, almost panting, even though he was still sitting in the same position on the ground. He wiped the back of his hand across his forehead.

"Seriously, Jake, are you on something? Are you okay?"

He got up and started pacing again, tree to tree to tree, but always keeping his eyes on her. "I thought this would make things different. Make it all clear. It's not working."

She moved over next to the statue, trying to get out of his path. "I'm sorry our talk's not living up to your expectations. You've hardly said anything that makes sense. I can't help you if I have no idea what's going on."

"I'm trying. It's just these spots I'm seeing. They're distracting. But it's a lot better when you're here. Just being near you is better." Jake's semi-circle was getting smaller with every pass, closing in on her.

She couldn't take this much longer.

She decided to give it one more shot. "Describe the spots again. Tell me everything about them."

The tree trunks flickered in and out of view as Jake walked. "I'd rather talk about you."

"Your five minutes are almost up."

She looked up at the sky. Pure blue, a little white toward the horizon. She wondered if Alex was awake yet. She wanted to get back before he realized she was gone. She was planning to tell him about her talk with Jake, but not until later. Next year sounded about right.

"That eager to get back?" Jake said.

He'd stopped pacing. Evelyn didn't like the way he was looking at her. Those almost-black irises, unfocused like he was staring through her. Or at the other side of her eyes.

"You and Evans, huh?"

"What's that supposed to mean?"

"I kissed you and you flipped out like I was a perv for even touching you. You acted so pure. And then you do *that* with him, three days after he made out with Caitlin? I don't think I'm the one who needs professional help."

The air shot out of her lungs, as if he'd pushed her. "That's private," Evelyn whispered. "You can't know that. There's no way you could know that."

He shrugged. "It's obvious, at least to me. Because I know you. I saw what you'd done when I looked at you through your kitchen window this morning."

Her jacket was unzipped. She pulled each side of it across her chest. He couldn't possibly know that she and Alex had slept together. It was just a lucky guess. But he was standing here looking at her like he could see straight into her mind and her heart and—

No. He wouldn't do that to himself. That was way too twisted, even for him.

"You haven't given me much credit since Evans got back," Jake said. "You always think I'm sick in the head.

Like everything you've done the past few days has been so rational."

She backed away from him. "Jake. You wouldn't do that, right? Tell me you didn't do it."

"Do what?" He smirked as it he said it. He knew exactly what she was talking about.

Darren's crystal serum. He'd injected himself with Darren's serum. And that meant he went back to the underground lab to get it.

"Did you take Darren's key from my room? From that box in my closet?"

Jake shifted his weight onto his toes. His arms hung by his sides, slightly out from his body, his fingers tensed. One of his hands flinched toward his pocket.

"Did you take it?"

He lunged and pushed her sideways against the statue's base. Evelyn's head bounced against the stone. Jake reached into her jacket and grabbed at her shirt. He pulled up the fabric on one side. She tried to push his hands away but he easily broke her grip. He pinned both her arms in place.

She felt a sharp, cold pinprick at her waist. The cold turned quickly into painful heat as it spread. Jake stepped back.

A syringe dangled from his fingers.

36

"WHAT DID YOU JUST DO?"

Her hands shook. Her entire side was burning. "Jake, what did you *do*?"

He looked at her with his mouth wide open, like he was equally shocked. "This is the only way. You'll forgive me when you see."

Jake dropped the syringe onto the grass. Evelyn slid down the base of the statue to the ground. Outlines of people emerged, moving so fast their faces blurred. But somehow, these figures were also standing still. It was like looking at a time lapse photo: long streaks behind the people, with sunlight and car headlights blending into a haze of yellowish-white around them. Evelyn felt thousands of different voices speaking to her at once from all over the park, overlapping one another, growing in intensity every second as the drug coursed through her body.

And yet, she could sense that this was only the tip of what lay beneath. She could feel so many more voices, more memories, prying at the edges of her mind. She wouldn't be able to take it if all that came rushing into her at once. But somehow she managed to keep it back. She heard a calming sound, a kind of hum, coming from somewhere near.

Her hand moved toward her pocket. The hum was coming from Mimi's quartz crystal. Evelyn touched the smooth surface of the rock, and the blurred images faded a bit.

"It's okay," Jake said, "it's not as high a dose as Darren gave us before. You'll get used to it."

She looked toward him. The air around Jake pulsed, thickening with his thoughts and emotions. He was desperate to connect with her like they'd been down in the tunnels, their minds linked by the serum so that neither could hide anything from the other. He thought he was in love with her, and that *this* would make Evelyn love him back.

"You see it now." Jake's smile made her want to scream. Blank white teeth beneath his empty, dilated eyes.

"You don't love me." It was hard to talk, hard to breath with the air so choked full of other people's emotions. "You don't even love yourself. How could you go down there? In that awful place?"

He didn't respond out loud. He showed her, in his mind.

He'd started slowly, going to the stable in the gardens, sitting at the base of the stairs with his back against the cold metal of the locked door that led to the underground passageway. It was terrifying at first, being so close to where it happened. But it got easier. And he thought if he could just see the door to the lab itself, the nightmares might stop. If it became a real place again, instead of the grotesque thing it had become in his mind. So one afternoon, one of the few times he'd been over at Evelyn's house, he said he had to use the bathroom and went into her room instead to find the key.

As soon as he had unlocked that outer door and stepped into the passage, he'd known. Seeing the door to the lab wasn't enough.

He spent weeks figuring out how to cut through the welds Alex had made that sealed the door. Jake rented the equipment he needed and snuck over to the gardens in the middle of the night. And when he finally got the door open...

Evelyn jerked her mind away from Jake's. She doubled over as nausea ripped at her insides.

"I don't want to see it. I want to go home, Jake. Please."

I want Alex. I need Alex.

"You don't need him. Listen. Everything was exactly the same as I remembered. The tables with the straps hanging down. The vials and syringes, just sitting there. There was this rank, rotten smell, so thick I could taste it. Sickening and sweet. I guess that's what people are talking about when they say a place smells like death. Sometimes I wonder how we don't smell it up here. We're standing right above it now."

"Jake, *stop*."

"You have no idea how good it felt to see that tarp rolled up against the wall." He touched her leg. She slapped his hand away. "To know Darren was in there. Every time I go down there and see it, it gets a little easier. I'm so close, I just need a little bit more and I'm sure the nightmares will stop. I know it'll work this time."

She knew what Jake really wanted now. He saw that she understood, and he nodded.

"It took me a while to figure it out," he said. "It won't work unless everything's the same. I know it seems scary right now, but I promise it will be good when we're there. You'll see. Just trust me. It'll make things better for you, too, and then you'll want us to be together all the time, like I do. So we can both feel safe."

Evelyn leapt up and ran in the direction of her house. But Jake was too quick. He blocked her way.

"I'm not going back in that lab," she said. "Not ever."

"Why won't you just *trust me*?"

They each tried to read the other fast enough to get one step ahead. She dodged him and ran toward Byrne House. He hadn't expected her to go there because that was the way to the lab. Evelyn really, really didn't want to go there. But it was her best hope to surprise him.

She bolted through the trees and reached the edge of the park. Jake panted close behind, his feet pounding into the grass. Evelyn stepped off the curb just as he grabbed her around the waist. Her ankle rolled when it landed on the street and she screamed, lurching forward. Jake pulled her back onto the sidewalk.

"Evelyn!"

She turned toward the voice. Ms. Foster and her sister Mimi stood on their front lawn. Both wore gardening gloves. Mimi was holding a spade.

"Evelyn!" Ms. Foster yelled again. Mimi took a few steps toward them.

"Please!" Evelyn tried to run to them, but Jake kept hold of her waist, lifting her off the ground.

"Quiet," Jake said, "do you want everyone to know about this? Do you want her to call the cops?"

Mimi started to cross the street, holding her spade up in front of her. Ms. Foster was right behind.

"Let me go, Jake."

"Please. I need this, we both do."

"Evelyn, what's going on?" Ms. Foster jogged toward them. "Jake Oshiro, you let go of her right now!"

"Wait," Mimi said, grabbing at her sister's jacket. "There's strong energy around them. It might not be safe."

"Do you really want them involved in this?" Jake hissed into Evelyn's ear. "They don't know what happened to us. They don't even know about the tunnels. They won't understand."

Jake let go of Evelyn's waist and held onto her wrist instead as Ms. Foster approached. Mimi hung back, still scrutinizing them, clutching at a green crystal that hung from her neck.

"What on earth has gotten into you two?" Ms. Foster asked. Her face was bright red. "You're fighting in the middle of the street. Evelyn, are you all right?"

Ms. Foster was terrified. One minute she'd been planting bulbs in her yard, the next moment she'd seen chaos. She was every bit as frightened as she'd been over the summer, that morning when she discovered her house had been ransacked. The place she felt safest, violated for reasons she still couldn't understand. Her sister's visit had helped, in spite of her protests. Ms. Foster had finally started to feel like the horror might be over, and now it was happening again, everything she thought she knew spinning around and ripping apart until she couldn't recognize it anymore.

Evelyn wanted to make Ms. Foster feel safe and normal again. She could deal with Jake on her own.

"We were just arguing and got carried away."

"Are you sure?" Ms. Foster asked.

Mimi still held the spade tight in her fist. The handle wobbled in her grip, and the metal tip blurred slightly from the movement.

"I'm sorry we upset you both," Evelyn said. "Everything's fine."

Jake pulled her by the arm into the street. Toward Byrne House.

"Goodbye, Ms. Foster. Bye, Mimi." She let Jake lead her away. The two women receded behind them.

"You're always protecting people," Jake whispered in her ear. "I know how strong you are. That's why I know you can do this."

They walked through the gate and around the side of the house. Part of her prayed that someone inside Byrne House would see, would stop them from going into the gardens. But if William or Mrs. Evans saw her, what would they think? Especially when she and Jake both looked so wild—sweating, pupils dilated. She had to talk Jake out of this before they got caught.

Evelyn stopped walking. Jake was still holding her wrist, so he was forced to stop too. For a moment, he considered hefting her over his shoulder like Alex had the other day. But he wanted her to go to the lab on her own. So he could tell himself that she'd really wanted this, too.

Evelyn sat down against the side of the mansion. Uneven stone dug into her back. He sat down beside her, still holding onto her arm.

"Why won't you listen to me?" she asked. "You really think you know me better than I know myself?"

He was truly convinced that he did. He thought Evelyn was the one who was confused. But his resolve wavered. A little.

"Jake, *please*. I can't go down there." She tried to push all her fears up to the forefront of her mind. She couldn't go back to Darren's lab. The serum would force her to relive every terrifying minute of that day in August. She didn't think her mind could take it.

Jake wiped a tear from her cheek. "I know you're scared. But I'll be there, just like you were there for me. That's the whole point. We'll be there together. It will be all right."

"These flashes I've been having—they changed something in my head, Jake. This is *not* like before. What if I snap, like Ada did? What if my nose starts bleeding and it won't stop?"

The air around him shifted. His plan was already messed up; none of this was going the way he'd expected. He didn't want to hurt Evelyn—he loved her. He'd have to adjust. But he wasn't giving up. His aura brightened with a new idea.

"Okay. We'll go someplace else, just the two of us together. It'll still be the same. That's the important part. Just us, together. This time I won't leave you."

He gripped her upper arms and pulled her to standing. She was already so exhausted. She couldn't keep fighting him.

Jake pulled her along behind him. "That's perfect. We'll go there."

"What? Where?" She hadn't been thinking of any place. Not consciously.

But Jake had a clear new path in mind. He paused by the patio to make sure no one was outside. Then he ran for the iron archway into the gardens, dragging Evelyn along by the arm. She nearly tripped on the flagstones trying to keep up.

They passed under the arch and ran by the rose garden. Jake didn't stop till they'd gone around the labyrinth. Now they were deeper in the gardens, out of sight of the house.

"Where are we going?" she asked.

Jake left the brick path and started wading through the brush. She didn't understand where he was taking her. Then Jake turned sideways to squeeze between the bushes, and she knew. He yanked on her arm. She had no choice but to follow him through the narrow gap.

They were in the clearing with the stone marker.

Jake went around to the back of the stone and stuck his fingers into the seams, feeling for the groove of the latch.

Evelyn saw fourteen-year-old Daniella, her image overlaid with Jake's, both of them finding the catch and swinging the face of the stone wide.

"I'm not going down there with you," Evelyn said.

"You were here with *him*." The thought made the colors around Jake turn to livid orange. "You fell here when you were little. You and Alex, together. That's why you care so much about him." Evelyn had never told Jake that story. But now he saw it all.

He would take Evelyn down there. He would take Alex's place.

Jake and Daniella bent down to open the trap door in the floor.

Evelyn ran for the gap in the bushes. She already knew Jake would reach her before she made it, but she still tried. She kicked and screamed and thrashed in his arms. He held her off the ground and carried her down the stairs into the room below.

37

THE ENTIRE ROOM WAS GLOWING.

"Do you see that?" Evelyn whispered. Streaks of light danced up the walls and writhed along the ceiling. They collapsed into shapes and faces before dispersing again, like fireflies disturbed from a nighttime field.

"I can only see it in your mind," Jake said. "I can see people moving in the shadows but it's not like what you see. Are you okay?"

Evelyn let Jake slip his hand into hers.

"I'm not sure." The lights were starting to separate into distinct voices. She could see the layers now, feel how they overlapped one another into an intricate maze. She could get lost in the spaces between them if she wasn't careful. The pull was so intense she was surprised she wasn't lost already. She stuck her hand into her pocket and closed it around Mimi's crystal. The pull of the glowing lights lessened a bit.

She felt Alex, just a child, with a blood-soaked jacket pressed to the gash in his cheek. Beside him, her six-year-old self coughed and cried out into the dark.

"Darren was here too, wasn't he?" Jake asked.

Evelyn nodded. She watched as Darren crawled through the dark, searching for a way out. His sister had coaxed him into climbing down a rope ladder she'd made, and he'd descended through the hole in the ground to find treasure. But then she'd left and he was hungry and scared. He'd found stairs, but they seemed to lead nowhere. At first, he'd thought that nobody had answered his screams. But there *were* things down here. Ghosts and monsters who pretended to be people. They were whispering to him. Inching closer.

Jake shivered and pulled Evelyn to the other side of the space.

"Does this connect to the tunnels?" he said, pointing to the archway.

Before he'd finished asking the question, he felt the terror rising in her. A memory, both inside Evelyn's head and coming from the passageway itself. Imprinted there.

"You're afraid of that door?" Jake asked. "But you don't know what's past it."

"I don't want to find out."

He put his arm around her shoulder. "We don't have to. I'll stay here with you."

This was exactly what Jake wanted. To feel like Evelyn needed him. He pulled her closer, and she couldn't help but cling to him. Because Jake was right. His touch disgusted her, but not enough to make her want to bear all these memories and emotions alone.

"I'm glad this is working out for you," she said bitterly.

"It would work for you too. If you'd let it."

He tried to put his cheek against hers, and she turned her head. "Are you finished now? Would you please let me go home? I don't know how much more of this I can take."

"Not everything down here is bad. That's why we have to do this. I figured it out in the lab. At first when I went back there, it scared the crap out of me. But I remembered how you were there, with the light around you."

He gripped her by the shoulders, looking down at her. She kept her eyes on the dirt floor.

"Now you can see it around me." Jake lifted her chin. Evelyn closed her eyes, focusing on everything else in the room instead of him. "Why won't you *look*? Why are you fighting this?"

She reached for a spot of warmth in the room that wasn't Jake. She let that memory pull her into its current, away from him.

Madeline stops in the middle of the room and sets the lantern on the floor. Sam is already here, waiting tensely for her in the dark. The lantern makes strange shadows of her nose and mouth.

She hugs her arms, thinking of the poor children who fell here a week ago. Alex just got out of the hospital and is on his way home to New York right now. She's tried calling Evelyn's mother, but the woman won't respond.

"How is your niece?" Madeline asks.

Sam rubs his jawline. "She's still recovering. Vivian's angry with me, but I'm sure it'll work out fine. Evelyn's a very brave little girl."

"It's just awful. I feel responsible somehow, though I had no idea this was down here. I didn't even know about the old mine shafts. Reginald doesn't tell me anything." She doesn't think Reginald knows about the secret stairs, though. He hates underground places. Even the storage rooms in the basement give him the creeps, and he avoids them at all costs.

"Maybe we shouldn't have come," Sam says, resting a warm hand against the skin of her elbow. "If it's making you upset."

Sam was the one who climbed in and got the children out of this room. He was also the one who found the trap door in the stone marker a few days later. He went to Madeline first, and she asked him not to tell anyone else. She's claimed this room as her own. It's one of the few places she can be truly alone.

Madeline has come down here several times since, thinking of Sam, agonizing over what she should do. Down here, in this space meant for secrets, she's admitted to herself how much she wants him. But she still isn't sure if Sam feels the same way.

She can't see the jumble of emotions that play across Sam's skin, infusing the room with chaotic energy.

"I wanted to make sure we could talk privately," Madeline says. "Reginald refuses to get rid of Walter's journals, and now he seems to be watching me all the time. Daniella and Darren won't listen to me. It's stifling in that house."

Her smile is pure sorrow, like a dark cut spreading in the upside-down light. "You're the only one who listens, anymore."

Sam moves closer to her. He knows this is trouble, this flirtation between them. But he can't seem to step away. For Sam, it's a familiar problem—a gamble with stakes high enough that they're too far to see.

"We'll figure something out," he says. "I'm sure the two of us can come up with a plan."

"The two of us?" Madeline asks.

She leans toward him, glancing longingly at his mouth. It's all too easy for Sam to close that last inch between them. Too easy not to think about what this really means.

Neither of them has noticed the moonlight falling across the top of the stairs. Neither of them hears the dry, reedy intake of breath when they kiss, or the faint click of wood against stone as the trap door closes.

Daniella runs toward Byrne House, her small feet nearly silent in the grass.

38

"YOU'RE BACK," JAKE SAID.

Evelyn's head hurt. She had to close her eyes and rest her forehead on her palms. Trying to think through the pain.

"You're bleeding." Jake lifted the end of his shirt to wipe her face.

"Stop, I'll do it myself," she said.

They heard a noise and Jake froze, still holding the bottom of his shirt in one fist. He and Evelyn both looked up as sunlight punctured the dark at the top of the stairs.

It was the sunlight that confused her most. She'd thought it was night outside, like it had been in the vision of Madeline and Sammy.

She blinked and held a hand in front of her eyes. Alex walked down the first few steps, ducking so he wouldn't hit his head.

"Evelyn? Are you down here?"

Alex's mind registered what he was seeing: blood running from her nose and down her chin. Evelyn's hands pushing Jake away. And Jake's shirt pulled up, exposing bare stomach muscles and the waistline of his jeans.

The air around Alex clouded over with dark grey, like a growing storm.

"What the hell's going on?"

Jake opened his hands and held them up. His wrinkled shirt fell back down into place. "Calm down, Evans. She's fine."

Evelyn tried to get up but fell to one knee.

"It's the drug," she said, "the one Darren gave us, I can't take anymore of this, please—"

The grey around Alex started to go black in narrow strips, like electric lights sputtering out one by one.

"You're dead, Oshiro," Alex whispered.

Jake jumped to his feet. Alex bounded down the stairs past Evelyn. He leapt on top of Jake, whose head smacked onto the ground. Alex straddled the other boy's stomach, raining blows. Bright pain blossomed around Jake. Duller pain came from Alex's knuckles.

Jake's fist shot up and hit Alex just below the middle of his chest. Alex cried out. Jake bucked and tried to push Alex over, but Alex found his balance and dropped his weight forward. He clapped his hands on Jake's neck and squeezed. Jake flailed his arms, hitting Alex in the face and chest.

"Stop!" Evelyn screamed at them both. "Stop it!" Alex didn't hear her. He couldn't see anything through his rage but Jake.

Jake's eyes bulged as he tried to pry Alex's hands away from his neck. He kicked and arched his back and grabbed at Alex's face. Unbearable pressure started to build in Jake's chest and throat. Alex lifted Jake's head and slammed it back onto the ground.

"Alex, no!" Evelyn looped her arms around his bicep and pulled. He was sweating, his hair hanging down in his eyes and sticking to his forehead.

Alex bumped her out of the way with his elbow. She stumbled back onto the ground and landed on her hip, on something jagged and hard. It wasn't on the floor—it was in her jacket pocket. The crystal.

When Evelyn looked up, Jake had gotten hold of Alex's hand and yanked it from his neck, twisting Alex's wrist at an angle that made her stomach lurch. Alex went over on his side, yelling and cradling his wrist while Jake coughed and retched.

Jake scrambled up onto his hands and knees in a cloud of dust and brought his fist down on Alex's ear. He pushed Alex face down onto the ground and fit his arm around Alex's neck. The inside of Jake's elbow clamped over Alex's throat like a vice.

Jake wanted to kill him.

She had to do something.

Evelyn pulled the crystal from her pocket and ran at Jake, dropping to her knees beside him. She raised the crystal above her head with both hands. Too late, Jake realized what she was doing and tried to turn. But her arms were already arcing down. The crystal caught him just above his eye, splitting the skin. Then the rock dropped onto the floor and rolled away into a corner.

Blood spilled into Jake's eye and down his face. "You stabbed me!"

Alex dragged himself up and stood, panting and swaying on his feet. Jake saw him and forced himself up, too, pressing his hand to the cut on his brow. They both gave off so much light she had to squint against the glare. They were going to start fighting again. Neither of them had any intention of stopping until the other one was lying in the dust, unconscious. Or worse.

Evelyn thought they were circling each other. But then she realized they were standing still—it was the whole room that was spinning. The firefly glow was now a blinding sea of yellow-orange flames covering the walls. Fire licked at the air around Jake and Alex.

The pink crystal was on the other side of the room somewhere. She couldn't see it anymore.

"Alex. Something's wrong, I can't—"

She fell to her knees. An image burned in her mind.

A door made of rust and gold.

It was the locked door at the end of the passageway. She blinked and a red film covered the room. Everything she saw burned with crimson. In her mind's eye, she'd passed through the door at the end of that hall, feeling the metal effervesce against her skin like boiling water.

She was inside.

Golden-colored mechanisms covered the walls, stained red from the blood in her eyes. Gears and levers, locked together in intricate patterns, spanning the length of the room, reaching up across the ceiling. A motionless pendulum hung on one side. Poised. Waiting for the trigger that would set it all into action. She could see the pathways of energy and thought running through them, cause and effect, beginning to end, the product of a twisted but vastly brilliant mind.

She understood it all. And she'd never imagined anything so incredible.

Or so monstrous.

Alex and Jake called to her from the other place, where she'd been before, but she couldn't reach them. She was trapped in that room, its clockwork poised like a deadly spider ready to strike. Her chest wouldn't breathe. Her eyelids wouldn't blink. She couldn't look away.

All was red, endless red and gold.

PART 3
THE GOLDEN CLOCKWORK

39

EVELYN'S HEAD FELT CLEAR. EMPTY.

More quiet than it had in weeks, maybe even months.

The mattress gently resisted her hands as she pushed herself up. She was in a sleigh bed next to a wide span of windows, all with their curtains drawn. A tapestry of a tree hung over the headboard.

Daniella's bedroom at Byrne House.

Alex sat in a chair on the other side of the bed, opposite the windows. He got up and lay down next to her on top of the blankets. He had a purple bruise on his cheek, next to his scar.

"How're you feeling?" he asked.

"I feel really good, actually. What happened?"

The door opened, and Daniella stepped in from the hall. "You're awake." She walked over to the bed, smiling. "How much do you remember?"

"Well…" Evelyn hated that question, and she knew the irony better than most. How would she know if she'd forgotten something? She thought of the bruise on Alex's cheek and wondered what he'd told Daniella about that. She remembered Jake and Alex fighting, and her arm making a curve in the air right before she hit Jake. But after that, everything was dark until she'd woken up just a couple of minutes ago.

Not exactly dark. She remembered pain. Pain painted red, with streaks of gold underneath.

"I was in the gardens with Jake, after he drugged me. And then Alex was there."

"You remember a lot, then," Daniella said. "From what Alex told me, you blacked out not long after that. Alex brought you to me."

"He did?"

He was still lying next to her on his side. A grave expression was on his face.

Daniella went to the windows and pulled back the curtains. Sunlight filled the room. "It's a very good thing, too. I was a little worried the antidote might not even work. But the bleeding stopped immediately and you were breathing normally again, and within just a few minutes your skin took on color. It was truly incredible to watch."

But how long had she been out? How much had she missed?

"What day is it? My mom——"

Evelyn tried to get out of bed, but Alex rested his arm across her stomach, holding her in place. "It's only been a couple hours since I brought you here from the gardens."

"I spoke to your mother," Daniella said. "So don't worry about that. Though of course I didn't tell her everything. She thinks we're all catching up like old friends."

Evelyn couldn't believe her mom would buy that. "I really need to get home."

"Of course," Daniella said. "But I'd like to talk to you for a few minutes before you go. Alex, if you don't mind?"

He shrugged. "Say what you need to say."

Daniella glanced over at Evelyn and lifted her eyebrows. Her eyes were bright, dancing with reflected sunlight. She tilted her head, trying to communicate something without speaking. Evelyn's brain was still working a little slow.

"I meant alone," Daniella explained.

"No way," Alex said.

Evelyn touched his arm. "It's all right. I'm fine."

After some more grumbling, Alex agreed to step into the hall. Daniella shut the door behind him and turned around.

"Thank you for what you did," Evelyn said. "I don't know what would have happened to me otherwise."

"I wish you didn't sound so surprised. I'd do anything to help you, Evelyn. You can trust me."

She didn't respond. The truth was, she did want to trust Daniella, as foolish as that seemed. Daniella had likely saved her life. For the past couple of weeks, Daniella had only tried to help her. Yet so far she'd asked for so little in return.

"It does seem strange that you had that extreme a reaction to Walter's serum, though. You were hemorrhaging. I can't explain it."

A little of the old anger resurfaced. Evelyn remembered how Daniella knew so much about that serum. Convenient that she called it "Walter's" serum and not Darren's.

"I think it was because of the flashes," Evelyn said. "A side effect from when Darren injected me with his drug." Her pulse was throbbing in her temples. She had to stay calm. Lashing out at Daniella again wasn't going to solve anything.

"Flashes?" Daniella sat in the chair beside the bed, leaning toward her.

"The past few months I've had these flashes of other people's memories. Things that happened in the past, in whatever place I happen to be. I think it had a multiplying effect, sort of, when Jake injected me with the drug this morning." Somehow, Mimi's crystal had kept the worst at bay—until she'd lost it. She'd have to get it back somehow, though she wasn't eager to go down there again.

"Fascinating." Daniella was staring like Evelyn was a guinea pig, and she was already thinking of the next experiment she wanted to run.

Evelyn shifted back on the bed. "But I feel really different now, like I can finally think without anything else whispering in the back of my mind. It must have been the antidote you gave me."

She hoped she was really rid of the flashes. Sometimes it wasn't so bad—seeing Alex's aura, for example—but she was tired of other people's emotions hijacking her mind. Then again, if not for the flashes, she'd never have known about her uncle's death. Daniella could still hold the answers to that mystery.

Evelyn glanced over at the windows. The curtains were open to a view of the gardens. They looked warm and inviting, as if spring were already here. But true winter hadn't yet started. More snow was bound to come.

"Have you been able to consider what I showed you last night?" asked Daniella. "In Walter's journal?"

"A little."

"I've been eager to hear your impressions. I thought it might be easier without Alex here. He's obviously very skeptical."

"He made that pretty clear."

"But what do you think?"

Evelyn hugged her knees to her chest. "Anything's possible."

Daniella smoothed back her long hair. "I've always felt the same. My mother is like Alex—a pessimist. She thinks I'm wasting my time chasing Walter's research instead of going back to my grad position. That's why she won't tell me the rest of what Simon wrote in his journal. She wants me to let go of Byrne House and get on with my life. You understand why I can't."

"Why does it matter to you what I think?"

"I can't get my mother to tell me what she really knows. But she might be willing to tell you."

"Me? Why?"

Daniella smiled, her eyes moving over Evelyn's face with something that looked like affection. "I knew my mother would like you. I think you remind her of herself when she was younger. Not like me. I don't even think she entirely trusts me. But you, she wants to trust. She will, if you give her a reason to."

"I don't know." It seemed so dishonest. Getting Madeline to trust her just so she could get information. All the while, Evelyn would be hiding the fact that she already knew so many of Madeline's secrets. Hiding what she'd done to Darren, her son.

Daniella got up and perched on the arm of the chair, looking down at her. "I'm willing to offer you something new in return. More than what I've already given you, which I think anyone would agree is a lot."

Evelyn's eyes flew up to Daniella's. "Information about my Uncle Sammy?"

She tensed. "I *told* you, I don't know anything about that. I'm offering something else. Your mom mentioned your dilemma to me. About where you'll live next year?"

"She did? When?"

Daniella casually shrugged one shoulder. "On the phone this morning, when I called to tell her you were here. I think she doesn't have many people she can talk to."

And Daniella was eager to take advantage of that. She really was convincing, if she could get Vivian to open up to a member of the Byrne family. Or maybe Viv was just that lonely.

"How would you feel about living here, at Byrne House?" Daniella asked. "I'm sure I could work things out with your parents. You'd be able to see all your friends, go to Castle Heights High for the rest of your senior year."

"Live *here*? What about Alex?"

"He'd be here, too. I'd settle everything for you both. You could see each other every day, have dinner together every night. There's plenty of rooms to choose from. Mrs. Evans will be back in New York; trust me, she won't interfere." Daniella's voice was velvety soft, soothing Evelyn's nerves though she knew she should stay on her guard.

"I'd be happy to give you and Alex all the privacy you need," Daniella added coyly. "I was seventeen not so long ago. I understand."

This is a distraction, Evelyn told herself. *You offered to help her in exchange for information on Sammy. Tell her no deal.*

But she couldn't say those words. Living with Alex—it really sounded possible when Daniella described it. So perfect and so tempting. They'd pick a room in some distant corner of the mansion, a place they could create good memories to replace the bad. And they wouldn't have to resort to getting married, which Evelyn was firmly against.

But would their families really let Evelyn and Alex live in the same house, essentially without supervision?

"William doesn't want Alex here," Evelyn said.

Daniella laughed with her lips closed. "Don't worry about William. Like I said, I'd settle everything. I can be very persuasive when I want to be, Evelyn. I think you already know that. All you have to do is talk to my mother. Find out what she's keeping from me."

Daniella smiled for another moment, still sitting on the arm of Evelyn's chair. Then she slid down, walked to the door and opened it.

"You can come in now, Alex."

Alex was leaning against the opposite wall with his arms and ankles crossed. "No thanks. I'll wait until Evelyn's ready to leave."

"All right," Daniella said. "You've been pacing out here in the hall the whole time we were talking so I assumed you wanted to come in. You clearly don't like to be separated from Evelyn. It's very sweet."

She turned and smiled at Evelyn again, that same smile with her teeth barely showing. Like she thought she'd already won. "Think about my offer."

Alex and Evelyn watched her walk away and go down the stairs.

"What offer? What did she want?"

"Weren't you listening at the door?"

"I tried. The wood is too thick."

"She wants me to talk to her mother for her." Evelyn took his hand and headed for the stairs, but Alex pulled her back.

"Hold on a sec. I know I should wait until later to ask these questions, but I can't really stop myself."

She knew what he wanted to ask. This wasn't going to be pleasant or easy to explain.

Alex glanced down the length of the hallway. Then he turned back and said, "What the *hell* were you doing with Jake?"

He shook his head, then lowered his voice. "When Ms. Foster called and said she saw the two of you fighting near Byrne House, it made no sense to me. I thought everything was right with you and me after the past couple days—and nights, especially—and I thought she had to be wrong. At least until I saw it for myself. Why would you go anywhere with him?"

"Jake said he was going to hurt himself. I was worried about him."

He let go of her hand and rubbed at the scar on his chin. "But why would you care, after all he's done?"

"Alex." She sighed. He would never understand it. Every time she looked at Jake, she saw him lying next to her on that table in Darren's underground lab. Glassy-eyed, his chapped lips partly open. Like he was dead.

She couldn't leave Jake there. She just couldn't do it.

"I wanted to save him," she said.

Rationally, she'd known for a while that she couldn't. But only now did Evelyn truly believe it. "We have to tell his parents he needs help."

"Ms. Foster already called them," Alex said. "Now, it's out of our hands."

⁂

At Evelyn's house, Alex called the shower first and ran upstairs. Vivian was sitting at the kitchen table with a pile of papers when Evelyn came in.

"Have a nice time with the Byrnes?" Viv asked. "I got an odd call from Daniella, saying the two of you were bonding? She seems eager to get on my good side. And yours, apparently."

"She and William eloped." Evelyn sat down beside her.

"Ah. No wonder she needs allies. If I was Alex and William's mother, I'd be on a war path."

Viv's eye moved to Evelyn's left hand. Her mouth crooked in a slight smile when she saw the infamous ring was no longer on Evelyn's finger. But she wisely chose to stay silent.

Viv straightened the edges of the papers and pushed them aside. "You had a visitor while you were gone. Jake left that here."

She pointed to the kitchen counter. Darren's key was there, next to the sink.

"Did he say anything?"

"Nope, just shoved it in my hand, went back to the car, and left. Looked like his mom was driving. What's that key for, anyway?"

Evelyn went over to the counter and stared down at it. This small little key had caused so many people so much pain. "Something Jake wanted me to have. It's not important."

Part of her wanted to get rid of it—both this key and its duplicate waiting in her keepsake box upstairs. She never wanted to go into those tunnels again.

But Evelyn knew she still might need these keys—at least, if she agreed to keep working with Daniella. And if she wanted to be with Alex next semester, what other choice did she have?

She dragged the key to the edge of the counter. It made a dry, scratching sound against the tile. Holding it with just the tips of her fingers, she stuck it in her back pocket.

40

MADELINE'S ROOM WAS TINY, JUST A DOUBLE BED with a simple rectangular headboard of wine-stained wood, a dresser with a dusty vase of white silk flowers, and a low-backed armchair. There was a book on the chair, opened facedown.

"It's not much, I know. This was a maid's room, back in the day." She must have followed Evelyn's eyes on their path around the room. "But I'm not interested in pretending I belong here. I only came back to Castle Heights because Daniella asked me, whatever her reasons. I hadn't heard from her or Darren in so long, and now their father's dead, and Darren's taken off—it seemed like the right thing to do."

She sat on the edge of the bed, not quite facing Evelyn, but not turned away either. "Daniella sent you."

Not a question. No point in denying it.

"How'd you know?"

"Why else would a teenage girl on winter break with a boyfriend like Alex be here, instead of finding a way to be alone with him?"

A nervous laugh snuck out of Evelyn's chest. She looked down at the floor, trying not to think the thoughts that were automatically surfacing in her head.

"It's nothing to be ashamed of," Madeline said, laughing along. "I'm sorry, I shouldn't embarrass you like that. The truth is I'm a lonely old woman and the only excitement I ever get is vicarious."

"You're not that old."

She held up the end of her grey ponytail. "That's what the mirror tells me, anyway. Who am I to argue?"

Evelyn's bag fell on its side by her foot. She bent over to pick it up, thankful the mirror hadn't fallen out. She needed to talk to Madeline for a while first before getting to that. She knew that Madeline had lied to the newspaper reporter about what she'd seen underground. But there were many reasons a woman might lie. She'd been down there with Uncle Sammy.

Madeline might know what had happened to him.

"So what's she promised you?"

Evelyn stood up. "What?"

"Daniella. She never does anything unless she thinks she'll get something out of it, and she probably assumes that you're the same way. Because you're smart, like her. She tried the same thing on me, offered me all sorts of things to give her Simon Byrne's journal, and when she found out I'd destroyed it, she offered me even more to tell her what it said."

She hadn't expected Madeline to catch on so quickly. But the woman knew her daughter too well.

"I'm supposed to move away from Castle Heights after New Year's," Evelyn said. "Daniella's going to make sure Alex and I can both live here at Byrne House. So we'll be together."

"Then I'm sorry I can't help you. But I'm sure you'll manage to work things out next year." Madeline got up and went to the window. A car passed by on the street below. "It's a very special thing to be in love, and to be young and feel like there's so much time it's endless. Don't waste it."

Madeline was already talking like she was about to leave. "How do you know you can't help me?" Evelyn asked. "I haven't told you why I'm really here yet."

Madeline tapped her fingers against the window. "To find out what Simon wrote in his journal. Right? I already told Daniella she's better off not knowing. The same applies to you."

"That's what Daniella wanted me to ask. But I want to talk about something else."

She smiled and motioned for Evelyn to go on. "Be my guest." She took a seat on the bed, poised to listen.

Evelyn took a breath. She hoped she wasn't making a huge mistake.

"Sam Stanton."

Madeline looked at her for a moment like she hadn't heard. Or didn't understand. Then she said, "What about him?"

"Did you know he's dead?"

She closed her eyes, absorbing the news. Maybe she really hadn't known. Evelyn wanted to believe that. She hardly knew Madeline, but so far she felt inclined to like her.

"When? What happened?"

"You really have no idea?"

She threw up her hands, exasperated. "I assume you're here to tell me."

Evelyn stuck a hand into her bag and found the mirror inside. "I guess it's more show than tell."

She explained what the mirror could do. "I know it sounds crazy, but it's not a trick, or a sick joke or anything like that. It's real. You can try it for yourself."

Evelyn handed her the mirror. Madeline set it in her lap, eyeing it cautiously. "Tell me what you saw. Then I'll decide whether to believe you or not."

"I saw you with Sam in that hidden space under the gardens, a few days after Alex and I fell there. You kissed him."

Her lips shook as she smiled. "I was willing to give up everything I had for him, I was so starved for love. I hoped he felt the same." She turned the mirror over in her lap, and the smile hardened with bitterness. "I was wrong."

"What do you think happened?"

Madeline took a slow breath. "He showed up at Byrne House one morning and quit his job. Reginald didn't seem to care, but I was completely shocked. Sam promised to meet me later that night to explain. But he never showed. I found out he'd already run off. I found out he'd..." She shook her head, shuddering at whatever she'd been about to say.

"What?" Evelyn asked.

"He wasn't the person I thought he was. Let's just leave it at that."

Evelyn had no idea what that meant. But Madeline needed to know the truth. What would it do to her to find out what really happened to him, after believing for so many years that he'd run off without even saying goodbye?

Of course, Madeline didn't know about her son's death, either. At Evelyn's hands. But she couldn't confess about Darren. Not yet.

The mirror shifted slightly in Madeline's lap as she adjusted her weight on the bed. A sheen of light passed across the glass. "Why dig up these old memories?" she whispered.

Evelyn came over to the bed and sat beside her. "Because it's important to know the truth."

"What makes you think you want to know the truth yourself? There's plenty you don't know about your uncle. And it's not pleasant." She tossed the mirror onto the blanket and got up from the bed. Her eyes were hard and shining. "Sam could have found me, explained what happened. But he didn't have the guts to face me."

"It wasn't like that. He never had the chance."

"That makes no sense, he—" She pressed her fingertips to her mouth. She must have seen it in Evelyn's face. "You're telling me he died *that day*?" Madeline sank back down onto the bed. "Oh God. I don't understand any of this."

Evelyn put a hand on Madeline's knee, unsure of how to comfort her. They hardly knew one another. Madeline coughed and her chest moved up and down with three heavy sighs, like she was trying to push all the sobs back in.

"Was he murdered?" she finally asked.

"Yes."

She pressed her eyes closed and her chest heaved again. "And you saw it with that?" She pointed at the mirror where it lay beside her on the blanket.

"Yes."

Madeline slowly stood. She picked up the mirror by its gold-plated handle. "Then show me. I need to see it. I need to know."

41

MADELINE STOOD IN THE TOWER BEDROOM, WHAT used to be her room. She held the mirror for a minute or two. Then she ran for the bathroom, pushed up the toilet seat and vomited.

Evelyn went in and put a hand on Madeline's back, wishing there was some way she could help. But Madeline yelled at her to get out.

So Evelyn sat down against the wall outside the bathroom and waited, careful to avoid looking at the bed. The air in the room felt thick against her skin, dense with emotion. Her eyes squeezed shut, terrified she'd have another flash of Uncle Sammy. But nothing came. The flashes seemed to be gone.

This was the first time she'd been back to the tower bedroom since she saw Sam lying there in a pool of blood. Suddenly, she realized what should have been clear before: she might be able to find out right now who killed him. She no longer had to fear using the mirror. But seeing the murder itself, not just the aftermath…

Evelyn gagged and quickly covered her mouth.

The toilet flushed. But Madeline didn't come out. After a few more minutes, Evelyn pushed the door inward and peeked through the crack. Madeline was lying on the bathroom floor with her face in the crook of her elbow.

Evelyn had told her about possible side effects, but Madeline said she didn't care. Exactly what Evelyn had expected her to say, but still she wondered now if she'd done the right thing. She imagined her own mother on the bathroom floor instead of Madeline. Viv would be devastated to learn the truth about her little brother's death. Could Evelyn really do that to her?

Maybe it was easier not to know. And much, much easier not to see.

"I couldn't tell who did it," Madeline said.

Evelyn could barely hear her. She scooted to the doorway and looked in again.

Madeline was in the same position, facedown on the floor. "I kept seeing him die, over and over. But I couldn't see who held the gun. Do you know?"

"I didn't see that either—I think the imprint of Sam's death overwhelmed all the other memories in the room, even the moment he was shot. But I could use the mirror to find out."

Madeline dragged herself up to sitting. "In return, you want me to tell you what was in Simon's journal. Right?"

That had been Evelyn's plan until she'd seen Madeline fall apart. "I'm not trying to make a deal with you. I'll help you, whether or not you tell me anything. I want to know what happened to Sam just as much as you."

Madeline was quiet for a few minutes. Her face was streaked with red, puffy and soft-looking around the eyes.

"This isn't going to be easy, Evelyn."

"I know, believe me."

"There's something you *don't* know. It's horrible and disgusting so I'll just spit it out." She screwed up her mouth. "Daniella told us that Sam touched her. Hurt her."

"*What?*"

"Darren confirmed her story. I'd always believed that's why Sam ran—because he knew he'd been found out. That's why I left Castle Heights myself, a few months later. I felt like a failure as a mother. I gave up my children because I thought it was best for them. Now I have no idea what's true and what's not. But I have to know."

Madeline nodded at the mirror, which Evelyn held in her hands. "I can't do it, though. It'll have to be you. Are you willing to use that mirror to find out the whole truth, knowing what you might have to see?"

The thought sickened her. Evelyn had seen terrible things in the mirror, and she was already steeling herself to see Sam's murder. But something like that...Could her uncle have done something so evil? In her visions she'd seen Daniella's fascination with him. Sam Stanton clearly had a strong influence over Daniella. They'd had study sessions in private. But this couldn't be true. Evelyn had felt the last few wisps of emotion that left his body as he died. That kind of darkness would have shown through.

Wouldn't it?

"Tomorrow," Evelyn said. "I'll be ready then." She'd have to be.

42

EVELYN FOUND HER MOTHER IN THE LIVING ROOM, rearranging the pictures on the mantle. She'd drawn the one of her and Uncle Sammy—on Christmas day, as kids—to the front. The tree in the photo was nearly identical to the one in the corner of the room.

"Do you miss him?" Evelyn asked.

Vivian jumped in surprise. Her fingertips lingered on the frame a moment before she answered.

"Of course. It's hard not to think about him now that I'm planning to move away. We grew up here together." She rubbed a knuckle against the corner of her eye, smearing the tear there. "Some days, I hate Sammy for leaving us. Other times, I replay everything I said in our last conversation, wondering if it's my fault. But I always miss him. Every single day."

"Why would it be your fault?"

She glanced at Evelyn warily. "Why the sudden interest in your uncle?"

Evelyn retreated to the sofa, away from the intensity of her mom's eyes. "I miss him too. I've always wondered what really happened, but you refused to talk about it."

Her mom turned to the mantle. "We had a fight, Sammy and I. About...I guess you're old enough now. Sammy had gotten involved with a married woman. Madeline Byrne. He came to me for help, and I screamed at him. I couldn't believe he'd been stupid enough to get mixed up with those people, after all the warnings our grandmother gave us. He stormed out of this very room and slammed the door. That's the last I ever saw of him."

Evelyn wished she could comfort her mom. But if she hugged Viv now, she'd blurt out the truth.

"I just wish." Viv's voice broke, and she stopped to clear her throat. "I wish I knew that he was okay."

"What if he's not?" Evelyn said carefully, picking at the seam of the sofa cushion. "What if something bad happened to him?"

She spun to face her daughter. The tears were gone, and her eyes were hard. But her trembling lower lip revealed just how much she was fighting to stay in control.

"Evelyn, that's probably what *did* happen. Otherwise, why wouldn't he contact us even once in all this time? I even hired an investigator once, but nothing came of it. I'm sorry, honey. But you're almost grown now. I don't want to lie to you."

Guilt overwhelmed her. Evelyn couldn't look at her mom anymore. Viv came over and wrapped her in a hug. "Oh Evvy, I know that's difficult to hear. Maybe I'm wrong, maybe he's out there happy somewhere—that's what makes this so damned hard."

"But if he's not, if he's…Would you want to know?"

"Yes." No hesitation, no doubt.

Evelyn had her answer. As soon as she knew who'd killed Sammy, she would tell her mother the truth.

That night, Evelyn told Alex what Madeline wanted her to do. And what Madeline was willing to do in return. Halfway through, her hands started shaking. He gathered her into his arms.

"Give me the mirror," Alex said. "I'll take it over to Byrne House right now and find out. You've been through enough already."

"Sammy was part of my family. I need to do this for my mom."

Alex sighed. "You're doing so much for everyone else. What do *you* want?"

She wanted the courage to tell her mother the truth. And she wanted to clear Sammy's name, if she could. With Madeline's help, maybe she'd even find Walter's invention, if it existed. But that was too much to get her head around. Seeing the future—it was like thinking about having superpowers. It wasn't real to her.

Alex was real. Being near him and touching him was so real and so *now* that it filled up the moment and didn't leave room for much else. She didn't want that to end, and she was willing to do a lot to make sure it didn't have to.

"I want us to be together." The same thing she'd wanted for months.

"I know, but that's not what I mean. Out of everything in the world, what do you want?" He looked at her intently, like he thought he could give it to her if he just knew. If only that were possible.

"I want things to be like they were before."

"Before I left? Or do you mean your mom and dad?"

"No." She closed her eyes and pictured it. The lacy fabric of her dress, soft against her skin, and Alex in that green checked shirt that matched his eyes.

"The first time we kissed. *Really* kissed, and I knew that you felt the same way I did, and I was so happy and everything was so perfect for those few minutes. I finally knew the truth about what had happened to me. And I had you. I was sad, but it was a good kind of sad, you know? I wasn't alone anymore. I couldn't imagine ever worrying about anything again because I had you. That's what I want. To feel that again. And for it to last."

He rested his chin on the top of her head. She felt the vibrations in his throat against her forehead as he spoke, mixed up with the beats of his pulse. "That's how I feel all the time when I'm with you. Except I do worry about losing you."

"That kinda spoils the effect."

"Maybe. But I still can't imagine anything better."

They sat together until they couldn't deny how tired they were. Alex went up to use the bathroom, and then he came down and she went up. She changed into her sleep shirt and brushed her teeth, but instead of going to her room she went back downstairs to the couch. Alex was already dozing.

She nudged him. "Can I sleep down here with you?"

He smiled and lifted the blanket. She lay down on top of him, and he tucked the blanket around them. He folded his arms over her back. She could feel the tension in his shoulders when he moved, shifting beneath her on the couch.

"There's a lot more room in your bed," he said.

"But I think I can talk my mom down when she finds me on the couch with you in the morning. My bed, I have my doubts."

"What's this?" Alex asked. He hooked a finger through the chain necklace Evelyn was wearing.

Ada's ring hung on the chain like a pendant.

"I wanted to wear it," Evelyn said.

"But not on your finger."

"Not *yet*. But I will. Someday."

He smiled. "I can live with that." She settled against his chest and felt his heartbeat thump against her eardrum. In minutes, Alex was asleep. But Evelyn kept opening her eyes every time they closed, wanting to stay awake as long as she could.

She wanted to believe they'd be all right. That no matter what happened tomorrow, they'd find a way to be together. Even if Evelyn's mom reached her limit and kicked him out—even if Daniella broke her promises—this wasn't really their last night.

But as she lay there in his arms, peaceful and content, it seemed more final than that. Like after tonight, things wouldn't be the same, could never be as simple and as good between them as this one fleeting moment. Like she was in the middle of losing the one thing she'd ever really wanted, and she'd never get it back.

43

EVELYN PUSHED HER BAG UP ONTO HER SHOULDER and knocked on Byrne House's front door. The bag slipped down again onto her elbow.

"This would be a lot easier if I had two hands to work with," she said to Alex.

He held her other hand to his mouth to kiss it. "I told you. This one's mine today. You're not going anywhere without me."

Since they'd woken up that morning, he'd only let go of her hand long enough for her to go to the bathroom and get dressed. At breakfast, Evelyn's mom kept glancing down at the table, toward where their hands were locked together in Alex's lap. She finally stopped frowning when Evelyn told her they were going over to Byrne House. She probably thought Alex was going to talk to William about moving back.

Evelyn knocked again, louder this time. Madeline opened the door. "We'd best talk in private. Daniella is out with William, but I don't know when they'll be back."

"I hope it's okay that Alex is here. If it's not, I—"

Alex gripped Evelyn's hand tighter. "I know all about what's going on. I'm not letting Evelyn do this alone. I've left her too many times before when she needed me."

Evelyn tried not to roll her eyes.

"It's all right," Madeline said. "Of course you can stay, Alex. I wouldn't dare to separate you."

She led them to a large room on the second floor, where a couple of old school desks faced a dusty chalkboard. "I thought we should start here. If anything ever happened, if

Sammy really...well, it would have been here. I don't think they would have been alone together anywhere else. The staff would've noticed."

Evelyn took the mirror out of her bag and set it on one of the desks. "I'm going to need both my hands," she said to Alex.

"Are you sure it's safe?" he said. "What if the same thing happens as before, one of those flashes in your head at the same time?"

"Flashes?" Madeline looked from Alex to Evelyn. "What flashes?"

"They're gone, I'll be fine. Stand somewhere out of the way. I'll see what I can find out."

Alex and Madeline gave her room. She held up the mirror, aiming it at the chalkboard, and sought out the most intense emotion that had ever been imprinted here.

Daniella—a girl, no older than fourteen—appeared, talking to Uncle Sammy. He had on his tweed coat again, the same one he was wearing on the day he died.

Tears were streaming down Daniella's face.

She let the vision take control.

"You can't," Daniella says, voice as broken as her heart feels in her chest.

"I'm sorry, but I have no choice." Sam glances down at the small box of items on the desk—pens, teaching manuals, handkerchiefs, a stray necktie—that he's left in the classroom over the last months. The few hints of his presence here at Byrne House, and soon they'll be gone.

"Trust me," he says, *"it's for the best."*

"But Sam..." Daniella reaches out and brushes her hand down his arm.

He takes a step back. This is getting out of hand.

"Is this about my mother?" Daniella asks sharply.

Sam sighs. So she knows. The kiss with Madeline was a mistake. He's known since it happened—since before, really. But then he did something even more idiotic.

He told his sister, Vivian, hoping for advice.

Their fight was epic. Thank goodness Evelyn wasn't woken by their shouts. But Vivian was right—he can't stay here. He's made so little progress with the kids, and he's crossed the line in so many ways with the Byrne family. Daniella especially. It can't go on.

The classroom walls close in on him, strangely dark. He's never been here so late in the day, and he hardly recognizes the room in this light. Dirty streaks appear on the wallpaper, uneven planks poke up from the floors.

Daniella's face is different, too. A hardness around her eyes where before he saw only softness.

"It's partly about your mother," Sam says gently. "But not just that."

He's been a fool about Daniella. Those private tutoring sessions, the extra attention. Clearly she's gotten the wrong idea.

But isn't that his fault, too? Daniella's crush on him was obvious, but he did nothing to stop it. Instead he tried to use it—intimate smiles, occasional touches on the shoulder—hoping that she'd be more interested in her schoolwork as a result.

So, so stupid.

"I care about you, Daniella," he says. "As a student. I'm just not the right person to teach you and Darren. That's why I quit today. I need to get away from Castle Heights for a while, figure some things out."

Daniella feels like she's sinking into the floor. But Sam cares about her—she clings to those words like they're keeping her afloat. Sam is the only person at Byrne House who understands her, who wants her to be happy. This is all her mother's fault, going after Sam out of jealousy.

"You're a great teacher," she says. "The best. I'll work harder, I promise. I'll do whatever you ask me."

Sam picks up his box, head hanging, and starts for the door.

"No, you can't go." *If Sam leaves, she'll have no one, no escape from her brother's episodes, her father's distance, her mother's secrecy. Daniella blocks his path, pushing him back into the room. Her small hands grab at the lapels of his coat.* "I'll stop studying Walter Byrne's journals, like you wanted. Please—"

"Even if I believed you, it's too late."

"No!" *She pulls him down by the collar until his mouth crashes into hers.*

"Daniella, stop!" Sam thrusts her away from him so hard she bumps into her desk.

Shame floods her. She'll drown in it. She'll die.

The floor creaks. They both look.

Darren stands in the doorway, a short, dark silhouette in the fading light. He's seen what happened. He was listening for quite some time in the hall.

"What's going on?" Darren asks.

Sam smooths out the lapels on his jacket. "I'm packing up to go. I'm sorry Darren, it's just not working out. I already spoke to your parents."

A faint but steady voice whispers to Daniella: You can't let him do this. Why did Sam Stanton even come here, if he was just going to leave? Why did he work so hard to make you care? He's cruel, that's why. He should bleed, like you're bleeding now.

"He touched me," Daniella blurts out. "Mr. Stanton, he made me do things."

Sam just looks confused. "I what?"

"He hurt me," she says. That, at least, is true.

"I never—" Sam Stanton shakes his head in disgust. "That's enough."

Darren glances between his sister and his teacher. He never liked Mr. Stanton much. And he really didn't like the way Daniella fawned over him, as if their teacher was so cool. It hurts Darren that his older sister has been ignoring him lately—ever since Darren confessed to their parents that Daniella had been alone with cousin William on the day those little kids fell in the gardens. She called him a mean name: snitch. I hate you, she'd said.

He misses her. Darren wants his sister to pay attention to him again.

What do I do? he wonders. He looks to his sister for an answer. He doesn't want to make her mad again. He doesn't want to be a snitch. But Daniella nods at him, as if she trusts him. And everybody knows that if a teacher touches a student in a bad way, then you have to tell someone. They'd been kissing. It wasn't right.

"I'm telling our father," Darren shouts.

Darren is stocky, but his thick legs carry him fast. Sam runs after him, begging him to stop. This is madness, all of it. Sam's sister, his aunt, his grandmother—the women of his family have told him since he was a kid to stay away from the Byrnes. Why the hell didn't he listen?

Darren goes the first place he can think of: his parents' bedroom in the tower. "Dad! Help!" He's not here; he must be downstairs. Their mother left the house an hour ago—probably at the spa. Anything to avoid them.

Darren spins to go, but Sam bars the doorway. "It's not true. You can't honestly believe I'd do that. I've been a good teacher to both of you."

Daniella comes up behind Sam. "He's lying," she says.

Sam is trapped between them—the Byrne siblings, fury in their eyes.

"Get out of my way," Darren says. "I'm telling my parents whether you like it or not."

Sam glowers from one to the other. "I am not letting you do this."

Darren lunges for his father's nightstand. He has to help his sister. If Mr. Stanton really did hurt her, then he has to protect her. Darren digs into the nightstand drawer until he finds it.

His father's gun.

He points it at Sam's stomach. "Go away," he says, hands trembling. "Get out of here."

Daniella rushes forward, takes the gun away. "Don't be an idiot. Go get Dad, I'll keep Mr. Stanton here."

Darren takes off, and Daniella is now the one pointing a gun at Sam with a satisfied look on her face.

Sam barely glances at the gun. This has to be a joke, a dream. "Why are you doing this? Accusations like that could ruin my life, Daniella. And yours, when everyone finds out the truth."

"You're the one who's ruining my life."

Sam comes closer, holding out his hands like he's approaching a wild animal. "You don't mean it. You're angry and hurt, but this isn't you. I know you."

She braces both hands around the gun. "You don't."

Daniella thought he did. But she was wrong. No one really knows her, no one sees.

Sam takes another step toward her. "Put that down and talk to me. Scream at me, if you want. But when your dad gets here, you have to tell him the truth." He keeps his voice soft, hoping to lull her into calmness.

Suddenly he charges toward her, grabbing at the gun. They struggle over it, Daniella's fingers cramping under the pressure.

"Daniella, just give me—"

The gun bucks in her hands and makes a pop, like a champagne cork but louder, and Sam's eye is gone. Just gone. Like he blinked, and then there was a dark red and black circle underneath when the eyelid lifted. Sam falls backward onto the bed, his mouth still open from the sentence he didn't get to finish.

Daniella gags. The gun drops onto the floor.

No, no, she thinks. Please, I never meant to—

The blood is coming fast, soaking the white comforter in an expanding blot of red. Darren runs back into the room, eyes wide. He takes in the scene.

"But...what..."

Daniella turns on her brother. "Is Dad coming?"

Darren has his hand over his mouth. He can't stop looking at the pool of blood. Daniella comes over and shakes him.

"Is Dad on his way up here?"

"I...I think so. He was on the toilet but he said..."

They hear their father's voice calling upstairs. Footsteps running.

Daniella is thinking very fast. "We'll need his help. But you let me talk, got it?"

Darren is crying. "Mom," he's whimpering. "Mom." He wants his mother to hold him, hide his eyes. This isn't like how bodies look in his favorite superhero movies.

Daniella pushes her little brother into a chair. She wrinkles her lip at his smell. He's wet himself. "You're never going to tell Mom, you hear me? If you do, I'll make you sorry."

He nods vigorously, snot running down his lip. But she's already starting to plan. If he even hints at telling their mother again, she'll teach him a lesson he won't ever forget.

44

D<small>ARKNESS</small> <small>DREW</small> <small>ACROSS</small> <small>HER</small> <small>VISION</small> <small>LIKE</small> <small>A</small> blindfold. Her eye—white-hot agony paralyzed her, threatening to drive her mad. She'd do anything to make it stop. Her mind began to unravel, driving the pain far away and with it all coherent thoughts save one: *Vivian, my sister. I'll never see her again. Never say I'm sorry.*

She was dying.

"Evelyn? Can you hear me?"

"Please..." The word scraped her throat raw.

"I'm going to pick you up, okay?"

Slowly the room materialized. The four posters of the bed, the large round window. The pain in her eye receded. Just a memory. Her uncle's memory.

Alex scooped her into his arms. "I'm getting you out of here." They walked a short distance, and Alex closed the door behind him. "We're in the hall now. Can you stand?"

He set Evelyn on her feet. She opened her eyes. The hallway wobbled around her.

"I guess not," he said. He held her up by the shoulders, keeping her steady.

"I thought I was dead." She blinked a few times, breathing deeply. Her throat was so dry. *I'm okay,* she thought. *I'm alive. That wasn't me.* She sobbed as the grief came, the full brunt of what her family had lost. She wept for Sammy, for her mom, for herself.

"I shouldn't have let you go through that." Alex's hand shook as he brushed his fingers against her damp cheek. "It should have been me."

"I'll be okay. It's over now." She took a few deep breaths to calm herself. She remembered why she was here. "Where's Madeline?"

"I tried to explain how this works while I was chasing you down the hall and up the stairs, but she didn't follow us. I guess she knew where you were headed and wanted to stay away for that part."

"I don't really blame her." Evelyn leaned into Alex, letting him support her weight. "It was Daniella," she whispered. "She's the one who killed him."

"Ev." Alex nodded at something behind her. Evelyn turned and saw Madeline at the top of the stairs.

"Is it over?" she asked. "Do you know?"

She nodded.

They followed Madeline to her room. She sat soberly on the bed, hands clasped in her lap. Like she was preparing for the worst. Evelyn pulled back the curtain from the small window so she could see outside. She felt like she'd been trapped inside Byrne House for days.

"Sammy never touched Daniella," Evelyn said, "not that way. She knew that you'd kissed him, and she was jealous. She told Darren the lie on impulse to hurt Sam. But then she couldn't take it back, no matter how much she might've wanted to…after."

It took incredible courage for a victim to seek justice after an assault. Evelyn doubted that Daniella could have maintained the lie for even a little while, once the emotions of that moment had passed.

But that day, for Sam, time had stopped. The decisions of those few, short minutes could never be undone.

Madeline dropped her head into her hands. "And Sam's death?"

Evelyn shuddered. "Darren wanted to defend his sister. So he took his father's gun, and…"

"And?"

Evelyn's first impulse was to spill it all, the terrible truth — to punish Daniella for what she'd set in motion. She'd taken Sammy away, robbed Evelyn's family of so much.

But then she looked at Madeline's face. This woman with her haunted, lonely eyes.

Daniella was the only family Madeline had left. And aside from William, Daniella didn't seem to have anyone but Madeline, either. If Evelyn told the truth, she'd be punishing Madeline just as much as Daniella. Maybe Madeline had been right when she said it was this house that twisted people, turned them against one another.

Her own family would never be the same—wasn't that enough suffering because of one girl's horrible mistake?

"Darren followed Sammy," Evelyn said, her voice a monotone. As if she were reciting lines out of a book. "The gun went off. It was an accident."

Evelyn met Alex's eyes, and he nodded. He knew she was lying, but he must have understood why she had to do it.

Madeline fell back against the bed and turned over onto her stomach. Her shoulders moved up and down as she cried.

"Would you rather be alone?" Alex asked.

"Wait." Madeline rolled over, tears still streaming down her face. "I'll give you what I promised."

⚜

She took them to another small room, this one hardly bigger than a closet. It had simple white walls instead of the ornate wood paneling and wallpaper that covered every other room in Byrne House.

"Simon wrote in his journal about an invention of Walter's. Simon had never seen it. But Walter said it could make a man richer than he'd ever imagined. Walter said he'd hidden it to keep it safe—he was paranoid, and half the time he seemed confused about where or even *when* he was. He refused to tell Simon the invention's location. 'It isn't for you,' Walter always said.

"And then he died, having never given more than vague hints about where the invention could be. Simon looked around for it awhile, but he was much more interested in booze, women and cards. He quickly lost interest in Walter's secrets. All of this, Simon wrote down in his journal."

Madeline laughed ruefully. "I spent a little time looking around Byrne House for this hidden invention before I had the children, when I needed something to do. Reginald didn't like me to have friends, and I was lonely. But finally I made myself stop. I had to accept the fact that Walter was either lying or insane. At least, I thought so then."

In the small closet, Madeline knelt to the ground. She pulled up one of the planks in the floor, leaving a shallow rectangular gap. A lump of yellowed fabric lay inside. She carried the bundle to the bed and sat with it in her lap.

The soft, worn cloth fell away on either side of a glass-topped jewelry box. Two silver keys lay inside, along with a silver locket necklace.

"Walter left this to Simon in his will."

"Why would Walter leave Simon a jewelry box?" Alex asked. "I thought they hated each other."

"Oh, Simon didn't appreciate the gift," Madeline said. "The box is impossible to open."

She handed it to Evelyn, who turned the box over in her hands. There were scratches all around the lid, evidence that someone had tried to break or pry the box open. But there was no visible latch or keyhole.

Alex touched his finger to the glass. "Why didn't Simon just break the top?"

"I don't know what it's made of," Madeline said. "Even my diamond wedding ring couldn't scratch it."

Alex thumped his knuckle against the clear, glass-like material. It made an odd, dull sound.

"I'd assumed the box was another clue to Walter's imaginary invention," Madeline said. "His way of tormenting his brother from beyond the grave."

Madeline held out her hand. Evelyn gave the jewelry box back to her.

"Maybe the invention is real after all," Madeline said. "Who except Walter knows? It was only Simon's vices that saved him from that obsession. But that's exactly why I didn't want Daniella and Darren to ever see this box. If I had the chance, I would have taken it with me and destroyed it, too. But Reginald watched my every move. And then I left. I could barely sneak Simon's journal away, and only because I'd kept it in a sock drawer all that time."

Madeline wrapped up the jewelry box in the fabric. She handed the bundle to Evelyn.

"I've had a long time to think about all of Walter's clues, a long time with nothing else to do but wander around my memories of Byrne House. Simon may not have understood, but I think I do. There's a stone memorial in the gardens. The back of it has a secret latch, and a trap door to—"

"I know how to open it," Evelyn said. "I've been inside."

She nodded, unsurprised. "As far as I know, Simon never even realized that trap door existed. None of us did, until you and Alex fell into the room underneath. There's a passage that leads away from that room with a locked door at the end. I've gone over Walter's clues time and again, and I'm sure that's where these keys will fit. If you can open the box to get them out, that is."

The locked door beneath the gardens. Somehow, Evelyn had known that they would end up going back there.

"There's one other thing you could do for me," Madeline said. "Let me take the mirror for a little while. I need to see a few more things before I go. I don't think I can stay at Byrne House much longer."

"Of course." Evelyn pulled it from her bag. "Take as long as you need. Keep it, if you want to. I don't really think I want it anymore."

Madeline pressed her hands around the handle. "I'll bring it back. I won't be taking anything of Byrne House with me when I leave this time."

Alex and Evelyn went out to the backyard.

She felt uneasy. Madeline's story didn't add up. Why would Walter brag about an invention to Simon, only to never even let his brother see it? And if he was simply lying or mad, why the elaborate clues leading to that hidden door?

On the other hand, Madeline had no reason to lie about any of it, either. Evelyn was sure that Madeline had told the truth about Simon's journal. Her account of Simon's character certainly matched what Evelyn already knew about the man.

Evelyn turned the box over in her hands. Aside from the glass top, it was made of silvery metal. It had geometric, interlocking patterns carved into its surface. She pulled on the lid. How was she supposed to open it if no one else could in all these years?

"Do you think that's Ada's locket in there?" Alex asked. "Look at the pattern."

She angled the box so light shone inside. The locket had a delicate, raised pattern of vines running along its edge. She had seen this pattern before. She pulled the chain from inside her shirt and held up Ada's ring. The patterns were identical.

"A matching set," Evelyn said. "Definitely Ada's locket."

Perhaps that was why he'd given Simon the locket—to make sure Simon would never forget what he'd done to Ada.

"Simon had the ring at first, too," Alex said. "Well, sort of—it was inside that secret compartment in Walter's cigar box. His wife eventually gave the box to Clara, Walter's daughter—my great-grandmother. Remember the diary I told you about?"

Evelyn nodded. He'd found Clara's diary among his father's things in New York. So that explained why the ring and the locket were separated. But why would Walter choose to hide the ring, and yet display the locket in this way?

And the keys bothered her—assuming Madeline was right, and those tiny keys would unlock the secret room beneath the gardens. Why would Walter have wanted Simon to have the keys to unlock his greatest invention? He despised Simon. He wanted Simon to suffer.

Alex took the jewelry box and examined it. He turned it upside down, resting it against his palm. "This space is odd," he said, pointing at a circular depression in its base. Unlike the rest of the jewelry box, the round indentation was surrounded by the same pattern of vines as they'd seen on the locket and the ring.

"Evelyn, give me Ada's ring?" he said.

She took the ring off the necklace chain. Alex gently lowered the ring into the circular indentation. It made a tiny click. A perfect fit. Both she and Alex were holding their breaths.

Alex rotated the ring in its new home, and then there was a louder click. He turned the box over.

The glass lid popped open.

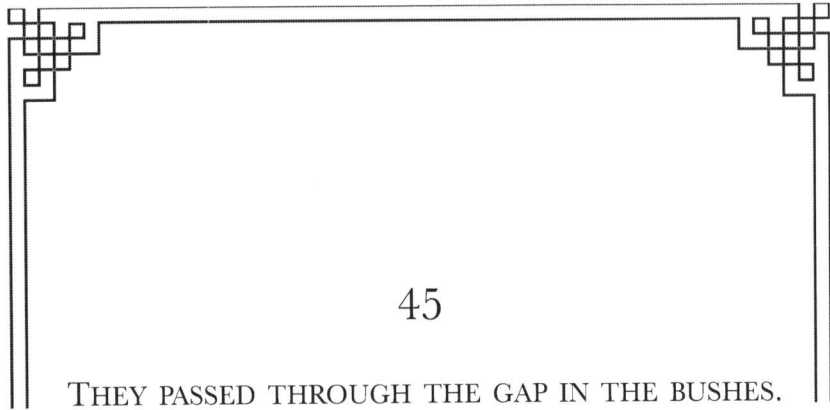

45

THEY PASSED THROUGH THE GAP IN THE BUSHES.

The stone marker was bone white, surrounded by damp fallen leaves. Evelyn felt for the latch in the back of the stone. It popped open, revealing the dark staircase inside.

Alex pulled a flashlight from his pocket. He'd borrowed it from the kitchen pantry on their way.

"I'm still not convinced this is the right spot to look," Evelyn said. "When I touched that door, it didn't feel like a place Walter would keep some great invention." She couldn't remember specific images, just a profound sense of dread. And still, inexplicably, the color gold.

"But you don't know exactly what you saw. I'm sure you sensed all the madness and grief that Walter felt after losing Ada. But you're not having the flashes anymore, and we're not using the mirror. You won't feel any of that again."

His reasoning made sense. But if she could just explain that intuition, the way it nagged at the back of her mind.

"We might as well check it out," Alex said, "and if it's not there, we'll keep looking."

"Going somewhere?" The bushes rustled, and a pale hand pushed the branches out of the way.

Daniella stepped into the clearing.

"You're not welcome here," Alex said.

"This belongs to me as much as you. I gave Evelyn the antidote yesterday. I saved her life."

"You only did that because you wanted something from us," Alex said.

"And you're nothing like that, are you Alex?" Daniella said, her voice lower and harder than its usual soft tone. "Evelyn, I thought we agreed yesterday that we'd work together."

Evelyn's hand went to her necklace where she'd tucked it beneath her shirt. She'd strung the two keys on the chain with Ada's ring. "I don't want any help from you."

Daniella laughed. "Don't be ridiculous. I'm sure my mother said all sorts of things to you about not telling me, but you can't pay any attention to that. She doesn't know anything about Walter's research or his inventions. Not like you and me."

Evelyn shook her head and didn't answer.

"I heard you talking about keys," Daniella said. "Did my mother give you keys to something down there?" She gestured to the stone marker.

"You *were* spying on us." Alex squeezed Evelyn's hand. His palm was sticky and hot.

Daniella's mouth cinched at the corner. "I knew you were upstairs with my mother. When you came down, I followed you. It's a good thing I did. I clearly can't trust you."

"And we should trust *you*?" Alex took a step toward her, tugging on Evelyn's hand to keep her next to him. "Your own mother should never have trusted you. You killed Evelyn's uncle!"

Daniella's face drained of color. "Did you tell my mother that?"

"We didn't," Evelyn said. "But you should. She deserves to know. If she hears it from you, maybe she can figure out a way to forgive you."

Daniella's teeth gleamed as she laughed. "What do you know about what she deserves? I don't want forgiveness from her. She's the one who should beg forgiveness for leaving me behind at fourteen. I had no one. Unless you count a father who packed us away to boarding school the first chance he got. Or my pathetic brother who was incapable of living a life of his own. It wasn't my fault."

"Poor Daniella the victim," Alex said. "You've never cared about anyone. All you've ever done is destroy other people."

Daniella stuck her fingers into her hair, breathing heavily. Her perfectly controlled facade was vanishing before their eyes, and beneath was something desperate and raw.

"You're every bit the smug, spoiled brat William always said you were. I will *never* let you live in this house. I'll make sure William never has to deal with your selfishness ever again."

"I'm not giving you the keys unless you tell Madeline what really happened to Sam," Evelyn said.

Daniella's shoulders hunched forward, as if she were about to lunge. Alex angled himself in between them.

"You're not getting those keys," he said.

"Fine," Daniella said, starting to smile. "I'll tell my mother the truth. I'll tell her what a whore she is for throwing herself at a man who was hardly much older than her children. I'll tell her how it felt for me to find out that Mr. Stanton, the only person who'd ever really seemed to care about me, planned to throw me away like a piece of trash. It's her fault he died, not mine. I—"

Daniella's gaze shifted past Evelyn. Her mouth snapped closed. Evelyn turned.

Madeline stood in the clearing. She had the mirror in her hand.

"I knew Evelyn was holding something back from her version of Sam's death," Madeline said. "Probably because she thought it was too cruel to tell me the truth. So I went back to the room where you killed him, and I found out for myself. I suppose I could have just come and asked you, Daniella. You seem to have no problem confessing it."

"Mother, I didn't mean what I said. Alex just made me so angry and I—"

"Enough. No more lies." Madeline's eyes, filled with despair, came to rest on Evelyn. "I saw you in the mirror, too. I saw what you've been hiding from me. I'm so sorry, Evelyn. You went through hell because of my family. Because of my children. I'm so deeply sorry."

She knew about Darren. She knew that Evelyn had killed her son.

Madeline swiped at a tear on her cheek. "Byrne House has destroyed everything I ever loved. There's evil here, corruption down to the very foundations. I never should have given you that locket and those keys. Please Evelyn, I'm begging you. Don't unlock that door. Leave the past in its grave."

"Come with us," Daniella said, her voice high and child-like. "You'll see all I've been trying to accomplish. How it will make up for everything."

There was so much weight in that word: *everything*. Evelyn suspected that Daniella was sincere. She thought Walter's great discovery would outshine all the darkness she'd caused.

"I want no more part of this," Madeline said. "I can't— I can't even look at you, Dany." Her composure finally broke. Sobbing, Madeline tossed the mirror onto the grass at Evelyn's feet and left.

Evelyn started to run after her, but Alex held her arm. "Just let her go. If anyone should go after her, it's Daniella. Not you."

Daniella turned away from them. She pressed both her hands onto the stone marker, supporting herself against it.

Evelyn wanted to hate her. But inside, Daniella had reverted to that wounded little girl. Evelyn could only feel sorry for her.

What did Walter's research or his inventions matter anymore, when compared to the terrible things that had happened in this house?

Evelyn took off the chain. The ring and the keys swung back and forth through the air.

Alex snatched it from Evelyn's hand. "We're not just letting her have it. This is ours too. We deserve to see what's down there just as much as Daniella does. More, even."

"You laughed when she told us her theory about Walter's invention," Evelyn said. "Something that could see into the future? Don't you remember how stupid you said that was?"

"But if there really is some amazing invention, why should we let her have it?"

"I don't care if she has it. Not anymore. Let's just go. If Daniella won't help us stay together next year then—"

"Evelyn, listen to me," Daniella said. She was still resting against the stone marker, looking down at her feet. Her voice sounded wobbly, like she was trying not to cry. "This all has to mean something. What we've gone through. It's led us here. Use the keys my mother gave you to open the door, and I'll do whatever you want. I'm sorry about what I said, Alex. I didn't mean it."

"Yes, you did." Alex put his hands on Evelyn's shoulders. "Look, this isn't just about her. I want to know what's down there. I've wanted that ever since we fell into that room, and I looked into that archway. We've both been haunted by that place. We need to know where it goes, once and for all, and then you and I can be done with this. Done with Byrne House."

Evelyn glanced over at Daniella. She was watching them, her face calm and white as the stone marker beside her.

"We don't even know what could be in there," Evelyn whispered. "Why would Walter give Simon the keys to his greatest discovery? It doesn't make sense."

"Most of what Walter did made no sense. But he was still a genius. Don't you want to see our future, living happily ever after?"

Evelyn bowed her head. Alex was right. She did want to know how all of this would turn out. Then they could leave Byrne House behind. Uncle Sammy, Ada, Darren—what happened to her in the tunnels—maybe Evelyn could finally let all of it go.

"Okay." She slipped her hand into his. "We'll do it. All of us together."

Without hesitating, Daniella started down the stairs. Alex and Evelyn followed.

At the bottom, Evelyn paused to find Mimi's quartz crystal. It lay against the wall, glowing a warm pink in the light from her phone. Its facets pressed into her palm as she gripped it. But she didn't feel the comforting hum anymore.

The others had already crossed the room, stepping through the piles of rubble that spanned outward from the dark outline of the archway. Evelyn hurried to catch up, tucking the crystal into her bag. Daniella went first through the gap. Alex lit the way with his flashlight.

They followed the curves of the passage. Then the flashlight hit the metal door at the dead-end of the narrow tunnel.

Daniella held out her hand. Evelyn removed the two keys from her necklace. Daniella picked one and tried it in the lock.

It turned.

46

THE DOOR SLOWLY SWUNG INWARD. NONE OF them had touched it after Daniella turned the key in the lock. Yet the door moved, as if pulled by an unseen hand from inside the room. It made a clicking sound as it opened. The noise echoed through the passage.

Alex pointed his flashlight into the room. A brilliant golden gleam responded, light bouncing off the uneven surface of the walls in every direction. A new clicking sound replaced the first, now faster and higher. A glow began to build in the corners of the room, starting at the edges and bleeding into the center. Flames began to dance in the glass oil lamps on the walls. As the light rose like a tide in the room, the shapes covering the walls came into view.

It was a sea of gold—layer upon layer of interlocking starbursts and thin bars of metal. Gears, like the guts of an enormous clock, were so thickly stacked Evelyn couldn't see the walls beneath them. Metal bars connected the gears to one another at their centers, forming a structure of criss-crossing lines that overlay the clockwork like a delicate spider's web.

The golden clockwork stretched up across the ceiling. It spread down onto the floor in the middle of the room, where a massive pillar covered in gears and metal webbing connected the floor to the ceiling. A pendulum, almost as tall as the room itself, hung motionless to one side of the pillar. It was suspended from a huge, spiked wheel that was attached to the ceiling.

In front of the pillar, just beyond the edge of the clockwork that carpeted the floor of the back half of the room, stood a table.

On the table sat a small box made of clear glass.

"This is incredible." Daniella walked around the other side of the door and peered behind it. "When I turned the key it must have triggered this pulley to open the door, and that turned these gears, which connect along here to the mechanisms that lit the gas lamps." Daniella traced a line in the air with her finger along the path of the levers and gears.

"It's like we're on the inside of a clock tower but there's no clock," Alex said.

He took another step into the room, pulling on Evelyn's hand. But she stayed in the doorway. Nausea inched up from the pit of her stomach. She felt like she was supposed to be remembering something, but it was still out of reach. As if the memory were a passage that faded out into darkness before she could see to the end of it.

"All these parts moving together would build up momentum," Daniella said. "It could probably generate a lot of force."

Daniella went up to a wall, leaning so close that her nose almost touched the metal. She gently lay the tip of a finger on one of the knifelike points that rimmed a huge gear. "Of course, it would also have to be extremely fragile. One pulley or lever breaks, one gear out of sync, and it would throw the entire thing out of whack."

"But the door worked," Evelyn said. "And the lamps. So whatever the rest of this is supposed to do, it could still work, too." The room had a purpose, though she couldn't yet see it. This place felt...*malevolent*.

"Oh, I'm sure it still does what it's supposed to do," Daniella says. "Whatever that is. Everything here looks completely untouched. I don't think anyone's been in this room since, well, since Walter left it."

Alex let go of Evelyn's hand. He walked along the edge of the clockwork near the base of the pillar. "Look at all this," he said. "It must have taken Walter years to put all this together."

"It took months," Evelyn said. "Three months, working day and night."

Daniella spun around, her eyes narrowing. "How could you possibly know that?"

Evelyn looked around the room, hoping to see something that would explain it, even to herself. She'd said the words without thinking. "I don't know. I just did."

This is a bad place, a voice inside whispered to her. *You shouldn't be here.*

"Just go with it," Alex said to Daniella. "Evelyn's been getting a lot of feelings about this place."

"Oh?" Daniella crossed her arms.

Alex had gone farther into the room. "Come look," he said, leaning over the glass box. "I think this is it!"

Daniella rushed over beside Alex. She gasped as she looked through the glass. "Oh my God. It is. It's what we've been looking for."

"Evelyn, you need to see this." Alex stepped to the side and waved her closer.

It was a handheld mirror in a silver frame—the fraternal twin to the mirror in Evelyn's bag—lying on a bed of maroon velvet. She walked over to the glass box to get a better view, her fear overcome by curiosity.

Inside the silver frame, frost clouded the sheet of crystal. Evelyn leaned in, her breath making a patch of fog on the top of the box. She realized the surface of the crystal wasn't really frosted—it was etched with minute symbols and numbers, so tiny and fine they blended together into a blur.

Daniella held up the key she hadn't yet used. She moved toward the glass box.

"Don't," Evelyn smacked her hand down. "Don't touch it."

Daniella recoiled. "What is the matter with you?"

"You can't touch that box. It's dangerous. I don't have a clue how I know this, but I'm *sure*." Evelyn's heart was speeding up, blood pumping faster as her body told her to run.

She turned to Alex. "Please, you have to believe me. We need to go—all three of us. While we still have time."

Alex nodded, his mouth creasing into a frown. "Okay, we can go. If that's really what you want."

"Yes, I—"

Daniella pushed her out of the way. Evelyn landed in Alex's arms as Daniella's hand shot forward. She twisted the key inside the lock.

"No!" Evelyn screamed.

Tiny gears inside the box began to turn. The glass lid ticked open on its hinge, exposing the frosted crystal mirror lying on its bed of red velvet inside. They all leaned closer, as if the mechanism were pulling them in.

They held their breath, waiting, unable to move.

The lid stopped, fully open. But there was still a faint whirring sound, like something else was moving but out of sight.

"See," Daniella said, "it's open and nothing bad happened. We're fine. Whatever Darren did to you down in that lab must have been worse than I thought because you're losing it." She reached toward the box.

Evelyn grabbed Daniella's upper arms from behind. "You can't. If you touch it, it'll be too late."

Daniella threw back her elbow. She hit Evelyn in the shoulder. "Get away from me. You're insane."

"Stop." Alex stepped between them. Evelyn struggled to reach Daniella again, but Alex held her back. "Evelyn, let's just go."

"We can't let her do this," Evelyn said to Alex. She had to keep Daniella from touching the silver mirror. But Alex wouldn't get out of the way.

"You just want to take it for yourself," Daniella said.

Alex glanced behind them, distracted by something on the floor. Evelyn tried to reach around him again. Daniella was already grabbing the silver mirror out of the box.

"Do you see that?" Alex said. "They're moving. The ones on the floor, they're starting to move."

Evelyn didn't have time to see what Alex was talking about. Daniella kept trying to push her away. She jumped, grabbing for Daniella's arm. Her hand closed around Daniella's wrist just as a flicker of light crossed the frosted surface of the silver mirror.

Alex and Daniella disappeared.

The room around them changed, somehow getting dimmer and glowing brighter at the same time, as if the gas lamps had gone out. But the golden clockwork was radiating heat and energy.

Walter stands before the pillar, framed in gold by the mechanisms lining the walls. His eyes, ringed with purplish-black beneath pale skin, burn with reflected light. His hands are tight claws at his sides, raw and stiff from hours upon hours of intricate work. His unlined face bears a strange, unnatural calm.

"Hello Simon," he says.

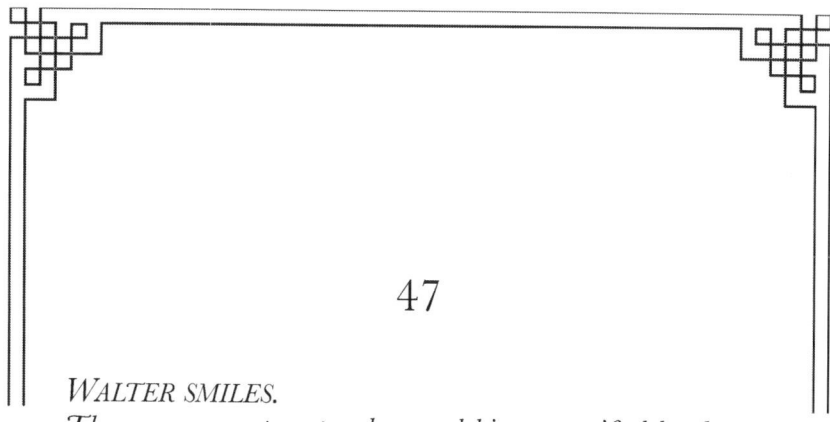

47

WALTER SMILES.

The room seems to expand around him, magnified by the rage that has so consumed him. Here, in this room, he cannot register anything else. Not even the pain in his hands or the unrelieved hunger in his stomach.

"If you're seeing this, brother, then I congratulate you. You must be very pleased to be rid of me now that I am dead, although I'm sure the bequest to you in my will was disappointing. A jewelry box holding a locket, once worn by the woman you destroyed. But you've understood the clues I left. I worried they might be too subtle, but I didn't want you to question my motives. I expected you to pity your poor, mad brother and descend like a vulture on the discovery I'd told you about. I expected I could rely upon your greed.

"And here you are."

Walter pulls a large brass pocket watch from his coat, along with a thin metal tool. He holds them in his cupped hand.

"I must admit to you, however, a small deception on my part. I suggested my invention would make you a very rich man, which it no doubt would, if you had the ability to master it. But I'm afraid you won't live long enough to pursue the opportunity. And yet I do have another opportunity to offer you, if you can pay close enough attention."

He uses the small tool in his hand to pry open the back of the pocket watch, revealing the movement inside.

"Have you ever seen the inner workings of a clock, Simon?" *Walter holds up the ticking object in his hands.* "A magnificent thing, the clockwork movement. The mainspring, here, is wound, ratcheting as it goes so as to forbid its moving backward. It cannot be unwound. An apt metaphor, don't you think? What we do, the choices we make, set certain things in motion that can never be undone. That thought has haunted me these past months. But it also inspires."

He replaces the back of the watch and screws it into place. Then he tucks the watch back into his coat, along with the thin tool.

"This room," *he says, gesturing around him as the walls and ceiling gleam like liquid gold,* "is a metaphor as well. Specially designed for you. A parting gift for my beloved brother. After you unlocked the glass box before you and removed the silver-framed crystal, the mechanism wound. It is ratcheting around you as I speak, like a noose tightening around your neck."

He steps to the side and turns, showing his profile. "The pendulum is here, just behind me. By now the gears have begun to rotate, setting others in motion, which triggered still others in their turn. The pendulum will soon begin to oscillate, swinging back and forth, keeping a precisely constant interval between each swing.

"The beat."

He takes the pocket watch out again and holds it up as he looks at the wheel on the ceiling, above the pendulum. "For you, my clockwork has already begun its motion. The gears are moving, cause begetting effect, toward the ending I've already predetermined. If I were a religious man, as Ada urged me to be, I would surely be a deist. The idea of God as a clockmaker does have a certain appeal."

He clasps his hands behind his back, the pocket watch held tight between his palms.

"The end is inevitable," *Walter says.* "This pillar beside me is part of the support system for the foundation of Byrne House. A system of my own design, the same one I used in the tunnels, inspired by the mining shafts that were our home before this house, when we still had nothing. Nothing but each other, I should say."

The madness splits open for a brief moment and sadness breaks through, like a beam of sunlight breaking through an overcast sky. Then his mind clouds over again.

"Once the pendulum begins to swing, and the gears have all begun to revolve in a beautiful symphony of motion, the force that travels and builds throughout the entire clockwork will culminate here, at the pillar. It will not be able to withstand the pressure of the mechanism I've created. The support system will fail, setting off a chain reaction. It will fall.

"And so will Byrne House."

Walter brings his hands to the front. He looks down at the brass pocket watch sitting like a closed shell in his cupped palm.

"But there is a small hope. Not for me, of course, but for you. The escapement. The lever turns the escape wheel, modulating the advance with each beat. One beat. One moment. That *is my great discovery. The possibility of unwinding that which has already been done, reversing what has already been set into inevitable motion. Only before the next advance, only before the next oscillation. A metaphor again, I know, but the principle is the same. The interval is the key. It is the reason I cannot get back anything that I've lost. For me, for Ada, it is much too late. But in that brief interval between moments, one beat to the next, is your opportunity. That is the true gift I am giving to you."*

He lifts his eyes, imagining he is staring into the face of Simon. The brother he once loved and now hates with a resolve and a passion greater than anything he has ever known. He did adore his wife; but even that devotion pales against the blinding glow of the walls in this room. He prays the hatred will subside before it destroys what of his mind is left. He only needs a short while longer before he can be with Ada, before he can rest.

"You can try to run," Walter says to his brother. "Try to save yourself. Or, you can use the opportunity I am giving you to unwind the clock. But you will not be able to save Byrne House, or anyone or anything inside of it, if that beat passes."

Walter's mouth moves in a grotesque imitation of a smile. "Be aware, the effort of it will likely kill you. But at least you will have the satisfaction of dying with the knowledge that you did a single selfless act, a single worthwhile thing just once in your wretched life.

"Goodbye Simon."

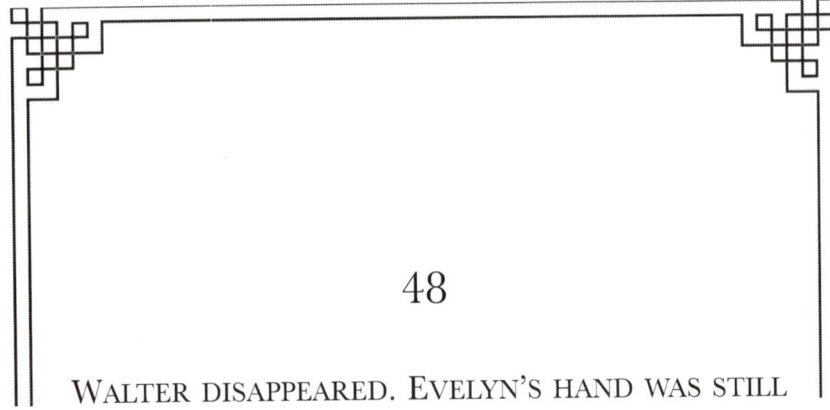

48

WALTER DISAPPEARED. EVELYN'S HAND WAS STILL clamped around Daniella's wrist. She let go and stumbled back into Alex.

"Did you see him?" Alex asked. "Did that come from the silver mirror?"

Evelyn nodded. She couldn't speak.

Walter had used the crystal to record his thoughts and emotions. The silver mirror had released the memory, as if playing a film reel, when they'd touched it.

A new sound filled the room, like the buzzing of bees. Hundreds of gears turned, the motion spreading up the walls and across the ceiling.

It's happening.

"Walter was telling the truth," Evelyn said. "I can feel it."

Daniella didn't move. She was staring down at the silver mirror in her hands. Then she began to laugh. "If I were you," she said, "I'd get tired of paying such close attention to my sad little feelings. You'll end up just as insane as Walter was."

Daniella looked up at the ceiling of rotating gears. "This is all crazy. All of it." She swung the silver mirror around her, pointing at the moving walls. They shimmered as if covered by masses of gold-plated insects. "It's all because Walter was *sad*. He wanted *revenge*. All of his talents, wasted. None of it means anything—the journals, the stupid clues. *None of it.*"

Nearly all the gears were moving now, picking up speed. The pendulum creaked as it started to swing upward, beginning the arc that it would soon carve through the air beside the pillar.

"What if Evelyn's right?" Alex said.

Do we run? Evelyn asked herself. Walter had said they had two choices: save themselves, or stop Byrne House from falling—and if Byrne House fell, the rest of the tunnels throughout Castle Heights could collapse, too. *A chain reaction,* Walter had said.

She followed the movement of the gears with her eyes, trying to understand Walter's plan. One gear moved another, then another, and another.

"We have to stop it," she said.

Alex turned to her. "Ev, tell me you understood what Walter was talking about. The stuff about the beats and the escape wheel and all that."

Daniella doubled over with laughter. "I'd actually convinced myself I'd be able to see the future. Now I know how you saw me, Alex, why you laughed like it was the funniest thing you'd ever heard. And it was! My entire life has been some kind of existential joke. I thought Walter's research really meant something, that it would give my pathetic, shitty life meaning, and it was all one, big, fat *joke.*"

"I don't have a clue what he was talking about. It made no *sense.*" Evelyn closed her eyes, trying to pry open that door in her mind that blocked the memory. It was there, she knew it. But it wouldn't come.

"Of course it made no sense," Daniella cried. "It was the ravings of a madman. And I've been listening to it. Maybe I'm the one who's insane."

Desperately, Evelyn ran through Walter's clues again. *My great discovery. The interval is the key. Refraction,* he'd written in his journal. *Reflection* and *refraction.*

The silver mirror, with its strangely frosted glass. The counterpart to Ada's gold mirror.

"Give me the silver mirror," Evelyn said. "That's what we're supposed to use."

Daniella grabbed Evelyn's shirt at the shoulder, clenching the silver mirror in her other fist. "You knew, didn't you?" Daniella said. "Your *bad feeling* about this place. You knew this would happen and you wanted to show me how stupid I was to believe, you wanted to stand there and laugh at me as my entire life crumbled into nothing."

She yanked Evelyn forward by her shirt, spraying her with droplets of saliva. "This is your fault. You've ruined everything."

Alex grabbed Daniella around the shoulders and pulled her back. She spun as he let go. Daniella slammed face first into the clockwork-covered wall. The gears shuddered but didn't slow. Daniella's arms pinwheeled out from her sides. She whirled around, her mouth curling into a toothy snarl. Blood began to seep from tiny cuts on her cheeks and nose.

She looked down at the silver mirror in her hand. Then she screamed, a primal cry of rage and fury. Her arm snapped back. She slammed the mirror against the clockwork. The silver mirror fell behind the top layer of gears.

"No!" Evelyn cried, hand outstretched. But the silver mirror was trapped, wedged into the mechanism.

"What did you do that for?" Alex said.

The gears kept moving at first—until the spiky edge of one of them caught on the silver frame. Then the gears started to freeze. A wave of stillness spread out from around the mirror to the edges of the walls. High-pitched keening filled the air as the gears struggled against the obstacle.

Daniella wiped at her face, smearing the blood that oozed from her cuts. She was giggling, quiet at first, but then she opened her mouth and it got louder, layering on top of the noise of the straining gears.

"I stopped it," Daniella said, still laughing. "I told you this whole damned thing was fragile. Walter was so obsessed with his ridiculous theories and metaphors about clocks he didn't bother to make something that actually worked."

They heard a crackling sound, like ice cubes breaking in water. It was coming from the silver mirror. Tiny fractures moved across the frosted surface of the crystal. The gears lurched forward, then stopped again.

Alex walked over to where the mirror was stuck in the wall. He peered at it through the gaps in the gears. "Maybe she did stop it."

Evelyn pulled Alex by the arm. "Let's go before we find out it didn't." They had no other choices left.

Alex started to turn his head toward her.

Then the mirror exploded with an ear-splitting crack.

A piece of metal sliced across Evelyn's arm. Shards of crystal stung her face. The gears sprang back into life, moving even faster than before. The pendulum swung wide, then arced back down to the other side, whooshing through the air.

Alex still faced the wall where the mirror used to be. His hands were up at his chest. His body swayed. His head lolled back.

"Alex?" Evelyn said. "Are you okay?"

Alex fell to his knees at the base of the clockwork. He tottered forward. Evelyn pulled him back by the shoulders so he wouldn't fall against the spinning gears. He collapsed into her arms.

A triangular shard of the mirror jutted from his chest.

49

EVELYN COULDN'T TELL HOW DEEPLY THE GLASS had penetrated. It seemed large, grotesquely thick where it entered Alex's chest. A circle of blood was spreading around the wound and growing fast.

Alex turned his head to look up at her. "Evelyn, it... I..." He coughed. His body tensed with pain as his chest moved.

"Help! Daniella, help, please!"

Daniella ran to them and crouched over Alex. A whining noise filled the room as the gears spun faster.

Alex's shoulders jerked back as he tried not to cough. A tiny bubble of blood popped on his lower lip.

"Don't worry," Evelyn said. "I'll get you out of here, I promise." It was getting hotter by the minute, the air stuffy and stale. Pinpricks of sweat broke out under Evelyn's arms and along her stomach.

The red circle on his chest grew, expanding so quickly it didn't make sense. How could there be so much blood, so fast? This couldn't be real. More bubbles began to appear every time he breathed, a froth of blood leaking from his mouth.

"Daniella, do something." Evelyn looked up at her. "You caused this. You have to help him."

"The glass must have punctured his heart. Maybe his lung. I don't think there's anything that we can do."

Alex coughed and sprayed Daniella's arm with dots of blood. She cringed and wiped them away with the back of her hand.

"What do you mean we can't do anything? We have to call an ambulance!"

"There's no reception down here," Daniella said scornfully.

The front of Alex's shirt was soaked now, the blue of the cotton turning to black. Alex shivered and rolled toward Evelyn, closing his eyes and putting his forehead against her stomach.

The shard of crystal stuck out from his chest, utterly surreal.

"This isn't happening." Her teeth clattered together, like her jaw was loose and she couldn't keep it steady as she spoke. "This can't be happening."

Daniella stood over them, shaking her head.

The gears rotated on the walls and ceiling in a blur, too fast, all of it going too fast. Evelyn couldn't think. She held Alex close, trying to keep his shoulders still when he coughed so it wouldn't hurt him so much. Her mind scrambled for some way to help. She had to stop the bleeding somehow. She wondered if she should pull the shard out of his chest, but maybe that would just make things worse.

"I don't know what to do!"

A horrible popping noise responded in the room. The walls and floor began to vibrate, then shake.

"We need to go." Daniella dashed forward, her eyes on the open doorway.

"Wait, you have to help me," Evelyn said. "We have to get Alex out of here." She tried to put her arms around him to pull him up, but a wet-sounding moan came from his throat.

"You think we're going to carry him out of here like that?" Daniella said. "He can't even stand. We'll never get out in time."

"Ev." Alex licked at his lips, leaving smeared trails of blood. He could barely make a sound, and even that seemed to take terrible effort.

"I'm not leaving without you." She hooked her arms under Alex's shoulders and tried to lift him again. Tears clouded her vision. "Daniella, *please*."

Daniella knelt beside them. "Evelyn, I'm sorry, but he isn't going to make it. Even if we somehow get him out of here before the whole mansion collapses on top of us, we won't get to the hospital soon enough. Okay? Do you understand what I'm saying? We have to leave him and go if we want to have any chance at all."

Alex looked up at Evelyn and nodded. Blood dribbled from his mouth and down in a curve along his chin.

Evelyn pushed Daniella away. "If you want to leave, then leave. Go tell William that his brother is dead because of you."

Daniella stood and backed toward the door. "I'm sorry." She turned and ran.

The gears spun so fast that the spokes blurred. A haze of gold seemed to hover in the room like fog, buzzing in a swarm of motion and sound. A gear popped out of place and clattered to the floor, then another. Waves rolled through the clockwork machinery around the pillar, sending down showers of gears and pieces of the metal web.

One of the lamps sputtered out, casting half the room in shadow.

"Alex, please, you have get up. You have to try." She bent over him, protecting him from the noise and debris raining around them, cradling his head in her arms. "Please, don't leave me. I need you."

Alex made a gurgling sound in his throat, like he was trying to speak. Blood slid in trails from the sides of his mouth. His eyes moved back and forth over her, glistening with tears in the lamplight. He reached up to touch her cheek.

He was saying goodbye.

Evelyn's entire body screamed—a piercing, inhuman cry—and the room turned white before her eyes. All the rage and grief she'd been keeping back exploded inside of her.

The barrier in her mind fell away, swinging open, the door unlocked.

She remembered. She understood.

The noise in the room quieted. Every particle of dust in the air seemed to slow. The air was thick. Alive with thought. She saw the pathways crossing and overlapping in the air around her, the patterns unfolding and unwinding, revealing their source. Cause and effect, beginning and end.

And Evelyn stood at the center of it all.

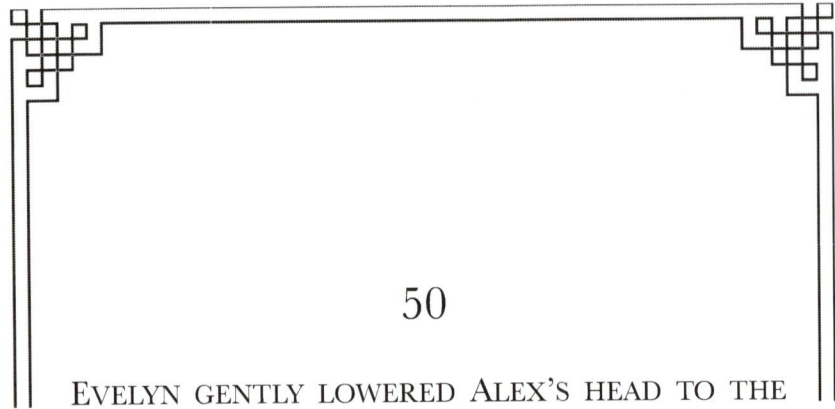

50

EVELYN GENTLY LOWERED ALEX'S HEAD TO THE floor. She scrambled onto her hands and knees. Hot metal stung her skin as she sifted through the debris, throwing fallen gears and pieces of golden metal out of her way. She spotted a large shard of etched crystal—an uneven triangle almost as big as her palm.

A pool of blood had spread out on either side of Alex, unfurling like red-stained wings.

Evelyn crouched beside him. She held the piece of crystal to her eyes.

The room changed, distorting out of proportion. As if Alex were at the bottom of a murky pond, and Evelyn was looking down at him. His body was relaxing into the floor, his breaths slowing. Giving up. She felt a sensation of weight, of falling, as if the crystal were pulling her downward, too. She fought back, keeping herself above the etched surface. She needed every bit of strength for this, every ounce of control.

Walter had meant for Simon to use this crystal to unwind the gears. It was the only way to stop the collapse of Byrne House. But he also knew that, for his invention to work, Simon would have to give everything he had. Otherwise, the mechanism would simply start again.

Simon would have to pay for his redemption with his life.

And that meant Evelyn might die in this effort, too. But she didn't care. She would save Alex, no matter the cost.

She focused all of her thoughts—all of her energy—through the crystal. The buzzing shifted to a lower hum. The gears on the wall behind Alex shook. He coughed again, an awful wet sound.

Evelyn concentrated on the gears, willing them to stop.

They resisted. She fought harder, grabbing at them with her mind. For a brief moment they still drove forward. Then their movement stalled, turning in a halting slow motion. Finally they paused. Evelyn's mind was holding them in place.

Blood ran down her throat, salty and metallic. She blinked and the view turned red.

The gears started to reverse course.

They inched backward, making a strange clicking sound. Like a knob turning on a wind-up toy. Gears and metal bars shivered on the floor, then arced upward towards the wall and ceiling, finding their rightful places with swift, graceful movements. The room cooled and the lamps relit. The clockwork slowly unwound, reforming, as the scattered pieces of the puzzle fit themselves back together.

Silver glinted in the air. The mirror reappeared, stuck again in the wall: first an outline of the frame and then jagged pieces of the crystal filling in the center.

The pool of blood around Alex shrank, his shirt going from dark purple back to blue. He breathed in, the air hesitating at first but then rushing inward. The sound smoothed out, dry instead of wet.

The shard of crystal pulled out of his chest as the circle of blood shrank into a point and disappeared. The shard turned end over end through the air. It lodged back into the silver mirror.

Evelyn pushed the gears back as far as she could. Her head was splitting from the effort. Blood caught on her eyelashes and poured along the back of her throat. Her ears itched like water was draining out of them, though she knew it wasn't water. The crystal almost slipped from her hands;

she was shaking. The gears had stopped again, straining against the mirror wedged deep in between them.

I can't do it. She couldn't hold them any longer.

The gears shuddered. Then they slipped back into motion, this time going forward instead of back. The last dregs of energy had drained from her body. She had absolutely nothing left.

She had failed.

The gears would begin to turn again. Byrne House would fall.

Evelyn dropped the piece of crystal. It sailed toward the wall, fitting back into the center of the mirror without a sound.

But maybe, she thought, *it can be different this time.*

Everything was still and silent for one stretched-out moment—the gap between the end of one breath and the start of the next.

The silver mirror exploded again. Evelyn fell forward to cover Alex with her body. She felt shards of crystal slicing her shirt, cutting into her back, but only on the surface. She couldn't feel the pain.

The gears were whirring again. Evelyn pushed herself up. She almost panicked when she saw a spot of blood on Alex's t-shirt, but then she realized the blood was her own. Another drop rolled off the tip of her nose.

She lifted the bottom of Alex's shirt and ran her fingers along his stomach. His skin was smooth and solid, all the way up to his chest. Perfect.

Alex's eyes flew open. "What are you doing?"

Joy awakened her body like the light of the rising sun. Evelyn laughed and leaned down to kiss him, leaving a circle of red on his mouth in the shape of her lips. She wiped it away.

Alex propped himself on his elbows. "You're covered in blood! Where's Daniella? What happened?"

The gears spun faster, the room filling again with golden fog and heat and the clatter of falling metal.

"You got hurt. But you're fine. Everything's okay now." Her mouth hurt from grinning. Evelyn sunk toward the floor. Her muscles wouldn't respond. She was too drained.

The whirring escalated to a high-pitched whine, and then the sound rocketed upward until it became a constant, overpowering shriek. Evelyn heard the cracking, popping sound again, like thick limbs snapping from a tree.

Alex scrambled up onto his hands and knees. "We need to get out of here."

The ceiling sagged. The clockwork fell away from the pillar in sheets. The pendulum made one last wild arc before the wheel above it dropped from the ceiling. Both slammed onto the floor, throwing gears and metal up into the air. Debris cascaded back down like rain. The pillar lurched, separating from the thick beams that held it to the ceiling.

Alex pulled Evelyn toward the door. "Come on. Let's go."

There wasn't enough time. They weren't going to make it.

She still had that feeling of clarity. All the pieces still fit together in her head, but the knowledge was fading. She had to get Alex someplace safe before the clarity disappeared completely.

The pillar lurched again. The ceiling and the wall behind it ripped open like wet tissue paper. White plaster showed through the opening, lit by the harsh glow of electric lights. The lights flickered and went out.

Evelyn picked up her bag from where she'd dropped it on the floor. She forced herself to stand, summoning the will from somewhere deep inside her. "Alex. The basement."

He followed her eyes and saw the break in the wall, but hesitated.

"Trust me, I know where to go," she said.

They headed for the tear in the wall, their shoes slipping on the gears on the floor. Some of the gears were still moving, grasping at Evelyn's feet like vengeful hands. Alex pulled her up into his arms and jumped through the gap into the Byrne House basement. Her feet touched back to the ground. Then they ran.

A terrific crash came from behind them. It reverberated through the walls, shaking the ground beneath their feet. The pillar had fallen.

"This way," Evelyn said. They didn't have enough time to get back to the main floor of the house and outside. It was too late for that. But there was one place they might be safe, one place that Walter wouldn't have wanted to destroy.

White walls flew past them, dotted with the gold that still echoed in Evelyn's eyes. Chunks of plaster and brick dislodged from the ceiling and fell around them as the hallway convulsed. She reached the end of the hall and turned into the storage room, pushing furniture and kicking boxes out of the way to reach the riveted metal door in the far wall.

Evelyn dug her hand into the pocket of her jeans for Darren's key. *Thank you Jake*, she thought. She shoved the key into the lock and threw open the door.

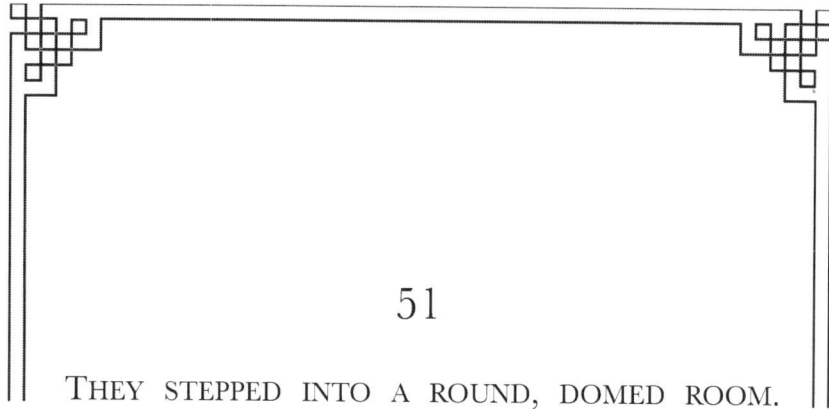

51

THEY STEPPED INTO A ROUND, DOMED ROOM. Ada's tomb. Where Walter Byrne came to die so long ago. Evelyn could feel the floor vibrating through her joints and into her head.

"You think this place will hold?" Alex pointed up at the ceiling. A fine network of cracks was spreading in the plaster.

"Walter would have wanted Ada to be safe."

A piece of plaster broke loose from the ceiling. Alex pulled her out of the way. It crashed behind them onto the floor, exploding in a cloud of white dust.

Alex crouched on the floor in the lee of the stone table, and Evelyn huddled next to him. He tried to wipe the drying blood from her face, then gave up.

"You look God-awful. What happened back there?"

She couldn't even begin to explain it. Seeing Alex with all that blood around him, and the gold of the room reflecting in his eyes when he thought she'd leave without him...It already seemed like just a nightmare. Or a flash of a memory that had belonged to someone else.

A rumble started, distant at first but then louder, building until the sound was so massive she could see it vibrating in the walls. The room shook and they shook along with it. She could feel the terror of the people still inside Byrne House. Her mind slipped away from her, like it had in that terrible golden room, and suddenly she was far above them. In the tower room on the third floor.

Madeline lies facedown on the bed as the house trembles. She's been here since she left Daniella in the gardens, lying in the same place

272

Sam died. The room that once belonged to her at the top of the tower. The house had been silent while she lay there, the only sound the muffled sobs in her chest, until the bed started to move and the crystals on the light fixtures jingled. She didn't understand it but it seemed as if the grief inside her had turned inside out, projecting into the room around her.

She hears the door open.

"Madeline, hurry." It's William. Her son-in-law.

More footsteps follow. "Mother, get up," Daniella shouts. "The house is collapsing. You have to come with us, now!" She leans over the bed and tries to grab hold of her mother's wrists. Madeline turns over onto her stomach, folding her arms beneath her. "Mother, didn't you hear what I said? We have to go."

"I don't care," Madeline says. "Let me stay here. This is what I want. Both of you, go. Do that for me, please."

"Mother, you're being ridiculous. William, go. Wait for us outside."

"I'm not leaving this house until you do."

Daniella turns back to her mother. She's desperate. She'll say or do anything to get her mother out of the house. This isn't what was supposed to happen, none of it. She's so sorry for what she's wasted, what she's destroyed for no reason at all. She can't let her mother die here. She has to do this one thing.

"I'm sorry for everything. I'm so very sorry for what I did. Please don't leave me. Don't leave me alone."

She's that girl again, the fourteen-year-old girl who only wanted someone to love her, to see her for the good person she could be. "You asked me to come with you that night before you left, and I said no because I was so sad and so ashamed of what I'd done. And I thought maybe you'd stay if I refused. But I wish I'd gone. I wish so much that I'd gone. I'm so sorry I did that to you. Please, don't do it to me."

Madeline stretches out her hand and Daniella takes it. "I'm sorry, too," Madeline says. "I wish it could be different. But it will never end, and it will never change. Sam's dead. Darren is dead. Both of you, both of my children, became monsters. Because of me. I can never go back and undo any of it."

She squeezes her daughter's hand and pulls it to her mouth to kiss it. Then she lets it go. "I thought I could escape Byrne House,"

Madeline says. "But the past eleven years—none of that was real. I never left. I've been the one lying on this bed, dying, all that time."

The framed mirror above the dresser falls, shattering into a thousand pieces.

William pulls Daniella toward the door. "We might not get out of here as it is."

"Momma, no. Don't do this to me, please."

William holds her around the waist and drags her from the room. Fallen picture frames litter the hallway. The paneling on the walls has cracked, and splintered pieces of wood grab at William's arms as he runs for the staircase, pulling Daniella, still screaming, along with him.

Madeline turns her head to the window. She closes her eyes and thinks of the people she lost. Handsome, good-intentioned Sam, who she's wrongfully despised all these years. Her sweet, imaginative son. Daniella as a girl, laughing and innocent. She worries that she won't be able to remember their faces, but then they come to her and she holds onto them.

The door in Evelyn's mind swung shut, and she came back to the sound of metal screeching and wood snapping.

They grabbed each other. Evelyn straddled Alex's lap, squeezing her thighs against his hips, clinging to his neck. He held her tight around the waist. They bowed their heads together as plaster and bricks fell from the ceiling.

There was a noise like a tremendous wave crashing onto shore. The house was buckling under its own weight, like a horse with a broken leg. The supports beneath the house were failing, one by one.

Daylight broke through above as the cracks widened, spilling down dirt and bricks. Alex pulled her under the table, crowding next to Walter, and pushed the skeleton out of the way with his foot.

Sound blended with movement into one thing that shook the room in its fist, and she knew the dome was collapsing. Everything was falling—Byrne House, the rest of Castle Heights.

The whole world, collapsing in on itself.

Her whole body clenched as she tried to fight with all her will, refusing to accept the truth of it, holding a barrier of resistance tight around her heart. But it kept coming. Unstoppable. Undeniable. There was nothing she could do.

Alex felt it too. "It's okay." She felt his lips against her ear. "We're together. Whatever happens we're together."

She pressed her nose and mouth against his shoulder, trying not to breath in the white dust that billowed from the growing cracks in the walls and ceiling. Alex buried his face in her hair. She relaxed against him, letting go of everything but the feeling of his arms around her and his heart beating against hers.

Then, after one beat and before the next, it was quiet.

They were still here. The dome had held, and it was over.

⁓ᏋᏋᏋᏋ⁓

For ages, she clung to Alex. As if she was holding the room together by holding onto him. But eventually, she lifted her head and looked around.

"Guess we're still alive," Alex said.

"Seems that way."

She peeked out from under the table. There were cracks in the dome spilling sunlight into the room, enough that they could see, although there was so much white dust clouding the air it wasn't easy. Dirt showed through bare spots in the walls where the plaster and brick had fallen away. The door had a huge dent at the bottom, a wrinkle in the metal like some heavy thing on the other side had slammed into it.

"Not so bad," Alex said. "Though Walter has looked better."

Evelyn glanced at the skeleton and quickly turned away. Falling bricks had shattered half of Walter's frame, and the bones on the other half didn't look like they were in the right places anymore. She saw the journal he'd clutched in his hands lying up against the wall, splayed open, pages torn. Her bag lay beside her, sagging open, with Mimi's crystal and the gold-framed mirror inside. The mirror was miraculously still intact. A useless relic, a sliver of the past.

"What happened back there?" Alex asked. "In the clockwork room?"

"What's the last thing you remember?" Though she knew the limitations of such a question.

He considered. "I was looking at that other mirror stuck between the gears in the wall, and then I was on the floor and you were feeling me up. I'm guessing I missed something in between."

She rested her head against the cool stone of the table. "Yeah. Something."

She was so exhausted it hurt to blink her eyes, so she closed them. Alex pulled her forward, and her head fell against his shoulder. She ran a hand along his chest, still making sure. She'd never felt anything so good as his heart beating, sure and strong, beneath her palm.

Sirens trilled through the cracks in the ceiling. "How long do you think it'll take them to find us?" Evelyn asked.

"Who knows. There's probably a lot of mess out there to dig through."

"Oh no, my mom. What if she's hurt? And Ms. Foster?" She started to climb out from under the table, but Alex pulled her back into his lap.

"There's nothing we can do. We just have to wait and hope everyone's okay."

"But I hate not being able to do anything."

"I know. But that's how it is."

The dust was settling down, the air clearing. Alex's hair was white from all the plaster dust. Hers probably was too.

"Talk to me," he said. "That's something you can do. You can distract me while we're waiting."

"I don't know what to talk about."

"Well..." He shifted his weight beneath her. "We could talk about something better than this. Which is pretty much anything. But that might be depressing because it'll make us think about how much we want to get out of here."

She rested her cheek against his. "Is there another option?"

"We could talk about something worse." She felt his hand on the back of her waist, his fingers spread wide. "The worst thing, for each of us."

She couldn't think of anything worse than seeing Alex in that golden room, gears spilling from the walls as blood poured out of the hole in his chest and bubbled out of his mouth. How could she possibly describe that to him, what that had been like?

"I don't think I can," she said.

"Give it a try. I'm here. I'm listening."

She closed her eyes so she wouldn't see the rubble piled up against the walls. She couldn't tell him the very worst thing, but she could tell him about the tunnels. It wasn't like seeing Alex almost die in front of her, but it was close. He knew what happened, but the way it felt to be down there by herself—she hadn't been able to talk about that before.

"When I was in the tunnels, after...after what I had to do, I was all alone. Except for things that weren't people anymore."

Ada. Darren.

"I hurt so much I couldn't do anything but lay there and think." She remembered lying on the cold ground, afraid that Alex would never know what happened to her or how much she really loved him. It was the same feeling Uncle Sammy had breathed into the room in the Byrne House tower before he'd died, the same shreds of emotion that still hovered there after he was gone—love for Vivian. For his niece.

"What did you think about?" Alex asked.

"I thought a lot about Ada. But after a while I could tune her out, and I just thought about you."

His fingertips dragged over her hair, brushing away dust and bits of plaster. "About me? What?"

She sat up so she could see him. "Everything. How you look and smell and taste and feel."

He smiled. The tears she'd been holding inside rose up, and she hugged him close again so he wouldn't see.

"Did it make you feel better?" he asked.

"Yes and no. It made me miss you so much it felt like dying. But it also gave me something to try to stick around for. So I could get through the waiting. I didn't know for sure you were coming, but I figured I should be there if you did."

"Good," he said against her ear. Evelyn could barely hear his voice above the sirens. Her cheek slipped against his, hot and wet. She couldn't tell if they were her tears or Alex's. Maybe both.

"I want to say that my worst thing was not knowing where you were that day in August," he said. "I couldn't find you and I knew something bad must have happened, and I felt totally helpless. Your mom said you hadn't come home, and I was looking everywhere I could think, and then Jake showed up, looking like he'd been buried alive and had to dig himself out. And then he told me he left you down there in the tunnels. I thought I might strangle him right then."

"You want to say that's the worst, but it's not?"

Alex wiped at his cheek. "That was really, really bad, but not the worst. The worst was the night my dad died."

"Tell me," she whispered.

"Things seemed so dark. I felt trapped, like I'd never get free of that pain. You know the weirdest thing? My scars hurt, like all those wounds had opened up again. And I started to think about that day I fell in the gardens. I hadn't really thought about that—thought about you—for a long time up to that point. Not in any detail. I couldn't even picture what you looked like. I just remembered being so scared I thought I'd suffocate down there. But you were scared too, and I had to stay strong for you. And..."

Alex put a hand gently against her cheek. "That night, after my dad died, I pretended you were there with me. It helped. Just the idea of you was enough, for that moment at least, to make me not feel so alone."

Evelyn felt for the chain around her neck. She unlatched it and let the ring fall onto her palm.

"Give me your hand," she said.

Alex held out his hand, and she slid the ring onto his pinky.

"What's this for? Are you asking me to marry you? If you are, I don't know, I'll have to think about it..."

"Not marry. That's not enough. It's a bigger promise than that."

"Bigger, huh?" He curled his pinky finger over the ring. "Okay then. I promise we'll always be together. Is that good?"

"But we won't always. Sometimes we'll be apart from each other. We can't help that." She was thinking of the next semester. Maybe even longer, depending on colleges.

He twisted the ring around his pinky. "Tell me then. What am I promising here?"

"That you'll always come back." Her throat felt so full she could barely get the words out.

He pulled her to his chest. "I told you the other night, I'm not going anywhere. I wouldn't last very long without you."

Evelyn sobbed into the dust-coated fabric of his shirt, the dirt caking between her eyelashes.

"What is it? Did I say the wrong thing?" He laughed gently, kissing the top of her head. "I really didn't think I messed it up that time."

She couldn't stop crying. "Just promise, okay?"

There was no way he could really make the promise she was asking, but she needed to believe it was possible. It was too hard to imagine living every day knowing she could lose him, after coming so close to seeing it happen right in front of her. She didn't think she'd be able to live through that again.

He lifted her chin. He was still smiling. His thumb made a curve under each of her eyes, wiping away the tears.

"I'll always come back to you."

He held her hand up, took the ring from his pinky and slipped it onto her finger.

"I promise."

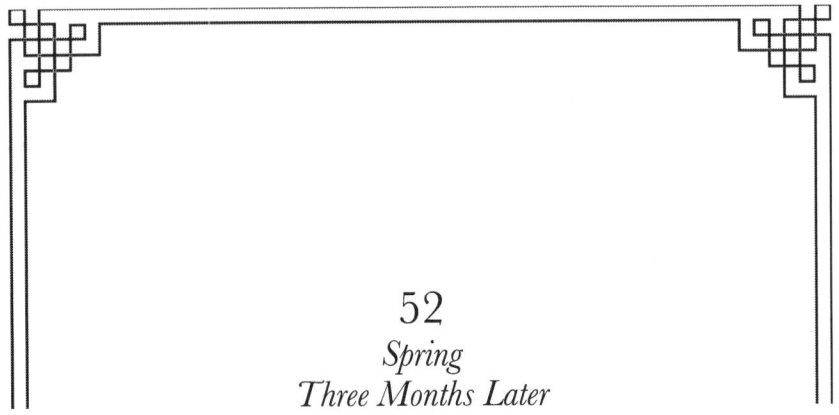

52
Spring
Three Months Later

"THAT WAS QUITE A STORY," MS. FOSTER SAID. "I'm sorry it took me so long to tell you the whole thing."

Evelyn picked up a crumb of the scone she'd left, half eaten, on her plate. They were sitting at Ms. Foster's kitchen table, midday sun shining through the translucent white curtains above her sink.

Ms. Foster glanced at the clock over the stove, and then at the teapot they'd emptied an hour ago. "It did take all morning, didn't it? It's nearly lunch time." She stood and took the teapot to the sink.

Evelyn brought their plates to the counter and watched Ms. Foster wash them. "I mean I'm sorry it took three months till I was ready to tell it."

"With all the chaos and the move, I can hardly blame you," she said with her back turned, rinsing suds off the dishes.

Ms. Foster was avoiding her.

After she got to the part in her story about Darren and the tunnels, Ms. Foster had slumped in her chair, looking down at the tabletop. She'd sucked in her breath a few times as Evelyn told her about Daniella's role and about what happened to Madeline, but by the time they got to the clockwork room, Ms. Foster fell silent. She'd kept her hand on the table, her fingers still.

Now, she leaned over the sink and squirted more dish soap into her hand.

"Aren't you going to say something?" Evelyn asked.

"I'm trying, there's just…It's so much."

Evelyn went back to the table and sank into her chair. "You don't believe me."

The water stopped and she turned around, drying her hands on her yellow cardigan. "I want to." She shook her head, bunching up her cardigan in her hands. "No, I do believe you. I do."

Ms. Foster came over to the table, sat down and took Evelyn's hands. Hers were still damp, a little sticky from the soap she hadn't completely washed away. "Of course I believe you. All I have to do is see the cracks in my dishes from when Darren threw them on the floor to see it's true. The ones that didn't break, anyway. Or look out the window, for heaven's sake."

Evelyn nodded. "I haven't told many people the whole thing. It's not easy."

She'd told Alex about a month back, on a Saturday when he'd been visiting Seattle for the weekend. Her mom had been out for the afternoon, and they'd been alone in her room in the apartment—technically against the rules, but Vivian had been pretty lax about it. Evelyn had been lying on the bed turned away from him, staring at the pink quartz crystal on her nightstand. Her good luck charm.

Alex's fingers had been running up and down the skin of her back. The words just poured out of her. The whole story of what really happened in the clockwork room. When she finished, he'd gently pulled her shoulder until she rolled over to face him. His eyes were shiny and wet, like hers. Then he'd put her hand, palm flat, on the middle of his chest, over the spot where she'd looked a dozen times for a mark even though she knew there wasn't one.

"I'm sure it wasn't easy for you to tell it to me," Ms. Foster said. "It wasn't easy to hear, either. What you went through in those tunnels. I can't even fathom it." She closed her eyes a moment and pressed her thumbs to the corners of her eyelids. "I'm glad that horrible man is dead."

Evelyn nodded. Not long after the city began digging out the ruins of Walter Park, they'd found Darren's body. According to the rumors, the police suspected homicide, but the collapse of the statue and the park into the underground lab had destroyed most of the evidence. And with half the streets in Castle Heights crumbling into the tunnels beneath them, along with several of the houses, the police hadn't devoted many resources yet to the investigation.

There'd been other bodies, too. The remains of Ada and Walter Byrne in their tomb. And Evelyn's uncle, Sam Stanton.

"But what about the last part?" Evelyn said. "The part with Alex and the silver mirror, what I did…"

"How you saved his life?" Ms. Foster's eyes shifted away, thinking. "I'll admit it's difficult to imagine how such a thing could be possible. Turning back time. My sister Mimi wouldn't doubt it for a second. I suppose that old quote from Hamlet would be appropriate here, 'more things in Heaven and Earth,' but that's a tad cliche, isn't it? I do think there are extraordinary things in this world that most of us can't begin to understand, but a few have seen them. People like Walter Byrne. And you."

It wasn't really an answer. Evelyn didn't blame her for not knowing what to think. Alex said he believed it, but sometimes she could hardly believe it herself. She was the only one who'd seen that pool of blood shrink back into his body. Seen the shard of crystal pull out of his chest.

The only time Evelyn had spoken to her on the phone, Daniella had claimed not to remember Alex getting hurt. And of course, the silver-framed mirror was in a million pieces, crushed beneath Byrne House right now. What was left of Byrne House. Which wasn't much.

"It's going to be so strange with you gone," Ms. Foster said. "I keep thinking about things getting back to normal, after all this construction is finished and we can actually drive on our streets again, and then I realize that even when it's all put back together you won't be here."

She brushed at her eye, smiling with her lips pressed tight together, and reached for Evelyn's hands. "I want you to know you're very special to me, Evelyn. Very special. You tell me if you ever need anything in Seattle and I'll move heaven and earth to get it to you."

Evelyn got up and hugged her.

In the last few months, she and her mom had settled into their Seattle apartment. The new school wasn't so bad; Evelyn had made friends. But the changes all felt temporary, with Castle Heights still such a mess. Their house still held most of its furniture and keepsakes. That was why they'd come back to Colorado for Evelyn's spring break: to make the move official.

Most of the houses here in Castle Heights were still empty of people, even though the city lifted the evacuation order weeks ago. The neighborhood finally had running water and electricity again. The Castle Heights schools were shut down, her classmates scattered among various other Denver high schools. But slowly, the city was putting the buildings and streets back together, filling in the tunnels, carrying away the ruins of Byrne House piece by piece. According to Alex, William was even talking about rebuilding the mansion. Eventually it would all be finished, the cracks healed, the scars erased. Like none of it had ever happened.

But Evelyn wouldn't be here to see it. After this week, she wouldn't have a home in Castle Heights anymore.

Ms. Foster squeezed Evelyn's left hand, the one wearing Ada's ring. "And you have to promise me that you'll tell me as soon as you set a wedding date."

Evelyn laughed and pushed at the ring with her thumb. "That will be a while. We both promised our moms that we'd graduate from high school first. But at least we'll be together next year—whether it's New England or California." They'd gotten into schools in both places—not all the exact same ones, but they had enough choices that they could at least be in the same region. If they could just agree on which side of the country was better.

"Alex doesn't want to be too close to Will and Daniella in San Francisco," Evelyn added, though she hadn't conceded that argument yet. She preferred the milder winters and sunshine.

"He's still not speaking to his brother?"

"Nope. Daniella and I have, but it's awkward." Daniella had called, wanting to talk about her mother, but it was too hard for Evelyn. Madeline was the only one who didn't make it out of Byrne House. Evelyn had promised Daniella she would try again in a few months, after the events at Byrne House didn't feel so close anymore. She hadn't forgiven Daniella for all the things she'd done—maybe she never would—but it hurt too much to keep the anger going. And Daniella had lost so much herself.

Ms. Foster walked her to the door. "Be careful on your way," she said. "I don't trust those makeshift sidewalks."

It looked a lot better than it had when the rescue crew pulled her and Alex out of the chamber beneath the gardens. It was night by the time they were found. The street had been a rocky trench, fractured by the spinning lights of the helicopters and emergency vehicles. Walter Park had looked like a black pit that swallowed the earth above it whole.

Evelyn and Ms. Foster hugged again, saying goodbye. Then she walked—very carefully, because Ms. Foster was still watching—down the recently reconstructed front steps and along the plywood-lined sidewalk. Right now, the street itself was a muddy field of broken concrete and toppled trees. But most of the houses still stood.

Vivian was out in front of their home, directing the stream of movers carrying furniture and boxes. The moving van was parked a couple of blocks away, on one of the streets open to traffic.

Evelyn kept her eyes down as she passed Byrne House. She hated seeing those piles of shattered stone and splintered wooden beams. The empty frame where the stained-glass window had been.

"Where were you?" Viv called. "Dad said he couldn't find you."

"I was saying goodbye to Ms. Foster." She walked across the filled-in dirt that now made up their front lawn.

"Silvia and Milo are here," Viv said. "You need to get in there and help."

Evelyn glanced down the street, to where the ground wasn't in such bad shape. Some of the houses down there still had actual grass and flagstone sidewalks.

She spotted a familiar figure hovering in an alley, someone she hadn't seen in months.

"I'll be there in a sec, Mom, I just need to take care of something first."

She found Jake leaning against the slats of a wooden fence in the alley. "Hey," he said. "Is it safe?"

Evelyn rolled her eyes. "Yeah, Alex didn't see you or anything. How're you doing?"

She had been in touch with Jake's mother, enough to know he was finally in therapy. And she'd gotten some e-mails from Jake himself over the past couple months. He'd apologized in vague terms for "what I did to you." But to him, she had not written back. She was still working through his betrayal. Yet part of her did want to reach out to him, to try to heal that broken part of him that she could feel within herself.

Jake wandered over to the other side of the alley and kicked over a plastic crate someone had left by the dumpster. "I have a girlfriend now. A girl from East High."

Evelyn's chest loosened. She smiled. "That's great. Wonderful. I'm really happy for you."

He frowned and looked away, like that wasn't the reaction he'd wanted. "Just so you know, in case you thought this was...Anyway. I just wanted to say I'm sorry one more time. Before you go, since we'll probably never see each other again."

Evelyn felt tempted to say it was okay, tell him he was wrong about never seeing her. Something nice, so this didn't feel so awful. But she figured it was better this way. Smarter, at least.

"Probably not," she said.

"Well. Okay then. Goodbye." He turned and walked out of the alley. She stayed put. Then he paused and looked back over his shoulder, like he expected her to come running after him to give him a dramatic hug and cry and say she forgave him. But she didn't move, and he kept going. She stood there and watched until he turned the corner, and then he was gone.

She found Silvia and Milo in the kitchen, passing out burritos from paper bags. Alex was there, too, bent over his elbows on the kitchen counter. There was a rising sensation in her chest when she saw him, a feeling of being in exactly the right place. Alex turned his head and grinned, one side of his mouth always a little higher than the other because of the scar.

"Hey," he said, "I've been waiting for you." He looped his arms around her and rested his forehead against hers.

Evelyn ran her thumb along his scar, from just below his eye down to his chin, and stretched up onto her toes to kiss him.

"We're trying to eat here," Milo said. From the corner of her eye Evelyn saw Silvia elbow him, but he was already laughing.

"I was at Ms. Foster's," Evelyn said. "You're supposed to go say goodbye to her, too."

"What about our project?" Alex asked.

"It can wait."

He nodded, grabbed two burritos and some napkins from the counter, and headed for the door. "Ms. Foster likes Mexican, right?" he asked from the entryway. She heard the door close.

Milo held out a foil-wrapped burrito. "Lunch?"

Evelyn took it. "Thanks. I think we're almost finished."

Silvia abruptly sobbed and launched over for a hug. Evelyn squished her burrito in her fist as she held it away from Silvia's hair.

"I can't believe it's really happening," Silvia said.

"We can still talk every day, just like we have been," Evelyn replied. "But I'm gonna miss you like crazy."

Silvia nodded, still sniffling. Her cheek was damp against Evelyn's. "I was going to say you better not forget about us, but I know you wouldn't do that."

"No way. There's definitely no forgetting."

She could never forget any of it.

Milo stood in the entryway, hesitating. Evelyn let go of Silvia, handed her the half-crushed burrito, walked over and put her arms around his neck. He patted her on the back with his arms stiff, but as she held him tighter, he relaxed.

"We can come visit you, right?" Milo asked. "It's okay if Alex is visiting too, as long as you can make him shut up occasionally."

"Come whenever you want. Although I can't make any promises about what Alex says."

Evelyn told them they'd talk more later and went upstairs to find her mom. Vivian was in the now-empty den, sitting up against the wall and staring at something in her hands. She looked up when Evelyn came in.

"There you are."

They'd both said it at the exact same time. Evelyn laughed, but Viv's face crumpled. Evelyn slid down the wall onto the carpet next to her mother.

"Mom, what's wrong?"

She shook her head, trying to smile. "Nothing. Everything."

"I know what you mean." Evelyn peeled away the foil from the top of the burrito and took a bite, then held it out. "Hungry?"

"Sure. Trade you." Viv took the burrito and handed Evelyn the little piece of plastic she'd been holding. It was a clear plastic hourglass with white sand inside. "I found it under the couch in here. Remember that board game you used to love playing? We never figured out what happened to that timer, but I guess it was under there, the whole time."

Evelyn tipped it upside down and watched the sand leak into the other side. "It was your game. I found it in that box of your old stuff, from when you were a kid."

"Maybe. I can't remember. Funny how time does that." She stretched out her legs on the floor. "You've changed so much in the last year, Evvy. I know part of it's meeting Alex, but I can tell there's a lot more. There's so much that's happened to you and sometimes I can see it in your eyes, and you look so sad and so grown and I hate that I don't even know what it is."

"Mom…" Evelyn wished she could tell all of it, like she'd told Ms. Foster. But that was impossible. When she'd tried to imagine explaining the mirror and Darren Byrne and the clockwork room to her mother, the words just wouldn't come.

Vivian knew that Sammy was dead. The police had found his body in a far corner of the tunnels. Evelyn claimed that Madeline Byrne said he'd died in a terrible accident, and that she took the blame herself. The decision had been a difficult one, but she was sure that Madeline would have preferred this story over the truth about Daniella's part. Besides, what proof did Evelyn have? A vision in a magic mirror?

She didn't want anyone else to know about the terrible crystals that Walter Byrne had found. There had been no strange reports or unexplained sicknesses to come out of the excavations of Castle Heights so far. Evelyn hoped that the last traces of the crystal had finally been buried or destroyed. Walter's research was better off forgotten.

As for Sammy, the Ashwoods had held a small memorial service for him, and as soon as the police released his remains, they planned a gravesite with a view of the mountains. Evelyn and her mom were both still grieving his loss, but each day was a little easier.

"I'm not asking you to tell me what really happened," Vivian said. "That's what I'm trying to say. I know you're almost grown up. You have your own life. Or you will, soon. I'm just grateful you're sharing some of it with me."

The top stair creaked and footsteps tread on the carpet in the hall. Evelyn's father poked his head in. "Silvia and Milo are still downstairs hovering in the kitchen," Toby said. "I think they're waiting to say goodbye."

Evelyn stooped to pick up the plastic hourglass and stuck it in her pocket. "I should probably go down."

"Hey, hold up," he said. "Hugs first. I'm not missing any more chances."

Evelyn sat down on the dusty floor of the basement in front of the brick wall. Silvia and Milo had left a little while ago, and Vivian and Toby were finalizing things with the movers. Now, she was just waiting for Alex to come back.

He'd know where to find her. He always managed that.

The basement was empty except for her keepsake box, a bucket, and a trowel. Plus the small stack of bricks Evelyn had bought at Home Depot early that morning, before she went to Ms. Foster's. She hugged her knees to her chest and stared at the black rectangular hole near the bottom of the wall.

Alex jogged down the stairs. "Got everything?"

"Yeah, except the water." She brought the bucket over to him. He took it and ran back upstairs. She heard rushing in the pipes overhead.

Alex came back down, water sloshing in the bucket with every step. He set the bucket beside the bricks. Evelyn ripped open the bag of mortar and up-ended the contents of the bag into the bucket.

"Want to do the honors?" She handed him the trowel, and he kneeled over the bucket to mix it.

Evelyn held up the glass-lidded jewelry box. The same one that Madeline had given her several months ago. It now held the keys to the tunnel doors, Ada's letters, and Ada's locket. Evelyn set the box inside the alcove.

"See?" she said, more to herself than to Alex. "That wasn't so hard."

She picked up the mirror, which was inside its black velvet bag. She held it in her hands, feeling the weight of it. The weight of so many things.

"You don't really have to do this," Alex said. "If you don't want to."

"But I need to."

She tossed the mirror through the hole. It thumped onto the floor.

Alex picked up the brick at the top of the pile and spread a layer of mortar onto it. He fit it into place, then started on the next. She watched the hole begin to close. Before long, he was picking up the last brick.

"Wait a sec," Evelyn said, stopping his hand.

She pulled her mom's little plastic hourglass out of her pocket and tossed it through the hole. She didn't hear it land. Maybe it had fallen on top of the velvet bag. No going back now. No changing her mind.

It was a good feeling.

"I'm ready now."

He smeared mortar onto the last brick, fit it into the hole, and used the trowel to clean up some of the mess.

"It looks like crap," he said.

She giggled. "Yeah, it kinda does. But that's okay."

There wouldn't be anyone here to complain, anyway. Vivian had decided not to sell the house for now, and Evelyn doubted anyone would have bought it with the neighborhood such a disaster. Eventually, they'd put it up for rent. But Evelyn wouldn't let herself imagine coming back here yet. She needed finality, at least for now.

Alex dropped the trowel into the bucket and wiped his hands against his t-shirt. They scooted over to the other part of the wall and sat with their backs up against it, their sides pressed together from shoulders to hips. Alex gathered her hands in his and pulled them into his lap. His fingers were tacky with drying mortar.

"You all right?" he asked.

"I'm good. Really good, actually."

When he kissed her, she felt the curve of his smile on his lips. "So when's the caravan leaving?" he asked.

"Pretty soon. I think the moving van is going now and we're supposed to go back to the hotel to pack up the rest of our stuff so we're ready to go in the morning."

"Did you ask your mom about staying with me tonight?"

"She burst out laughing. I think that was a no."

He leaned his head against the bricks, his hair falling across his forehead. "We could come back here," Alex said. "This doesn't have to be goodbye."

"True." But it might never be home again. Predicting if she'd ever return to Castle Heights was like trying to fathom the workings of another person's heart. Like peering into something vast and unknowable.

She had no idea what the future held. And she was okay with that.

Alex put his arm around her, and her head fell onto his shoulder. She closed her eyes, inhaling the dust that the movers had stirred up, mixed with the muddy smell of drying mortar and the sweeter scent of sweat evaporating from Alex's skin. Her nose itched, and the dust scratched at her throat. But she didn't mind it.

"I just want to stay here a little longer."

The End

Thank you

I hope you enjoyed the conclusion to Alex and Evelyn's story. I'd be so grateful for a quick review on Amazon and on Goodreads. And if you'd rather not leave a review, leave a rating. Every single rating or review helps this book connect with new readers. And many thanks to my growing team of advance readers—your support and your feedback mean the world to me!

To read a free novella from Alex's perspective, *Between Dusk And Light* (Byrne House #1.5), sign up for my e-mail list: http://eepurl.com/g3ox8r

Next from A.N. Willis
Coming October 2020:
HOW MUCH IT MAY STORM

Colorado, 1943: With a brother gone to war, Dinah must learn how to fend for herself. She spends her days scouring the old mine for ore and her nights longing to escape her dying town.

When Dinah sees a young soldier out in the snow—a soldier who looks just like Edward Gainsbury, a man who supposedly died in 1918—she follows him into the woods. But what she discovers will force Dinah to confront the true history of her town and the dangerous darkness hiding inside those she least suspects.

A chilling ghost story that spans two world wars, two brave young women, and the terrible secret that binds them...

About The Author

~⚜~

A.N. Willis writes books for teens and adults—sometimes sci-fi, sometimes supernatural, always with heavy doses of action and romance. She loves the creepy, the suspenseful, the otherworldly. She blogs about writing in the Mile High City on anwilliswrites.com. Follow her on Instagram @morningcoffeeforwriters, on Twitter @anwilliswrites, and on Facebook.com/anwilliswrites.

To hear about my new releases, sign up for my e-mail list at: http://eepurl.com/g3ox8r

Printed in Great Britain
by Amazon